Single Black Male
Addicted to Females

D1193335

Single Black Male Addicted to Females

KeAughn Caver

To everyone who wants to tell a story, but is still keeping it locked inside. Use the creation of this novel as proof that your story encourages optimism even in the face of adversity.

With all our horrors and faults, somewhere in us there is a shining.

—John Steinbeck

Prologue

The first court day with Veronica.

Keenan weaved his car carefully through Atlanta's streets as the torrential downpour slowed to a bone-chilling mist. Rain pooled against the curbs of the street, and women tip-toed across intersections, hurrying to get out of the winter rain. He spotted a place to park in front of the now-discarded Atlanta Underground, so he took the time while sitting in his car to gather himself before entering the century-old Lewis R. Slaton Courthouse across the street.

Thumbing through his phone, he saw some recent photos of his two teenage sons. One grinned from his bike, the other, older, was focused intently on a video game. He thought again of the $1,500 that could have gone to his sons for Christmas and instead was being wasted on a lawyer and court fees. Emotions had over-ruled reason, and he was paying the price.

He got out of his foreign sedan and stood on the sidewalk. The trees were lined up like a group of sages, with their branches shaking like bony fingers, delivering admonishment over his cleanly shaven head. The hindsight of knowing better than to get into this type of disagreement annoyingly settled into the pit of his stomach.

As he walked this gauntlet, he mused on his own history of relationships and his lack of understanding of the current dating world. From ages twenty-three to forty he had been in just two relationships—a total of seventeen years straight. He had missed out on the Roaring Twenties of dating, and navigating the world of dating as a grown man made him feel like he was herding cats. He felt the sorrowful realization that his memory and interpretation of expectations and display of accepted chivalry was quite frequently considered outdated.

Yet, he reminded himself, even though he had found his own idealized "Claire Huxtable" early in life and made two beautiful children together with her, the relationship didn't last. Even when he found another woman to spend seven years with after his marriage ended, that didn't end in a rose-petaled walk down the aisle. And now, here he was about to walk down another aisle—in a courtroom—to face down an ex-girlfriend who had inexplicably turned into an enemy.

Veronica.

He had been with her for only eight months, but he had been infatuated since the beginning. In the cold morning, it was easy to wonder at how sincerely he had felt love for her. The emotions she stirred up in him were so deep that her absence made him feel as if his heart had been ripped out by one of the walking dead. There was a hole and an emptiness within him, as much as he tried to ignore it.

At a point he considered the beginning of the end, realizing that their relationship was growing toxic, he had sought the advice of a relationship coach and matchmaker named Layla Hazel. She advised him to take a thirty-day break in contact with Veronica—and anybody else—so he could detox and have a fresh start. It was easy to regret that he hadn't taken her advice now, or maybe just not spoken to her about Veronica at all and let her set him up with someone who would be happy to have him. But he knew it wouldn't have done any good, as he was too head over heels with Veronica to think about someone else.

Nearing the stairs, he paused to put on his reading glasses, adjust his tie, and smooth the lapels of his brand-new black suit. His nerves caused him to stroke his neatly groomed mustache and goatee, which brought him some sort of comfort and raised his confidence. He knew that two things were for certain: thanks to Omari Hardwick, light-skinned brothers like him were bound to stay in demand, and he would be damned if Veronica won this case!

Keenan rushed up the courthouse stairs and walked through the arched doorway. The security checkpoints bustled with nervous energy as court guards checked in impatient visitors. He chose the shortest line possible. The scrawny woman in front of him with the crooked bright red wig flashed a quick smile at him as she placed her knock-off designer-inspired bag in the dark-gray plastic bin. He returned the smile, thinking, *At this point, there really isn't a reason to avoid humility.* He breezed through security and approached the elevator bay to discover that Veronica and her mother, Ms. Rubio, were in front of him and also waiting for an elevator.

Great.

The awkward silence filled the compacted elevator space as they all rode together to the third floor.

"Good morning," he said to Ms. Rubio, his old-fashioned manners betraying him again, but she remained silent. Actually, she inched closer to her daughter and avoided any eye contact with him.

Despite himself and the situation, he felt a bit stung by this gesture because it spoke to her feelings toward him. Veronica and her mom had been notoriously at odds and estranged for years, and their strained relationship was something that Veronica had routinely vented to him about while they were together. She even went as far as to ignore her mother's phone calls and prevent her from interacting with her grandson on video chat. It had been hard for Keenan to watch, as close as he was to his own children.

But now he saw the new cohesion between Veronica and Ms. Rubio. He guessed they had allied against an outsider—himself. Did Ms. Rubio even remember how Veronica had stopped payments on the Charlotte home where she resided while she was struggling to earn her degree in counseling?

Veronica adjusted her glasses over the broad ridge of her nose and turned her head slightly to glance at her mother. She wore contacts mostly but donned the glasses when she wanted to appear sophisticated and credible. Keenan remembered the times he nuzzled his own nose against hers after a long night of lovemaking. Those almond-shaped brown eyes held worlds inside of them. Her shoulder-length hair grazed her neck like Cleopatra's crown of glory.

The elevator doors opened to a mostly empty hallway as Veronica straightened her attire and put on her Rutgers Medical School and New York Medical College airs. This was the "don't mess with me because I am more educated than you" attitude. Keenan had seen it before. He remembered how he lost several debates while they were dating with her last words being, "Do you know how many letters I have behind my name, Key?"

The formidable force that could wipe the puzzle word board game clean before any opponent and give Ken Jennings a run for his *Jeopardy!* title strutted inside the courtroom with boldness and an attaché of doctored-up documents. She was ready to financially, socially, and emotionally cripple a brother like Kunta Kinte in his iron slave collar.

Keenan surveyed the dated wood-paneled courtroom and didn't see his lawyer. He frantically tapped out a text message, feeling sweat gather on his brow. *Where was he?*

Standing alone in the back of the courtroom, he watched as Veronica placed her evidence on the table, meticulous as always, stopping every so often to crack her knuckles. *She was planning to represent herself?* The notion shocked him. Like a black-widow spider, she had gathered her defense so she could trap him with verbal blows and then belittle him to an unpleasant and calculated death.

A warm layer of sweat gathered on the back of his neck as the judge repeatedly called for his case. His relief at finally receiving a reply text was offset by the judge's response to hearing the chime of his phone.

"Mr. Green, approach the bench," the judge said through gritted teeth.

Keenan trudged up the long aisle, feeling Veronica's eyes upon him. The judge scowled thunderously.

"There are at least three signs throughout this courthouse indicating that cell phones must be silenced in court. We will be confiscating yours for the duration of the trial. You may pick it up at the front desk after we adjourn."

Veronica snickered. The snarky laugh added salt to his wounded ego. He slunk back to his seat as his lawyer rushed into the courtroom.

"Double booked," he murmured.

"Today?" Keenan asked, but his relief was real.

While his lawyer prepared his documentation and opening statements, Keenan glanced at Veronica one last time and emotionally fortified himself for the circus of a case to begin.

How the hell did I get here?

Section One

Catching Koi

One

Shooting, Fishing, Fire, Divorce

THERE WAS TROUBLE in the Green family, though Keenan was far too young to know it. Nate, twenty-five, and Mary, twenty-six, had four young boys. They lived in Detroit, but Nate was spending a lot of time in Texas, where Nicki was. The last time he went down to see Nicki, Mary was nine months pregnant with Keenan. Then he left for a full week, and Mary started thinking seriously about California. When the job at Soledad Prison came through, she decided to take it.

Soledad Prison—the home of Sirhan Sirhan and the Soledad brothers. The idea of working with that population was intimidating, but she needed a fresh start, if not for her marriage then for herself.

As she suspected might happen, Nate wasn't interested in relocating, and she left Detroit for California with just her four young boys. To her surprise, though, Nate visited her in California not long after they moved. He liked it. With him right there, she remembered the good times. Then he left again, and she decided, this time really, *The end.*

She settled back into her life, making new friends and working her regular shifts at the prison. One day after work, the phone rang. It was Nate.

"I want to come out there," he said. "For good."

She told him, this time, he could come and live with her as a friend. He could get set up, get on his feet. "And then we are, you know, that will be it," she said.

He agreed.

She was seeing somebody else, but it wasn't serious. It was just a relationship because the guy was married. She wanted to see what it felt like to be on the other side of it. So, that's what that was about. The funny thing is, it was just okay. The excitement that she had expected to feel wasn't really there.

When Nate came out to join her, she was living in an apartment complex in Salinas, an agricultural center made famous by novelist John Steinbeck. At the center of Salinas was a bustling, old-fashioned downtown where people still did all their shopping, surrounded by an expanding boundary of tract homes and apartment complexes, where they lived. Beyond that were the unending fields of lettuce, strawberries, and stinking broccoli.

The long, machine-perfect rows of green flipped by as Mary drove down the 101 to her work in Soledad. It was windy sometimes, but never too hot or too cold. The climate felt like a reward for her courage to move.

Salinas had always been a place for working people to start over, and Nate was one of them. He stayed with Mary while he was looking for a job. He applied with the county sheriff's office and police department, but they wouldn't take him because he couldn't pass the background check. Finally, he was able to become a corrections officer and started working at Soledad, the same as Mary.

Mary was still seeing her other friend, and even though Nate was living with her, she wasn't about to break it off. This was her new life she was living, whether Nate was there or not.

She left with her friend for a weekend soon after Nate moved in. Nate watched them pull out of the parking lot from the door. When they came back, Nate spoke to the man privately at the door while Mary unpacked. She heard the front door close, and then Nate walked into the bedroom.

"What was that about?" she asked, putting away her things.

"I told him that I wanted to try and make our marriage work."

She thought of the boys. "Okay," she said. She didn't try to get in touch with her friend again and didn't take his calls. She tried to make the marriage work, and it did — for a while.

A few months later, they took a weekend shopping trip to the massive department store downtown to buy shoes and pajamas for the boys. The children's department was in the basement. Nate turned his head suddenly to look at a man walking toward the elevator with his wife and kids. Mary saw his glance and followed it. She didn't know the couple, but she saw how pretty the wife was — tall with long hair, big legs, and a big smile. Nate's type.

And then he called out her name. "Hey, Cathy," he said.

She turned her head, recognized him, and lit up the room with: "Hiiii, Nate!"

That's how she knew he was messing around again.

But Mary didn't let on. She chatted with the family at the elevator after Nate dragged them over to say hello, and found out that the husband was Nate's friend Base from work.

From that moment on, she watched with increasing suspicion

as the three of them spent more and more time together. Nate even joined the National Guard because Base suggested it. Like he'd done in Detroit, Nate started spending more time away from home. Instead of with Nicki, though, it was with Base and Cathy.

"It's all in your imagination," Nate said when she fussed about it. "What do you think I'm doing over there with a man and his wife?"

"I can take a couple guesses," Mary said under her breath. She had a strong feeling they were into some freaky stuff.

Then Mary started having bad dreams—dreams where she shot Nate. She even told Nate about the dreams, worried, but he just laughed it off. Even so, she took a prayer of protection and put it in his wallet. Surely the dream was a warning about some force that was coming for him.

She didn't know how right she was.

Mary signed up to do a double shift the night before Easter, but her heart wasn't in it. Her mind kept going back to the new waterbed they had just bought and how nice it would be to roll around on it with her man. When she got close to finishing eight hours, she made a sudden decision to go home instead, expecting Nate to be there.

"Hey," she called out as she opened the door. But no one answered her, and the apartment felt empty.

She picked up the handset for the yellow phone hanging on the kitchen wall and dialed the neighbor downstairs. Yes, the neighbor mumbled through her sleep, the kids were there, also asleep. *Click.*

Now that she knew the kids were okay, Mary couldn't even realistically give herself the grace to be worried; she knew exactly where Nate was. She tossed an angry glance at the wall. The hands on the starburst clock said two.

I'm going to take a long, hot shower, Mary thought with careful precision, *and give him 'til three.*

After her shower, she changed right back into street clothes and saw that only forty-five minutes had passed. So she sat at the kitchen table and watched the minute hand climb back up to twelve, her anger right along with it, then shut the front door and marched out with her car keys in her hand.

In her own parking lot, she saw the distinctive lines of Base's Chevy van cutting through the light mist. It was one of those "boogie vans" that crawled over the Central California coastline and parked to the side of windy beaches, rocking.

For a boogie van, Base's was relatively understated. He kept the original gold paint job, a subtle gradation from yellow to orange with white pinstripes. Each side was windowless except for a tinted rectangle toward the back, about as wide as the cab-side window but twice as long. Two orange-and-gold bucket seats were in the front. The walls of the van were wood-paneled, and the floor was covered in thick, orange shag, with a leather-covered wet bar and a wraparound bench padded in crushed, orange velvet.

As it was dimly lit from inside, Mary could see Base and his wife in the two front seats, but they couldn't see her. Then, through the rectangular window toward the back, she saw the distinctive silhouette of her husband, Nate, on the wraparound bench with the bobbing head of some woman in his lap.

Mary turned abruptly, marched back into the apartment complex, and went straight for the bedroom closet. On the top shelf behind the Christmas wrapping was an aluminum-and-steel pistol.

"It's the latest in home defense," Nate had told her when he brought it from Texas. "Because it's a 9mm with a stagger-stacked magazine."

His words echoed in her head as she slid that magazine into place with a satisfying *click*. Mary put the gun in her right hand, sensing the extra width of the grip due to the fourteen rounds it was carrying. The handle was fat with bullets. She pushed the hammer back with her thumb and felt the trigger engage under her finger. *She was just going to scare him,* she thought. *She was just going to make him come back into the house.*

In a daze from rage and her own confused thoughts, she walked closer and closer to the van, gripping a fully engaged 9mm double-action pistol. When she was just a few paces from the driver's-side window, Mary heard Cathy scream, "She's got a gun!"

Base, sitting on the passenger side, broke out of the van like a jack-in-the-box and took off running down the unevenly paved parking lot. Through the corner of her eye, she saw him start to circle back, trying to get behind her. Mary walked the length of the van, pointed the gun at the back-side window, and pulled the trigger. It gave her enough resistance so that she had a heartbeat moment of no return, like at the top of a roller coaster. Then she heard the gun go *pop* in her hand, and the glass of the window exploded from the double round.

Nate jumped out of the wide passenger door on the other side, bleeding from the head and cursing. The girl busted out, too, screaming, and Mary could see from her teenybopper-tight microshorts, tube top, and wide, innocent eyes that she probably was no older than eighteen or twenty.

She sensed or heard Base's steps; it was hard to tell. Adrenaline throbbed in her like an electric current. Everything was very bright.

"Base, don't come up behind me," she said, "because I don't want to hurt nobody. Just get away from me."

Then everything went from bright to blurry. She knew the

neighbors were calling the cops. The van sped away—with Nate and the girl in it. Probably Base and Cathy, too.

She suddenly didn't care. Unsteady, she went back in the house, hid the gun under the bed, and went to sleep. The phone woke her up. It was some reporter. "Do you know your husband's been shot?" he asked.

"Of course I do," she said. "I've got the gun."

Mary hung up the phone and laid back down, but this time her eyes didn't close. She stared at the ceiling. Two tears leaked out and fell down the sides of her face. A calm voice in her head said, "Lawyer." So, she opened the top drawer of the nightstand on her side of the bed and pulled out the directory.

Mary started flipping toward the yellow pages and paused. She had a name for a lawyer; it was someone's connection from work. She skipped over to the white pages and looked him up, making sure to memorize his information.

For the bail bondsman, she chose a company that had bought a quarter-page ad. Then she called her neighbor, telling her that the kids needed to stay there at least another night.

First steps taken in dealing with the mess she had made.

Mary put the heavy directory back in its drawer and closed it as a police siren wailed in the distance. She brushed her teeth, put on her shoes, and heard the unmistakable sound of a cop knock on the door. They were both white, but to her surprise, one was a woman.

"Ma'am, we've had a report of a disturbance involving a gun," the policewoman said, her face expressionless.

"That was me," she said. "Do you want the gun?" She turned toward the bedroom.

"Just tell us where it is, and we'll get it," the male officer said, quick and stern. The female officer handcuffed her while her partner retrieved the gun, and they marched her out of the complex to a black-and-white police car. As they pulled out, from the back window Mary could see shards of tinted glass scattered all over the pavement, soaking wet in the mist.

To her relief, she quickly learned that Nate hadn't been shot, after all, just hit with broken glass from the van window.

Before the trial, Nate moved his stuff out, took Keenan, and went to LA to live with Nicki. At the trial, Mary found out that her suspicions had all been true: Base was gay. Cathy was bringing men to their house to have sex with so that Base could get off on it and maybe participate if the right man came along. Nate wasn't the only one; he fell right into that trap.

She was still facing assault with a deadly weapon, though, and that would cause her enough trouble. She avoided serving any time, but lost her job, and then came the divorce papers from LA.

Mary traveled south to deal with it. She booked a roadside motel off Interstate 10 and called Nate. "We've got to get this paperwork in order," she said.

"Just sign the papers," Nate said.

"You can't file," Mary told him. "You haven't lived in LA long enough."

He didn't believe her, and the conversation turned ugly. When Nate finally said, "You tried to kill me!" Mary slammed down the phone. The next morning, when she tried to book one more night, her credit card didn't work. Neither did any of her other ones. Nate had canceled them.

"So, you're going to leave the mother of your children on the street," she said from a payphone in the parking lot of the motel.

"Why don't you just sign the papers," Nate said.

She explained again that she was the one who had to file under the law. "I personally don't care who files," she said. "I'm doing what my lawyer told me to do so we can be done." Her voice cracked a little.

Nate sighed. "I'm tired of this."

"Me, too," Mary said.

"Let's make this easier on each other," Nate said. "Stay here until we fix your credit cards. When you go back, start the divorce paperwork."

"Okay," Mary said, a little surprised.

"Also, Keenan stays here for now."

Mary's heart sank. *Her baby.* But then she thought of the family that was already in LA—Nate's sisters and their kids Q', Reese, Kizzy, and Mike—compared to her, one woman, no family, broke, and trying desperately to find a job.

"I need to always know exactly where you are," she said, "and he can't call anyone else 'mom.'"

* * *

Keenan woke up early that Saturday to the familiar sounds of his aunts chatting with Nicki, Dad's common-law wife, in the kitchen of their apartment. He could hear the playful screams of laughter from his baby sister Aesha, just two years old.

They lived in University Gardens, and his playground stretched from Figueroa to Jefferson and Vermont. The vanilla-colored building stretched out over a plot of land near the 110 Freeway. At night, he would hear the cars speeding by and the near misses of accidents with their screeching brakes.

The Gardens' location was a plus for any child under the age of twelve. It was right in the backyard of the University of Southern California, and often the children of the neighborhood spent their time running through its then-open campus, as well as any other part of South LA. Sometimes Keenan, his cousins, and the other kids from the neighborhood ran through the Natural History Museum, and other times they wandered through the science exhibits in the California Science Center. The security guards knew them, and it wasn't a big deal at that time to see children by themselves in every part of the neighborhood. The times were different, and they didn't have the same sense of danger that later generations would know too well every time they left their apartment.

South Central Los Angeles in the late '70s—or South Los Angeles, as it is now called—was not yet in the throes of what most people saw in the late '80s. Keenan was not exposed to crack or gang wars, and was too young to be aware of the Crips and the Bloods, who were just starting to form along their color lines. Children in his LA neighborhood played in the wide asphalt streets much the same way young African American children played in the streets in any inner city: Chicago, Harlem, Atlanta, Richmond, Boston. It was all the same.

This was a time when people still knew each other in the neighborhood, and didn't mind speaking out when they saw something wrong or someone doing wrong.

Keenan yawned as he walked into the kitchen, and his youngest aunt greeted him casually, "Are you gonna sleep all day? Q's waiting for you to wake up."

The apartment was cozy with bright light, plants, and a turnstile of family members coming through the door each weekend. Both aunts at the kitchen table lived in the same complex, and they each had two children, a boy and a girl. Keenan never considered what it meant to be alone or to have to play by himself. His years were built on laughter, hours of play, and an extended family, like most African American families, and his cousins were more like siblings because they played together, got spanked together, and were growing up together.

His favorite cousin, Q', burst through the door without knocking. He looked disapprovingly at Keenan in his pajamas. "I've been waiting for you all morning. Let's go!"

"Where do you want to go?" Keenan asked.

Q' and Keenan spent their weekdays after school running through the streets of Los Angeles and finding meaningfully mischievous things to do with their free time. Going to the museum was a breeze and a low-key day for Keenan and Q'.

But today—Saturday—was exceptional.

Keenan dressed quickly and followed Q' out the door and down the hall to his aunt's apartment. They grabbed a couple handfuls of bologna from the refrigerator, picked up their makeshift fishing poles (just a couple of sticks with some fishing line), and headed off to the park. With their poles over their shoulders, they looked ready for an adventure that didn't really fit the South Central Los Angeles locale.

As an adult, Keenan often wondered why no one ever stopped two boys walking down a street at least twenty miles from any beach with makeshift fishing sticks and a cooler full of water, to inquire just where they intended to occupy their time.

This Saturday, they walked past dozens of people peacefully strolling or sitting in the gardens, until they approached a circular pond made from dark stone. The flowers in that area of the park were well maintained, and today they saw more than the usual number of hummingbirds jumping from one bud to another. People huddled under the oaks for a picnic or just some relief from the California sun. The trees' shade covered large portions of the walkways and, taking advantage of the shade, Keenan and Q' stopped to bait their hooks with the bologna. The pond was only a few feet off, and it was filled with koi.

The boys dropped their hooks in, watching the giant fish drift through the shallow waters, twitching their graceful tails. Most were bright orange, looking like goldfish who had experienced a fairytale transformation into exaggerated versions of themselves. Others had different and more exotic markings and patterns on their bodies with long, trailing fins. They bumped into one another and moved their mouths in a motion that made it seem like they were kissing the very water they swam in. It was amazing to Keenan that they could be so content in that shallow, crowded pond. Their beauty and shape made him want to be close to them, to have them for his own.

Without worrying about who was looking, Keenan and Q' threw their lines in over and over and watched as the fish darted to the hook and gobbled the meat. Before even ten minutes had passed, Keenan had one with its jaw snagged on the line. Feeling the thrill of the hunt, he reeled the fish in and popped it in the cooler full of water. He studied it, looking for something special which would allow him to take it home and christen it as his new pet. Something in him wanted the prettiest, the biggest, and the one that didn't jump too far out of his hands.

"What are you going to do with it?" Q' asked. "Eat it?"

"No," Keenan said, and reached back into the cooler. The wounded Koi flopped in his hands as he threw it back, and as always, he recognized with some guilt that his dalliance of sport was actually causing it some harm. In fact, the koi never made it back to his home. Q' was fishing just to fish, but Keenan was sure that one day he would find the perfect one to take home to put in a tank and keep forever.

Ignoring the disapproving looks of those walking by, they fished all afternoon. Maybe it was better, in these shallow waters, to fish just for the fun of it.

* * *

Keenan's flip phone buzzed incessantly on the nightstand but could not break into his sleep.

"Keenan, your *phone*," his wife said, and his eyes blinked open.

Without turning over, he reached for it and mumbled, "Hello." Then his body stiffened and he woke completely.

His wife also woke up and watched him snap shut the phone and begin to pull on his clothes mechanically, his face a mask. "What happened?" she asked.

"There's a fire at the shop," he said. "I think it's all gone."

The next hours were a blur of ash and smoke as he looked over where his beloved shop had stood. He had come to Clark-Atlanta for college, stayed because of the opportunities, and made good. He had a wife, two amazing sons, and a thriving screenprinting business that he built from the ground up thanks to his side hustling while in undergrad.

And now it was gone. The income that put food on the table and supported his wife and two kids had literally gone up in smoke.

He drove home slowly from a day that had wiped him out, and fell into bed exhausted. As he spent the next day going through his paperwork and realizing what little he would be able to salvage from this economic disaster, the phone rang again with more tragedy. His beloved cousin Q' had died in the streets of LA.

He spent the next few weeks in a daze. One night, his wife asked him, "So, what are you going to do?"

Still stunned with his losses, he answered, "I don't know. Sit around a little. Figure things out."

She stiffened. "You're not going to sit around here and loaf off of me," she said.

And just like that, Keenan's love for her died.

There was little to be negotiated around a "no income, no us" declaration. He wondered, *How does marriage, a covenant from God, turn from a "yes" to a condition?* Her declaration sent numerous thoughts tumbling through his mind night after night as he contemplated divorce and the seeming end of his marriage. This was not something he wanted, but circumstances had developed in such a way that the death of the relationship could not be ignored or denied. He thought he was building forever and that this was a snag in the road. However, what for him was a snag had turned into a deal-breaker.

But his first goal was to get back on his feet. Inside him was still a determined entrepreneur who voiced that he had gone through too much to just let it all go. He decided to do both: move forward and restart his business with a focus on software development, another area of expertise for him.

Friendship Community Church had been a client for several years, and they hired him to do software-development work, paying him enough to put a deposit down on a new home. It was a rental property in a nice, gated community called the Gates at Bouldercrest; he resigned himself to begin divorce proceedings and move out.

He had met his ex-wife at the age of twenty-three. Now at age thirty-two, he was moving alone into a semi-furnished townhouse near East Atlanta Village. He dragged his bed and some other furnishings into what would become a newly minted bachelor pad, and set up the screen-printing equipment from his previous business in the garage.

And, he wondered to himself, *What next?*

Beyond the current pain and confusion he felt about the marriage ending, he felt the first stirrings of a need to meet someone, to find a partner . . . or at least a date. It was easy to tell someone that, yes, he enjoyed cooking, traveling, simple evenings at home, jazz concerts, and staying active. But he knew that may describe the vast majority of American men who live close to urban, metropolitan areas. He just believed that there was a chip inside of him that could connect with someone else and open a door to a relationship that he knew that he deserved.

His problem, as he saw it, was more centered on the fact that the last time he understood dating was when he was a young man. Sure, some things never change: pay the tab, treat her like a lady, invite her out to dinner. He was just used to being married and having someone there who already knew him. He was well aware of the stretch it would be to go from being a family man to being a single man in his thirties and relearning himself, as well as learning someone new. There were so many new things to sift through! Did he still like what he liked in years past, or should he try something different? How different should he go? Far right or far left? Where would the type of woman he was looking for place herself on a weeknight or a Saturday evening? Was he still sure that's what he wanted?

Keenan knew that the last thing he wanted was a counterfeit carbon of his ex-wife. Ideally, he wanted someone who possessed the same wholesome qualities: his ex-wife was nice, pretty, good with kids, and could cook. But there is always so much more to a woman than these general characteristics, and he was eager to meet someone with her own independent personality and experiences.

This algebra equation made him ponder exactly what he wanted in the months after his marriage broke up. He knew enough to look for a woman who was athletic and had her own interests, career, financial stability, and life. He also knew that he wanted someone who was ambitious and able to achieve her dreams with or without him.

Even though the problem of how he had changed and how

dating had changed still lingered in the back of his mind, it wasn't a stumbling block. It was just something to keep in mind. He knew enough about himself and enough about women to get out there and find exactly what he wanted, or even what he needed.

As the months stretched on, Keenan continued waiting for that type of love. When it tarried, he thought about searching for it. Where would he find a woman who was beautiful, ambitious, honest, and charismatic? Someone adventurous who wanted to explore new places? Someone active who would encourage a healthy lifestyle?

At church one Sunday, the minister seemed to read his mind as he praised the qualities of an ideal woman. That night, thinking of the sermon and his own loneliness, he switched off the TV and paged through his Bible to the scriptures that the minister had spoken on: Proverbs 31. As he read through the familiar chapter, he jotted down a list of her qualities. She was memorialized as a woman who:

- Makes sound business decisions
- Values and completes productive work
- Is aware of her ability to generate wealth for her family
- Knows when to rest and when to press through with a task, concern, or prayer
- Has her husband's full confidence
- Can select the best and is knowledgeable with her own skills and talents
- Knows how to cook and manage a household
- Has invested in property or some means of financial stability

Keenan continued reading, wondering how he could meet this

woman one day. He read about her compassion, her dignity, strength, and wisdom. Tall order or not, Keenan decided to begin his search. He felt an excitement at this new beginning similar to how he had felt those summer afternoons with Q': fishing pole over his shoulder, hook and bait, and the willingness to offer a comfortable new home to the one he selected.

Yet, as he remembered fondly their mischievous fishing trips, he chose to forget how he had always found some excuse to throw them back, and how happy they were to return to their natural habitat.

Francis

THE GATES AT Bouldercrest sat in tree-shrouded Southeast Atlanta and resembled the neighborhood Keenan always thought that he would move to when he was a child. Maple and crabapple trees lined a paved street that snaked through the gated community. There were A-frame brick homes with front-load garages, and children zipped by his mailbox on bikes and skateboards every day.

It initially felt abnormal for him to wake up alone in the house without hearing his sons crashing through the living room and taking charge of the hallway with their toys. But he soon realized, thanks to the former owners, that this quiet neighborhood was where he was supposed to reside for the time being. He was grateful for the blessing of moving into a house that the previous owners had left with furniture, a washer and dryer, and other household items he needed so much at this point in his life. He moved into a home that was waiting for him to stretch out and take ownership.

But that didn't make it easier. Once dusk fell and the orange glow from the streetlights clicked on over his driveway, he was always reminded that he was separated from his boys and from the relationship that he thought was solidly built.

Francis Moore lived two doors down from his townhouse, and Keenan used to see her by her mailbox, opening mail and then scanning through whatever was in the envelope. Some things she would toss immediately into a nearby trash bin. The important stuff was what she tucked protectively in her armpit before walking back to her front door.

He didn't even know he was watching her at first. She was just a neighbor out getting her mail. There were other neighbors, too: Mrs. Williams with the three cats, the young couple still clearly in the honeymoon stage of their relationship, the growing family two doors down.

And Francis Moore.

She was young, he realized, to be in such a family-centered neighborhood. A couple of weeks later, he found himself wondering if she had someone special in her life. *Damn*, he thought to himself. *Why am I always thinking about this girl?*

Driving to work one day, he heard the song "You Don't Know My Name" by Alicia Keys. He always liked the song, but now it made him think about his own situation, so close to this woman and yet completely invisible.

Now he couldn't lie to himself. He was hooked. Each time he saw her, his eyes soaked her in. She was tall, light-skinned, and more than fit: her long legs and trim waist gave her the wholesome, athletic look of a college track star. Her eyebrows arched perfectly over wide, brown eyes, and the apples of her cheeks gave her a smile that melted his heart.

Finally, one bright weekend day, he could stand it no longer.

21

He ventured out of his garage and caught her at the mailbox. "Hello," he said, smiling, trying to act natural.

Neighborly, even.

She studied him for half a second before responding to his greeting. Almost as if she wasn't sure if she wanted to engage with anyone.

"Hi," she replied with a hesitant smile that made him inch closer toward her.

They found that both hailed from California and had attended Clark-Atlanta, but she was an alumna who had completed her MSW.

Keenan felt captivated, but now that the thrill of the first hello was over, he turned cautious again. Still in the throes of working through a divorce, he didn't want to bring her into anything or start something which might or might not work, or become insanely complicated. It was the right move, because Francis was cautious, too.

So, their conversations over the next two months revolved around their hobbies and their common interests. They eventually began to go out and enjoy each other's company, and it was simple. Easy. Nonphysical. Nonsexual. Just two people appreciating another's time. They shot pool like brothers, played one-on-one basketball, jogged around Stone Mountain, and carried on as if they had known one another for years.

Other times, Francis would come over to his place and they would watch TV and talk about nothing for hours. He appreciated that she made room for him in her life, and he slowly accepted that this was a new chapter in his life that wouldn't hinder his current progress.

The first time they slept together, there had been no sex. He had volunteered to host a party for a friend's birthday. It was the first time he'd had an event at his home or hosted anything since the divorce, and he was touched that Francis had pitched in, made his friends comfortable, and helped him clean up afterward. Exhausted, they had both dropped onto the couch to watch a movie and fell asleep naturally, comfortable with each other. Keenan woke up to feel her next to him, and although they were still in the clothes they wore at the party, the intimacy of having her warm and beautiful body next to his made him realize how much he wanted more than just conversation and friendship.

He wanted Francis to be his lover. But did she want him?

He wondered, but he didn't plan anything, especially when she laughed off their experience of waking up with each other and didn't seem to feel any one way about it.

About a week after the party, she came over as usual. They set themselves up on the couch to watch a movie, but something was different. Last week he woke up with her in his arms, and it seemed to break some internal physical barrier that she had tended to hold between them.

He sat with his arm around her, and she cuddled into him as they watched. He found himself admiring her beauty all over again. Her T-shirt clung to her soft, round breasts, flat stomach, and narrow ribcage; her sexy, long legs were tucked up under her. Almost unconsciously, he began to stroke her collarbone and the side of her neck as she watched the movie.

"That's nice," she breathed.

Taking that soft affirmation as his sign to keep going, Keenan gently lifted her chin and pressed his lips against hers. She opened her mouth immediately, and all of the erotic energy that he had tried so hard to suppress as they slowly got to know each other came rushing into him in one giant wave. She had been so hesitant at first to get to know him, and their platonic stage had lasted a long time. But in this one kiss, he felt how much she wanted him, and encouraged by her passion, he finally allowed himself to stroke and squeeze her sexy breasts, rolling her nipples with his thumb and fingers while he kissed her, making her squirm.

To his shock and delight, she was the one to unzip his pants, but he wasn't going to let her lead from there. Instead, he quickly rolled them over on the couch, and while the movie played sense-lessly on, she wrapped her long, gorgeous legs around him and bucked up against him as he plunged himself into her, gorging himself on her like a man who has been starving for days.

He had been starving. Starving for love, for affection, for sex. He guessed she had been starving, too.

They couldn't get enough of each other. After that first explosive moment, he led her to his bedroom, and it was dawn before they fell asleep, exhausted, in a new role as lovers as well as friends.

It was passionate, but it was peaceful, too. They had opened themselves up to fully experience the relationship that they had been building for the past three months. They became a couple almost effortlessly, and Keenan loved that she had no qualms about partnering with him when it was his weekend with the boys. He soon began to rest in her affection, love, and presence in his life.

In spring 2006, Francis lost her job, and she decided to rent her house and move in with Keenan. They talked extensively about her next move, but her mind was made up to return to Emory University and pursue a second master's in public health and then switch careers.

This left most of the bills on his shoulders, but he didn't mind. He was thinking of what it meant to be a partner with someone, forever.

By June 2006, the solitaire engagement ring had been riding

around in the trunk of his car for about two weeks. Keenan was waiting and watching for the right moment to ask her to be his bride. The hard part was navigating around the emotions that constantly psyched him out of asking her. Something in her kept him from being able to go through with any proposal. Like clock-work, he would kick himself during the day while at work and try to raise up his courage while handling job responsibilities and going about his workday. Once he arrived home, he never felt comfortable bringing up the subject. He recognized his reluctance as a sign from his subconscious, but his love for Francis had turned him into a living, moving, breathing idiot of hope.

As much as he welcomed the opportunity to partner and share a life with someone new who supported him and allowed him to support her, he knew something was wrong. Besides just the worry that it might not be accepted, a heavy gut feeling was keep-ing him from a proposal. He pushed it back and pushed it back, but soon admitted to himself that there was real trouble.

Their disagreements were escalating into foreign territory that he didn't regularly see in his childhood home or his marital home with his ex-wife and boys.

One particularly hectic Sunday morning, he couldn't find something in the kitchen. She dragged by him and he gave her a once-over. *Moods are allowed*, he thought. *They come to the best and the worst of us.* Since he was aware that she had been in a considerably long bad mood (since Friday), he prepared himself to inquire her opinion instead of asking her to do something.

"Babe, I'm looking for the—" he began as she passed by him into the living room.

"Can't you just find it yourself? I swear, you have to be the most annoying thing in my life right now," she said, avoiding eye contact.

His first thought: *Is she crazy?*

His second thought: *No. Something else must have happened.*

"What's going on?" he asked, preparing himself for anything. She had become verbally abusive over the last couple of weeks, and he was treading lightly.

Francis flopped onto the sofa and scooted into the corner, content to finish watching an episode of a popular cooking show. "It would be nice if you just fucking left me alone for one minute. I don't have to talk about any and everything with you all the time," she said.

Keenan approached the sofa. In a bad mood or not, this wasn't going down. Absolutely not.

"You can talk a little more respectfully," he said as he stood near the sofa.

She didn't take kindly to his posture, his voice, the angle of the sun, or possibly the taste of the air in her mouth. Their argument escalated and moved back into the kitchen before she began to swing.

He dodged her swings and tried to calm her down, disturbed by how familiar these physical outbursts had become. This wasn't the first time. Sometimes he just walked away, determined to avoid an even uglier situation. These were exhausting arguments that felt like someone dumped hot slime on the top of his head.

She thought he said . . . he told her he didn't . . . he told her it wasn't . . . "You're playing games . . . "

And then she slapped him.

She actually slapped his face.

He focused his eyes on the cabinets over the stainless-steel stove and wanted to walk away. This time was different, though. He hadn't been in a fight in years, so he wondered, *How do you end up getting smacked in your own house by someone who just told you they loved you?* How did he even tell another man that every argument with this woman resulted in him being stole on like it was 1995 and he was standing in the parking lot of a downtown club?

He blocked the next swing and grabbed her by both shoulders. "Stop putting your hands on me," he firmly said. "I don't want to be slapped, so please stop doing that."

When he released his grip on her shoulders, she stumbled backward into the dishwasher, grabbing the counter behind her. She seemed stunned by the fact that he physically stopped her, and it did just enough to bring some sense to the situation.

The hitting and verbal abuse quelled after that point, but he never felt that reassuring push or release to move forward with any proposal. How could he authentically move forward with a proposal after dealing with any type of abuse in a relationship? That's a relationship and trust killer.

His frustration felt like a pressure cooker and he felt like, though there was now a brief respite, she would continue to cuss him out, call him out of his name, and even smack him whenever she felt frustrated.

What man can put up with that?

His friend Derrick encouraged him to end it, but he couldn't. He was cut from a cloth that boasted an allegiance to commitment, with covenant being the ultimate goal. He held to this ideology even if their covenant was nowhere near to being discussed.

Plus, he didn't exactly want to end up like Derrick, a serial dater who sometimes slept with five to seven women a week. So, it was hard to take his advice seriously.

He held on through Francis's graduation in June and hoped for the best.

Late June is exceptionally beautiful in Atlanta. The crepe myrtle and dogwood trees brag on their color, and the city has a sleepy

Southern wonderland appeal to it that begs you to sit in outdoor cafes and stroll just a little longer through the parks.

Enchanted by the evening weather report and the special close-ness that they were sharing after making up, Keenan called Francis from work and told her they were going out for dinner. The horrendous traffic that evening didn't sway them from laughing and having a good time. The stop-and-go maze of brake lights gave them extra time to laugh at some of the topics that used to taunt them into a full battle royale. The arguments had just about ceased, and a sweetness had returned to the relationship. He was convinced that this was further proof that no relationship is perfect and that each one goes through its own growing pains and cycles.

Once they arrived at the steakhouse on Piedmont Avenue, Francis and Keenan responded to each other as if they had just met. There was giggling, blushing, and all sorts of awkwardness that should have been a thing of the past. He watched her finish her wine and zeroed in on her lips, already planning in his head to make love to her for as long as possible that evening.

Why not watch her moan and grip the headboard with an en-gagement ring on her finger?

"I don't see any reason for us to not move to the next step in this relationship," he said as the waiter took their plates. He watched her eyes carefully for anything less than an agreement.

"The next step?" Francis replied, looking as if he asked her to go outside and push the car back to their house.

"Would you consider a marriage proposal from me?"

He had expected her eyes to swell with water. A deep inhalation. A change in body posture that lent itself to being overwhelmed.

"Don't you ever fucking do that," she quickly replied. "That's the last thing I want."

He blinked as he replayed the last two minutes of his life. Based on what he thought he heard, he wasn't sure if he had just suffered a mini-stroke.

"Wait . . . what?" he asked, glancing at the happy couples sitting nearby at their happy relationship islands of white-linen tablecloths. "Are you saying no?"

The waiter slipped the black-leather case with the bill near Keenan's water glass and thanked them for dining at the steakhouse. Keenan kept his eyes on the bill, too ashamed to look up and see if he had heard anything. One hand rested on the black-leather case next to his free hand. The other hand held the ring box in his jacket pocket.

Francis and Keenan held each other's gaze in a Mexican standoff.

"What do you want?" he asked, not really wanting to hear her answer. It was obvious that she didn't want to marry him. He just wanted to know the nature of his competition.

"I'm not interested in marriage, Keenan. I'm not—I'm just not ready for a family yet. You have traveled the world, and I haven't. You're seasoned in your career, and I am not. I want to experience life before I have a family. Let's keep it the way it is."

She shifted in her seat and glanced at the couple sitting near them. Keenan felt relieved that this also felt awkward to her as he mechanically paid the bill and peeled his tongue from the roof of his dry mouth. She started to say something else, but he slowly shook his head and passed the black-leather case to the passing waiter.

"It's okay. You ready to go?" There was no need to continue the humiliation.

The ride home was oddly pleasant because both acted like nothing out of the ordinary just happened. Something like, "I'll have coq au vin, mesclun salad, Pinot Grigio, and a strong middle finger to the nigga who thinks I wanna marry his ass." Neither one of them wanted to seemingly act like they just put their feelings on the table without any chaser.

He awakened the next morning way before her. As she slept peacefully, he slipped out of the bed and dressed in the closet. By noon, he had returned the ring and some of his feelings.

After she graduated, Francis secured a new job and she began to hang out with her friends every Friday and Saturday night. Keenan thought she would kick in financially around the house, but she was rarely home on the weekends. They used to work out together, but she found a personal trainer and stopped something they always enjoyed doing. She wasn't putting time into the relationship, and eventually that last bit of electric "something" that makes a relationship into a relationship cooled off into a slow, thick sludge that neither one of them wanted to address.

It stank. It was heavy, and it pulled you into something deeper if you tried to maneuver around in it.

One year later, Francis came home and told him that she lost her job. But he didn't get mad or hold it over her head. Change was already afoot because he had recently left his job at NBS TV station and shut down his screen-printing shop to work for a telecom company as a contractor. He had also just secured full custody of his boys, then fourteen and ten. He and his ex-wife had long ago agreed that when the boys grew older and needed a male role model to guide them into adulthood, it would be his turn to be the primary caregiver.

Once again, Keenan thought of how his ex-wife had spoiled him. They had never quarreled over their custody plans; they were partners in building their children's future and would never let their private feelings interfere.

Now the boys were with him, and even though Francis and

Keenan were practically living as roommates, they accepted her and loved her as part of their family. The house was in full upheaval, and they tried to adjust to this by becoming an even tighter family unit.

Or at least, he and the boys were.

"I applied for a job in North Carolina and I got it," Francis blurted out one night as they were unloading the dishwasher after dinner. The boys watched TV in the next room. He glanced over toward them to make sure they didn't hear anything.

"You're leaving?" he said, trying to contain his disappointment. He knew she was applying to many different positions in the area. Journeying out of state just wasn't something he thought she would do.

"Only for six months," she said as she touched his arm. "It won't be long, and then I'll return."

She cleared her throat as he stared at her, arms crossed over his chest and repeatedly glancing toward the boys in the living room. "So, this has nothing to do with me getting full custody of my sons?"

She grimaced. "You know, I thought you would say that, and I talked myself into believing that I was overreacting. Cheers to you for being so spot on," she whispered.

"I just find it amazing that you decide to run off to North Carolina two weeks after my sons move in." She wasn't going to be let off the hook that easy.

She tossed a dish towel onto the counter, and he kept an eye on her hands.

"That's not fair!" she said with her voice rising. "I applied to this position months ago, and I've been interviewing for at least three weeks."

Months ago. Okay. He cut her a side-eye glance and began to remove glasses from the dishwasher. "Francis, you haven't communicated much to me since you graduated," he spoke barely above a whisper. His full intent was to keep the incident muted so his sons could remain clueless and never have a memory of this night.

"I can send you child support to help out with the boys. You know I love them and that I'm only looking for a way to build and stabilize my career," she pleaded.

Seeing that this was going nowhere—especially since she already accepted the position—he simply said, "I understand, sweetie," and passed her a plate, signaling that the conversation was over.

Just as over as their sex life.

The next few weeks included them driving to Raleigh to help move into her apartment and sign the lease.

There was no tension, and there were no tears. It was what it was, and they once again pretended that they weren't just slapped with a cold, wet rag of reality.

They pulled up to the leasing office at Francis's new apartment complex, and Keenan was resigned to silence. She was clearly excited by the way her eyes twinkled and her lips turned up into her adorable smile. The small talk between them was silly, and it was one of their fun moments that he knew he would miss immensely after this weekend.

Mrs. Lewis, the perky, blonde leasing agent, re-entered her office with a stack of papers and two pens before sitting behind her desk.

"Okay, here we go!" she chirped as she placed a pen down in front of each one of them. She noticed that Keenan didn't pick up the pen. "Are you not signing?" Mrs. Lewis asked as she blinked and looked between Francis and him.

"It's just me," Francis quickly said as she began to flip through the leasing document in front of her.

"Oh, I'm sorry. I misunderstood when I saw both of you today!"

Mrs. Lewis was overly apologetic and blushed in embarrassment. Keenan settled into his seat like the spook who sat by the door.

"Well, either way, I have an eight-month lease with all the terms and conditions we discussed during the visit," Mrs. Lewis said as she pointed to the first signature line. "Please start by signing here."

Well, damn. What was happening to their relationship? Francis looked straight ahead. Keenan slowly moved forward in his seat and turned to face her.

"You told me that you would only be gone for six months," he said, careful to keep his tone casual.

Mrs. Lewis busied herself in the leasing document and then started to dig through a drawer in her desk, looking for something important.

"That's all that they had, Keenan," Francis said with the pen still in her grasp. "I felt like it was worth it to stay a bit longer and build a career. It's only two months, though. Not long."

Mrs. Lewis popped up from her leather swivel chair and said, "I think I left a page on the copier." She bustled out of the door and disappeared down the hallway.

"So, fuck what we have, right?" His voice trailed off as he mentally restructured what the rest of 2012 would look like. Actually, what the rest of his life would look like. Almost seven years, and he found himself here again. Starting over alone in a house that was meant to hold a family.

"Don't say that. We can see each other every other weekend," Francis said. Her eyes still pleaded with him. Was it because she wanted them to stay together, or that she didn't want Mrs. Lewis to put the apartment on hold? Keenan wasn't sure.

The idea of marriage was once again floating through his head. He loved her and didn't want to lose her.

Try hard, remember?

Be who you are, remember?

He was a man who loved being in a relationship and loved the woman he was bound to in his current relationship.

She signed the lease and Keenan took her out to dinner, helped her find a bedroom set, and held her in his arms for a while before his flight back to Atlanta that night. He wasn't sure if that was the last time he would see her or the last time they would share the dwindling bit of love between them.

"I don't want to be without you. You know that, right?" he said that evening as they said their goodbyes in the foyer of her new apartment.

"I love you so much. You know I want to be with you, but I have to get my life together," Francis said before she nuzzled her head into his neck.

"There's an online site that will allow you to design an engagement ring. Why don't you go online, design it, and let me know what you want? Sound good?" He felt that he had to at least try. Maybe this would change her mind.

She pulled away from him and beamed with a smile that he hadn't seen in a while. She nodded her head. "Okay, baby. Sure, I will."

Keenan held her some more and thanked God for working out another glitch. Sometimes you throw in the towel, and sometimes you keep fighting after the bell. This was one of those times where he believed he was going to keep fighting despite the bell's constant ringing. He was fighting his way to a TKO, even after the match was over.

Keenan left that evening fighting the urge to click his heels in the air. Still fighting.

They did indeed see each other every weekend for the rest of the year, but she never found the time to design the ring, or go online to the site, or even tell him when she would find time to do it.

In December 2012, they were driving through the streets of suburban Raleigh when she decided that she wanted to stop by the mall. It was a day of "looking" for them, as they drove through gentrified Durham and a multicolored leaf–ridden Raleigh.

The Raleigh-Durham area was beautiful in the winter, and it beckoned, in Keenan's opinion, for love to be solidified and lives to be built within its borders. He imagined them moving into a rehabbed loft in Downtown Durham, or him coming home to a brick colonial in Chapel Hill. He would walk into a kitchen that smelled like lasagna and garlic bread as the boys finished their homework and a newborn slept in a nearby crib. She would be busy working on her laptop and telling the boys to "Hurry up before dinner."

He turned the car around and drove to the mall, parking near a retail jewelry store. She wasn't aware of his plan or that they even parked near a store that could possibly hold the key to the next chapter of their lives.

He turned off the ignition and told her to look up.

She looked and turned her head, looking for the object of his focus. "What am I looking at?" she exclaimed before reaching into her purse and dabbing on some lipstick.

He kept the dumb grin on his face and pointed toward the jewelry store.

Francis looked around, chuckled, and said, "What are you doing, silly?"

He pointed again to the jewelry store. She turned her head and looked between the store and him before her smile faded. "Keenan, I told you . . . " she began gently as she zipped up her purse and put it on the floor.

"I know what you said earlier, but come on. We can at least look," he said before jumping out of the car and shutting the door.

The only issue is that she didn't move. Francis sat in the passenger seat, elbow resting on the passenger-side door window.

"Francis, get out of the car," Keenan said as he stood in front of the car hood. It was a windy day, and it felt like a sudden gust took the rest of his words. Did she hear him?

Her eyes went straight through him and stared at nothing in particular.

"Come on!" he shouted. "It's cold out here, girl."

He rubbed his hands together. His Clark-Atlanta sweatshirt wasn't created for this type of weather. Francis twisted the corner of her mouth and looked down into her lap.

"Francis, get out of the goddamn car!"

A family walking by turned in his direction and sped up their pace. He felt his face flushing pink in anger.

Francis shook her head and shrugged.

And just like that, the anger vanished. He was depleted. Done. Finished.

Fuck it. He could finally see what it was, and now that he was able to stand in this place again, he realized that he could move on knowing he did everything that he could.

He got back in the car and they rode in silence back to her apartment. Later that night, he told Francis that he no longer wanted a long-distance relationship and that he was ready to date and see other people. He told her that if she ever returned to Atlanta, they could talk then. At the moment, though, it just didn't seem like she was taking them seriously as a couple.

Keenan returned to Atlanta with a new outlook, one that didn't necessarily involve trying harder, and he was fine with that.

A couple weeks later he met Tanya.

Three

Francis v. Tanya

KEENAN'S CAREER BECKONED. There wasn't enough work at the telecom company, so he decided to look elsewhere in the metropolitan area and found a position with a pay increase and larger workload at a national department store's technology center in Johns Creek. It was a well-heeled city north of Atlanta that offered its fair share of celebrities, gated communities, and multimillion-dollar homes.

Keenan was still reeling from the break-up with Francis, but not so much that he couldn't find the strength to jump back into the dating scene. He was working crazy hours, and it was hard to find time to meet anyone. He missed Francis, and realized that he might have taken for granted all the help she provided him over the years with his boys. It softened him, realizing that her rejection had a lot to do with the fact that they were at different stages of their lives. Still, it was hard being a single parent with full custody, and his hands were full.

Keenan had always been one of the many people who shook his head at the number of people who get duped or murdered by the strangers they met online. He was well aware of the risks, but he figured that it couldn't be that bad. In fact, it seemed to him that a lot of people were jumping online to meet new people—it's just that no one was really talking about it. He had been so wrapped up with women he actually knew that it was never a thought to go online and sift through profiles of smiling women who may or may not be crazy.

He placed the remote on an end table and sat down in front of his laptop. He knew his life was either going to turn for the better or just crash and burn next to the ashes of his time with Francis and Tanya. He typed the online dating site into the web browser and began to fill out his profile. It was grievous to write things about himself, so he typed in his interests as quickly as possible: traveling, fishing, reading, laughing, dancing, sports, handyman jobs. His looks: five-foot-eleven, athletic and toned, with hazel eyes, black hair. No way on smoking, but a social drinker.

He searched his hard drive for the best two or three pictures. He had no problem describing himself, but he knew that love didn't always come in the same package. He knew from his past that he could fall in love with someone curvy, skinny, athletic. He wasn't sure what would grab his attention. *But how*, he wondered, *do you maintain an openness for something new and still lean on what you want?*

He returned to himself and delved into this new world that was nothing short of modern-day human fishing. He clicked everything: about average, curvy, toned; blue eyes, gray eyes, hazel eyes; light-brown hair; never married, widowed; definitely want kids, someday wants kids, not sure if she wants kids; Hindu, Jewish, Agnostic, Catholic, Christian Protestant, Islam; model, education, administrative, executive, government, and construction fields.

The dragnet was wide, but he kept the height, income, and smoking tightly wrapped around his preference. No smoking, and nothing under $50,000 per year, or shorter than five-foot-eight. He also stated that he was not fond of weaves or fake breasts.

He'd hardly begun to review the surprising number of active women on the dating site when he saw a familiar picture. Stacy was a friend he hadn't seen in years, and had lost her phone number. He messaged her through the system and she messaged right back. They agreed to meet up at an Italian restaurant a few days later. He arrived early and got a table, and when she walked up, he almost choked on his breadstick. She looked just like her picture from the neck up, but in person he could see that she was unmistakably pregnant. On a date!

She was an old enough friend that he felt comfortable jumping right into the issue. "So you having much luck being pregnant on a dating app?" he asked.

She shrugged. It clearly didn't bother her. Instead of answering him directly, she told him about the father. "He had so many girlfriends," she said. "I thought I would be different, but I wasn't."

They had a nice time catching up, and Keenan was glad to be in touch with his old friend. But when he opened the door to his house, he walked straight over to his laptop and disabled his dating app profile. Never mind.

One day he went to lunch at the health-food market near his office and ran into a former client. A sophisticated acquaintance of a certain age, she was delicately pecking at a salad heavy on quinoa at a booth near the cash registers. She saw him in line, smiled, and waved him over in a friendly but imperious way — her usual style. She ran an interior-design business and had hired Keenan to build a few websites for the company over the years.

Angela loved to matchmake, and had previously tried to fix him up with Lex, one of her daughter's friends, but he was married at the time. Tossing that aside, the friendship between Angela and him hadn't changed.

He joined her and they caught up over lunch. She was always something of a mentor and confidante, and he found himself telling her about his recent breakup with Francis, that he now had full custody of his two boys, and that it was extremely hard to keep up with their schedules.

"Enough about me," he said. "How are your two daughters?"

She smiled like the Cheshire Cat and replied, "You should call my daughter Tanya. You know she's single and carrying two kids on her own now, also."

Tanya. Keenan knew her daughter Tanya. Like her mother, she radiated sophistication. She was a little closer to his age than Francis, a parent who was doing well for herself as an IT exec in the technology department at a global payroll service company. Tanya managed to be both utterly professional and eye-poppingly glamorous.

She was also raising two kids who happened to have a former NFL running back as their daddy. Tanya not only knew what she wanted; she was quite used to getting it. It was hard for Keenan not to assume certain things about her, because of the stereotypes associated with baller chicks, but this was a new life for him, so he vowed to put aside any skepticism and get to know her a little better.

"Hey, this is Keenan," he said easily into the phone, having promised Angela he would call. "So, your mom is setting us up."

She laughed just as easily, and Keenan felt his last bit of concern drop.

With no effort, they arranged to meet at the popular restaurant, not linen-tablecloth type, but a nice, mid-ranged price place. She walked in radiating class, as always, and they chatted and laughed until they were the last people seated, with the waiters keeping a respectable but impatient distance. All of his preconceived judgments were quickly tossed aside.

Tanya became more important in his life, even though Francis had not fully disappeared. She would call from time to time, but it was increasingly important for Keenan to move forward. He'd never been one to remain stagnant, and every time he reminisced on the many times he sought Francis's long-term companionship, he felt a divine release to just let it go. He was coming to understand that there's a peace in due diligence.

Plus, Tanya was very insightful on parenting tips, and so he found value in what she had to offer through her conversation. And she offered more than just helpful tips; she knew how to get things done. As he told her about his struggles to not only be a good father, but make his house a home, she nodded sagely then whipped out her smartphone.

"I'm texting you the number of an excellent nanny," she said. "You need one."

Keenan interviewed the nanny that Tanya suggested and hired her that week. His life eased, and his appreciation of Tanya increased.

Toward the middle of January 2013, about a half a month after they met, he received a cheery morning phone call from Tanya as he sat at his desk.

"Let's go on a cruise to the Bahamas for your birthday!"

Wow. Keenan was a little overwhelmed by her enthusiasm. He knew she was used to ballers and football players who had a long budget, but he was not that guy. He did well enough with his salary, and he knew it was nothing to scoff at. But to just buy a two-passenger cruise during the height of cruise season for a woman he'd only known for three weeks . . . and for his own birthday?

Nah, that was a pass.

And it's not because he didn't like her. He was definitely interested; but he wasn't a birthday kind of guy. Birthdays had always been low-key days for him. This offer to have something new was great, but not that tempting. Yes, he was turning forty on February 5, but he could care less if the deal was going to end at five p.m. that day.

He never called her back and hoped it would blow over. It didn't matter, though, because his cell phone rang again shortly after five thirty p.m.

"I bought a package for a cruise to the Bahamas! Happy birth-day!" Tanya exclaimed.

Keenan leaned back in his chair and shook his head. She was definitely more excited about this than he was. But what could he say to a woman who just bought him something that he'd never had? Until that point, no woman had ever bought a vacation pack-age for him and done it just to celebrate a milestone in his life.

Even though he didn't understand the offer, he appreciated her wanting to spoil him. It was a new sensation.

They began to spend more time together, and the long dinners ended with long, sweet kisses in her driveway, then on her couch, then between her thousand-thread-count Egyptian cotton sheets.

Tanya made love like a French courtesan. Keenan had never been with anyone who shaved themselves completely bare; he didn't care one way or another, really, but the novelty of it turned him on. She knew all the moves, but even more, she knew how to do the wildest things with intimacy and style.

The new experience of Tanya's body and her skills created a whirlwind of days and nights that continued even onto the cruise. On the quick flight to Miami, they sipped champagne and gazed into each other's eyes. Then Tanya insisted that they take a limo to the port. Keenan didn't mind. As they checked in, he felt like a rock star.

"I have a surprise for you," Tanya said as they opened the door to their cabin, and Keenan saw that their unassuming room had been given the romance treatment. Rose petals sprinkled the bed sheets, and another bottle of champagne was waiting on ice.

Tanya plucked a chocolate-covered strawberry out of a waiting silver bowl and fed it to Keenan. "Happy birthday, baby," she purred, and he tasted the sweet fruit and chocolate while he felt her hands skillfully unbuckle his belt and her soft body slink against him, going down.

"What are you doing?" he said.

But she couldn't answer him at that moment because her mouth was full of his dick. He eased back a step so he could fall back onto the small double bed and let her do her best. She sucked his cock like the baller chick she was: lapping at his swollen head slowly and placing her lips lightly around the tip, then plunging down enthusiastically, sucking hard all the way. Her hand cupped his balls, holding them with the lightest touch while her soft, wet mouth rode up and down his shaft until he could feel the head of his dick at the back of her throat. He exploded in her and she gulped it down, then wiped her mouth off with her hand and smiled at him wickedly.

What could go wrong?

He was about to find out.

At dinner, full of endorphins and champagne, he almost missed the importance of Tanya's oh-so-casual statement: "I'm not seeing anyone else, you know."

"I didn't know that," he said evenly, suddenly thinking fast. So, the ride was over. Tanya wanted him to be her man. Keenan wasn't ready for that type of commitment with her. It had only been a month, and he felt like it was too soon.

For one, he was still talking to Francis quite frequently, so he couldn't guarantee that his heart would be completely with Tanya. Second, it seemed like Tanya never asked him any questions about himself, and he wanted her to truly know him. A month had passed, and she had never even been inside of his home. She was moving too fast, and he was moving too slow.

It also seemed like she mentioned her child's father in every conversation. Also, even though she made love like a goddess/demon, she was also a little too good . . . too performance-oriented. Like she was doing it for herself and her ego. And, her fake breasts had kind of turned him off. Who puts implants in their body?

He tried not to let it get to him, and on the surface, the romance continued. Mind-blowing sex, sweet moments, fun in the sun. But he could tell she was waiting for an answer, that she wanted more.

So, in the hope that they could work things out and be honest adults with each other, he explained his feelings to her as they sat on deck one night in a secluded spot. To passersby, it looked like they were having a romantic evening. If they looked closer, they would have seen Tanya's tears and wilted shoulders. They couldn't come to an agreement, even though each was convinced they were right.

"We don't know each other well enough yet," Keenan said.

"I think I know you," Tanya countered.

"Oh, yeah? Then what's my favorite color?"

Tanya paused. "Champagne," she answered, and they both laughed.

Keenan was a little on edge when he woke up the next morning, but as he shaved in the tiny bathroom, he heard Tanya wake up and sing out the sweetest "Good morning." They were on their way to go ashore at Nassau and rent jet skis on Goodman's Bay Beach. Who could stay mad while jetting through the clear, turquoise water, with the wind and spray at their faces?

After an hour bouncing on the waves, they turned toward the shore, cutting the speed to a crawl and gently easing back to the beach. From the shore, they saw their jet-ski vendor beckoning to them.

"So, is this where we leave them?" Tanya asked.

"Not sure," he replied. As they were talking, they slowed their jet skis and were taken by surprise at the sudden instability of the machine. Both capsized at the same moment and fell into the warm, crystal water that suddenly turned dark and cool. Reflexively, Keenan kicked out for the light and saw Tanya do the same. They surfaced in a flash, but as quickly Keenan realized that they both lacked the selflessness essential to be in a committed relationship.

"Let me get on my jet ski first," he said, "and I'll pull you up." It only took a second for him to stabilize his machine. He helped Tanya up to hers, and they rode in.

They settled on the beach for the afternoon, lounging on sand as soft and fine as sugar. Tanya, in her tropical-print bikini, looked sexy as hell, and Keenan shook off his gut feelings. He'd have time to think about their relationship later.

"They're doing a salsa night tonight onboard," Keenan said, his face turned sideways in the sun.

"I like the music, but I don't know how to salsa," Tanya answered. She was on her elbows, absorbing the sun on her over-sized cabana stripe beach towel. A beach hat and sunglasses were added now to her tropical bikini.

"I'll teach you."

That night, Tanya wore a short, sparkling cocktail dress that showed off her gorgeous legs, and Keenan taught her the basic steps. They held their own on the dance floor, swept back to their room on a cloud of sexual energy, and made love again in their tiny cabin.

Unfortunately, as the ship crept into the Miami port, he found that Tanya had other plans for them. They waited, luggage in hand, for the ship to give the green light for everyone to offload.

"I was thinking that maybe we shouldn't talk for a while," Tanya said out of the blue.

Keenan felt disappointed, but not terribly broken up. He did think they were at least building something. He just wasn't sure what that something was and if he wanted it long-term. He didn't know her that well; this trip was her idea, and it was basically decided for him that he would go.

This was awkward, and he could see that Tanya liked being in control and making snap decisions that suited her. What he felt and what he wanted had only been discussed with tears and arguments. Now that they were not supposed to communicate, it looked like the likelihood of a discussion was going to zilch.

"If that's what you're interested in, then I will comply," he said with concern in his voice. "I'm not so sure that this is a good decision."

She sighed in frustration. Like he was playing a game with her.

"Keenan, this is the only decision we have available right now."

He thought, *We? When did "we" become a factor in one of her decisions?*

To further complicate this trip, they had different flights back to Atlanta. So, once they came ashore, he dropped her off at the airport and continued to a roadside motel in Ft. Lauderdale, where he had booked a basic room. He had decided to take an extra day of vacation for his birthday and go deep-sea fishing.

The next morning by eight a.m., he was setting off on a forty-eight-foot sport fishing charter boat into the deep waters off the coast. The sea there was more blue than the turquoise water of the Bahamas, though still warm. He stood on the aft deck and watched the skyline shrink into the distance. The troubles in his life, too, became less dominant out here in the open air on the ocean. A cruise ship couldn't give you that feeling; it was too big and too much like a hotel on the water. In contrast, this forty-eight-foot boat was exposed to the wind, sun, and waves.

He grasped a fishing rod and watched its thin line trail in the water behind them as the boat churned through the waters. The railing had rod holders every few feet, and there was a fighting chair bolted into the middle of the deck, but so far he hadn't needed them. He hadn't even caught a grouper.

He checked out his rod and reel—just the standard issue that the boat offered, but still a fine fishing rod, especially compared to the homemade sticks and fishing line he and Q' had made for themselves many years ago fishing for koi.

He thought of Tanya, and how she'd been fishing for him all weekend. Now, it was his turn.

What would he catch in these waters? Maybe nothing but some sun, as an hour had passed with no fish. The three-man crew of the ship were friendly and encouraging, giving him tips.

"Just wait a bit," one of them said. "You'll get something."

Not too long after, he felt the first tug. It didn't seem like much, but suddenly the end of his rod dipped almost ninety degrees into the water. It was dramatic. What had he caught?

"Whoa!" he said.

"You got one!" his host said, and rushed over to help him get into the fighting chair. He braced his feet and stuck the butt of the rod in a rod holder. He was pleased to see that the crew were genuinely excited.

"You got yourself an apex predator on the line," one of them said.

It took a surprisingly long time to reel him in, but with some expert advice from the crew, he was finally able to look overboard and see the creature that he had yanked out of the blue depths.

It was a twelve-foot hammerhead shark. *What a beast.* Its sleek, long body was almost dolphin-like, only with distinctive pelvic and tail fins. And the head! He could see from the deck its wide, bizarre expanse, with the two liquid eyes, big and round as silver dollars, staring balefully to each side. Its slit of a mouth was open, and Keenan caught a glimpse of the sharp, triangular teeth, honed by millions of years of evolution to rip and tear the flesh of weaker creatures. This was no peaceful koi. What kind of a sign was it, he wondered, to catch a predatory creature at the start of his new year of life?

On the flight the next day, he mused over the weekend with Tanya. Did he allow what occurred between Tanya and him to happen? He was just trying to go with the flow, which was something that he didn't necessarily do while he was with Francis. What a strange experience to be the one who didn't want to move too fast. With Francis, he pushed when he should have waited and observed, so he was determined to do things differently this time.

Little did he know that once he arrived back in Atlanta, a whole new comedy of errors awaited.

* * *

"Keenan," Francis's voice said plaintively, "I've been in town all week and waiting to hear from you."

That was the first voicemail.

"Where are you?"

That was the second voicemail. There were five in total, with increasing levels of irritation at his absence. He called her back as soon as he was in his own kitchen.

"Hey, Francis, what's up?" he said, happy to hear from her in spite of the annoyance he'd heard in those last voicemails.

"I came into town to surprise you for your birthday," she said, "and now I only have two more days before I go back. Where have you been?"

"On vacation," he said. "I didn't know you were coming. Get over here," he added, smiling into the phone.

So, now that this circumstance was on his plate, he was forced to do what he knew to do: ignore the hell out of Tanya until Francis left town.

He knew it was not the most polite thing to do, but he had been banking on not hearing from Tanya anyway. She did just tell him to not call her for a while, and he'd only known her a month.

He quickly understood that Tanya had not meant one word of her call for a separation. He was sitting on the couch cuddled with Francis when his phone buzzed with a text. It was from Tanya.

"Where the hell are you?" he read on his phone.

"Who's that?" Francis asked.

"Some work shit," he lied. But he couldn't keep his phone away from her forever.

That night, after giving her a screaming orgasm, he fell hard asleep. Francis dozed, too, then walked off naked to his bathroom. When she came back, she grabbed his phone from his bedside table while he slept and began to scroll. When she found Tanya's text, she read it several times, her face blank. Tears came to her eyes. Quickly, she tapped in a response.

"I am with my lady right now," she wrote. Then she curled up on her side, tossed and turned for a bit, and finally went to sleep.

In the morning, they sipped coffee at his kitchen counter, a house she knew so well.

"Who's Tanya?" she asked casually.

Keenan paused. "She's someone I'm dating," he finally said

evenly. He watched her face. He could tell she was trying to keep a neutral expression, but her voice and her eyes gave away her hurt.

"So, you're dating," she managed. "I get it. Moving on."

"Yeah, Francis," he said gently but firmly. "What did you expect me to do?"

Francis sighed. "I don't know," she said. "I guess, this. It's hard after seven years."

Seven years. He'd known Francis a long time. If Keenan was honest with himself, he had to admit that she was still his baby and she had the highest priority at the moment.

None of this went over well with Tanya, as she was incredibly incensed by the time Francis returned to North Carolina. But Tanya wasn't his girlfriend, and he had the right to focus his attention on Francis. Plus, Tanya had specifically told him they were not communicating, then freaked out when he allowed himself to spend time with someone who was incredibly important to him. How inconsistent could someone be?

As Valentine's Day 2013 drew near, he found himself trying to figure out what he wanted to do. It was another topsy-turvy season in his life, as he was working seven days and seventy to eighty hours a week. Thankfully, he still had the help that Tanya had referred to him, the nanny that was helping him with his boys, Kelvin and Cameron. She was a Jamaican woman. She worked hard for the family, and he appreciated it and appreciated Tanya and her mother, Angela, for stepping in and giving him the referral.

Hard work had always been something he took pride in and strived to do so he could provide for his family. Juggling a demanding contract with a department store, two kids, a dating life, and his own separate issues and priorities left him feeling pulled thin. So, he was looking for anything simple at this point.

His "try harder" mantra was now reserved for Keenan and Keenan's career. So, the morning of Valentine's Day, he had no clue, but did what he thought would put a smile on Tanya's face. He dropped off a card and some flowers to Tanya's house. She seemed pleased but also a little disappointed. Not so disappointed that she didn't invite him over for dinner that evening.

He didn't put much thought into it and continued on to work. He also sent two-dozen roses to Francis at her job. In the middle of his workday, he was called to the front desk and found an edible-arrangement fruit basket and balloons from Tanya waiting for him. It was really big—a little too big. As a grown man, he wasn't crazy about receiving balloons. He dropped it off at his car to avoid embarrassment and thought that this was going a bit too far.

Feeling awkward, he called her when he returned to his desk.

"Tanya, thank you so much." He tried to sound sincere, but he could hear the pressure in his own voice.

She, meanwhile, sounded like she was curling into a mink stole.

"You are *so* welcome," she cooed over the phone. "I can't wait to see you later tonight."

"About that," he began and braced himself for tears or something worse. "I'm just not going to make it. Work is crazy, and I have to work late."

"You're not coming? It's Valentine's Day. What do you mean, you're not coming?"

Okay, so they crossed into something worse.

"Sweetie, I can't make it, and I really want to be there—"

"You have ruined my Valentine's Day. Isn't this about a bitch? You just decide at the last minute that you can't come and tear up the most romantic day of the year," she spat out.

He bit his lip and remained silent. This conversation couldn't go anywhere positive.

"I've been trying to make something special between us, and you just up and decide to do your own thing. Again."

Did she just say "again"?

"Don't you have anything to say? Are you even concerned about my feelings?" she screamed.

"I'm so sorry, Tanya. I didn't mean to ruin your day," he said carefully.

"You aren't damn sorry. You're just embarrassed, and this is some bullshit. Thanks a fucking lot. I gotta go." She disconnected the call, and he slowly returned the receiver into the cradle.

Winners. He was attracting winners, apparently.

* * *

For the next two weeks, he was lambasted and shredded with slick words and tension whenever he spoke with Tanya. Avoiding her calls was not an option because her text-messaged rants were laced with enough salt to irritate and infect whatever wounds of insecurity that he had felt comfortable enough to share with her. She even texted him that the nanny had revealed to her that he had another woman staying at his home earlier that month.

A spying nanny? Who had he let into his house? The betrayal of it made him feel a bit ill.

That was of no consequence to her, though, because it was always his fault and always something he did to ruin something in Tanya's life. He realized that he was being punished for not wanting to exclusively be her man. This wasn't necessarily a major indictment to him, but in her mind it was a deal breaker.

Yet, she continued to call. He didn't have the heart to tell her to go to hell. He didn't even have the heart to tell her that her consistent talking about her baby's baller daddy made it difficult to even want to hold a conversation.

How could he compete with a man who didn't even want the girl who was seemingly still in love with him? He didn't have a chance, in his opinion, to really get to know her without being held to a standard that was too high to even grasp.

In March 2013, Tanya called him and his first thought was to not answer the phone. The nice guy in him decided to go on and pick up the call. No more than two minutes into the conversation, the beautiful lady with the oily personality began to criticize him and call him a bad father, based on all of her juicy information from the in-house spy she had so cleverly inserted into his life. She eloquently laid out the reasons why he was a bad father, which mostly included him working too much and never spending time with his kids. It was as if she had practiced this monologue in the mirror. All that was missing was the slide presentation in her version of an expert speaker conference from hell.

Who did she think she was?

He quickly ended the call and deleted her number from his phone. He thought a moment, and proceeded to block her so that she would never be able to get through to him again.

Sure, he worked long hours, but he was no different than any other parent who has committed to providing the very best of everything to their children. He also fired the nanny for violating his family's privacy.

At some point, he decided, *you have enough and you decide to do something different*. Trying hard didn't work out well for Francis and him, but it did work out well when applied specifically to him. The only problem, he discovered, is that trying hard for yourself can often ruin a relationship.

Yet, he didn't think that he deserved to be roasted over coals for being a provider.

He chose to forget Tanya. There's more fish in the proverbial sea, and his track record showed that he was quite a skilled fisherman. He had been in Atlanta for almost eighteen years at this point and been in two long-term relationships for a span of sixteen and a half of those years. That was a pretty good record.

Not too long after Tanya's phone call, he stood in front of the television and channel surfed for something that would take his mind off of the drama spawning in his life. A commercial for an online dating app caught his attention with laughing singles, overly confident men, and the question that begged, "What are you waiting for?"

The messages and winks began to roll in within minutes of restoring his profile. He was mesmerized at this virtual nightclub and the forwardness of the women. Some were aggressive and wrote him witty opening lines and sent half-naked pictures. *Come and get it.* Then there were some who just sent a weird "Good morning" and nothing else. *Were they just used to rejection?*

He answered the same questions over and over: "No, I'm not from Atlanta. Yes, I have kids. Yes, they live with me. I've been single for a couple months. Yes, I go to church. I've been here a long time. No, I've never been to your hometown. How was your day? You're beautiful, also. Thanks for the compliment. How was your weekend?"

It was exasperating, but he kept at it.

In March 2013, Besaflor77's smile was a beacon of light drawing him in from the ebb and flow of the dating profiles. He had been surfing through on his lunch break, in the evenings, and even after midnight. She was often online searching in the middle of the night, as well. The sheer beauty of her picture intrigued him, and he wondered what treasures were behind that smile.

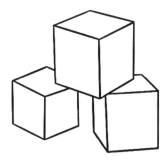

Keenan Falls in Love

The first court day with Veronica - Continued

HOW THE HELL *did I get here?* He thought again as he watched Veronica take the stand.

In spite of the encouragement of his lawyer, he was feeling sure that he would lose. But moment by moment, that feeling began to recede. This guy was good, and Veronica didn't seem prepared at all. In fact, he was making her seem kind of . . . dumb.

Was it even possible? The mighty and intelligent Dr. Veronica Rubio?

He could tell she was nervous from the way she played with her scarf. He remembered that scarf from her photos on an online dating app.

* * *

Her profile stated that she had been to different places. A

picture of her in Italy visually confirmed this tidbit of information. In the photo, she was smiling, holding a tiny porcelain espresso cup while seated at a wrought-iron table, wearing a soft, gauzy, white blouse, a colorful scarf in her hair. He could see the cobblestone street in the background.

He wondered if she spoke Italian like a true native as she strolled down the roads of aqueduct-filled cities. Was she a fashion maven who rocked Italian designers? He could only imagine the wind lightly teasing her dark, straightened hair while she lounged in a gondola.

He skimmed over the remaining bare bones of her profile: one child, lived at home, 5'8". Even though much was lacking in detail, he still wanted to get to know her. She was sexy as hell with nice-sized breasts—a dark-skinned goddess with long legs and a tiny waist. But he knew you can only tell so much with a few pictures.

He reached out to her on the dating app, and she seemed really impressed that he had full custody of his kids. He wouldn't have expected that fact to put him at the head of the line, but he'd take it. She asked him to give her a call, and they agreed to meet at Perimeter Mall with their kids to enjoy lunch.

As he drove through the parking lot with his son Cameron, he saw a pearl-white European sedan pass by. He told Cameron that could be her, but Cameron didn't think that was the case.

"She probably drives a low-end car," he said, laughing.

"Thanks for your input, Cameron," Keenan said dryly.

He eased his car into the parking space and walked with his son toward the restaurant entrance. Veronica came in the door with her nine-month-old son still in his car seat, and her thirteen-year-old niece Lauren.

They sat down and ordered food as Veronica sprinkled a few pieces of breakfast cereal in front of the little baby that she introduced as Mathew. Matt's chubby fingers grasped handfuls of the cereal and stuffed it all into his mouth. He smiled widely with a gummy grin, and crumbs trailed the corners of his mouth like flaky whiskers. He giggled as he moved each grain of cereal with the strategic ease of a chess grandmaster. Keenan moved another cereal toward the baby, causing him to pause in his game and gaze up at this new adult.

He was a round, light-skinned baby with curly, dark-brown hair and a joyous laugh. Keenan remembered his sons at that age, and he missed holding them in his arms while giving them a bottle. His children were entering the tween stage of their lives, a bittersweet moment for any parent. At least it was for Keenan. While it was exciting to see Kelvin and Cameron develop into the young men they were destined to become, it also meant that time was passing by and they were no longer infants who would hold his hand as they learned to walk.

Keenan found himself helping to feed him as a matter of course as he and Veronica participated in the conversational dance of getting to know each other. She said she was born in Buffalo, her mother was from the Dominican Republic, and she spoke Spanish and French fluently. Though she didn't share a lot of details, he could tell that she had overcome serious obstacles on her way to becoming a doctor and that she was clearly working toward the next level in her career.

Her drive and ambition charmed him. As a professional who made six figures annually, he often thought it would be nice to have a woman who was his equal financially and could hold her own. As they talked further, Veronica seemed to fit that requirement. But she was definitely a type-A personality.

They continued to engage in light conversation peppered with a little humor here and there. She asked his son questions, and he shared his interest in toy-building blocks. After paying for cheese-cake and buying ice cream for everybody, she took her son and niece shopping within the mall. When she had finished, they said goodbye and planned to link up later that evening for drinks downtown at an eccentric cafe.

He was sure that Veronica was feeling him, even if the conversations felt lukewarm and distracted on her end. She agreed to get her cousin to babysit for her, but she wanted to go to a girlfriend's birthday party in Conyers before they met up that evening.

Unfortunately, the meet-up never occurred, and he didn't hear from her the rest of the day. She sent him a text around two a.m. saying that she decided to not drive back downtown for their date. He felt like she flaked on him that evening and doubted that he would ever call her back. He really wanted to spend time with her that evening, and it seemed like the effort wasn't reciprocated.

Later that morning, he received an apology text from her. He thought for a minute and then called her.

"Hey," she said, and with that one word, Keenan felt himself pulled in by the melodic tone of her voice.

"I got your text," he said. "So, how are you?"

How could he resist her? Everyone deserved a second chance, right?

"I'm good," she said, smiling into the phone, and something inside Keenan switched on and lit up. They chatted for a minute.

"Do you want to meet for lunch sometime this week?" he blurted out. He hadn't really meant to set another date so soon, but something about this woman made him hungry to see her.

"Sure," she said. "That sounds easy."

They were able to meet for lunch during the workweek because she worked at a hospital and her office was relatively close to his office. After this low-key date, she swam around in his thoughts like a sea siren. As he spent his workdays maneuvering through the matrix code of programming, he wanted to take the blue pill and go down the rabbit hole toward Veronica's wonderland. This girl had his nose wide open.

At the end of the week, he scheduled a cooking class as their next date. Keenan had taken dates to classes there before and enjoyed the ambience, even though he always walked out after buying some random kitchen utensil he would never use. The cooking classes made every last cheese knife and pepper grinder so appealing, and the instructors were friendly and fun.

He arrived on time and walked in through the glass double doors under the black and white striped awning, glancing through the aisles of kitchen gadgets to see if Veronica had arrived. No sign of her, so he made his way to the back of the store where the cooking class was located and stood at his station, a waist-high butcher block table. He put on his apron and waited, trying not to eye the other couples with envy. Would she stand him up? To his relief, she finally arrived, extremely late.

The chef had just finished announcing the meal for the evening, steak and potatoes—a basic staple of American cuisine—when she breezed through the door and sat down next to him.

His hands were clammy, and he didn't know why he was so nervous around her. Then her arm lightly brushed his, igniting a chill down his spine. The scent of her perfume lingered around him, spiraling like a silky web and binding him with her sexuality.

They began to cook, and he could barely concentrate on the task at hand for looking at her. The swell of her breasts peeked through her clothing as she bent down to retrieve the pan for the potatoes. Her hair cascaded over her face like a curtain. He moved his hand toward it to push it back so he could whisper a sweet nothing into her ear. But his player move fumbled in execution when he knocked over her glass of wine.

She smiled like she knew what he was trying to do as she arched her back flirtatiously to grab the salt and pepper shakers that were on the right of him.

He tried to impress her by asking the instructor a lot of questions during the lesson. As they got into a rhythm of cooking, they completed their meal and found that they worked well together. He was a movement by himself in the kitchen, blending spices together that made one's tastebuds sing. But together, it seemed that the cooking class showed that he and Veronica were a force to be reckoned with.

When the class ended, he walked her to her car, and they were barely settled into their seats when her phone rang. She looked at the in-dash caller ID and sighed. "James. I wish he would stop calling me."

They spoke on the car's Bluetooth speaker, and the conversation was tense as she tried to get him off the phone. Keenan was perturbed that this guy called her and that she actually answered the phone while he was in the car. *If she really didn't want to talk to him, why not press the red button and send his call to the abyss?*

"You need to just stop calling my lady," he blurted out in agitation.

He heard him exclaim, "Oh, really?" before she disconnected the call.

Suddenly, an ominous feeling entered the space between them. They had just had a great evening bonding over food and domestic activities that spoke to them being a couple. Little did he know that the phone call was about to open the floodgates to an overflow of information about Veronica's past.

Veronica ran her fingers over her face in frustration. Her ragged nails proved she didn't take the time to pamper herself with manicures like most women he knew. She shifted her body and faced him. "Look, I have something I want to talk about with you."

"Go ahead and speak your mind," he said.

She inhaled and said, "Remember when we were supposed to meet up? I actually went out with James. He invited me out, and I thought he was a nice guy until he started making it an issue about me having a baby from someone who didn't want to have one with me. I thought it was just rude."

She stopped her car behind his, and he felt the whir of drama spin into gear. His mind began to race with questions. He was disappointed that she went on a date with someone else when she had actually told him that she was at her girlfriend's party. *Lying, already?* Also, she hadn't shared much about Matt's father, so he didn't find James' concerns out of bounds.

It turned out that Sam was Matt's father and a native of Brooklyn, New York. When they met on a dating site, he was working out of a coffee shop as an ex-criminal who helped credit-challenged celebrities get financed for luxury vehicles. His celebrity clientele, and even Veronica, would pay a little extra to get approved for an auto loan to an inside person to get her foreign car financed.

As she continued with the story, Keenan realized that this woman didn't mind being a little dirty. Her ex seemed to be a real-life drug dealing villain from a TV show.

Sam left her when she became pregnant, and moved back to New York. Then another man named Pete Wilcox entered the picture. This was Matt's so-called godfather. Veronica and Pete met on the dating site prior to Veronica meeting Sam. A major coincidence occurred when Veronica was dropping Sam off at the airport to move back to New York.

"Oh my God, it's you," Veronica blurted out in the terminal. There, waiting to check in some baggage, was Pete.

"Veronica! You're looking good," Pete said.

"Not feeling so great," she responded, walking with him on the other side of the rope as he moved forward in line. "Are you leaving town forever, too?"

"Nah, I'm just visiting some friends," he said. "Listen. Why don't you give me a call next week when I get back? I'll try to put a smile on your pretty face."

They went on a few dates after he returned and became a couple. At first, he agreed to help Veronica raise her child as his own and to also marry her. Somewhere along the way, he changed his mind, moved out, and eventually married someone else.

Any normal man would have decided to leave Veronica alone after hearing about her past with men. Any normal man would have cut his losses instead of following her home that evening to ensure her safety. He would have chucked up the deuces instead of going inside her house and talking for a little while.

But Keenan wasn't the typical male. And something about Veronica kept drawing him back.

"I'd like to take you out for dinner this weekend," he said. "Somewhere nice."

"Okay," Veronica said, smiling but still uncertain.

"No, really. Dress up. How is Friday?"

"Okay," she said again, and her smile got a little bigger. He kissed her on the cheek and drove home feeling nearly intoxicated with the taste of her soft skin on his lips.

That Friday during his lunch hour, he picked up his new sport coat from alterations at a luxury department store, then let the salesperson convince him to buy a new tie. *Why not?*

After that brief spot of fun, he returned to work and the afternoon dragged painfully on. He found himself reminiscing about Friday afternoons of his childhood, stuck at his school desk and praying for the weekend so he could hang out with Q' and fish for koi.

When work finally ended, he suited up and drove to Veronica's, and she met him at the door. Her face was fully made up, but a robe covered her dress and she still wore house shoes.

"Come in for a bit," she said with Matt in her arms. "The babysitter's not here yet."

She offered him a glass of iced tea in the kitchen, and he sat down at the table to drink it, placing his keys on the table next to his glass. When the babysitter arrived, she disappeared with her for a second, then re-emerged ready to leave.

Wow.

Keenan had told her to dress up, but he hadn't expected her to look so damn beautiful. The black, strapless cocktail dress embraced the curves of her body, and she wore shimmery, gold-tone, slingback designer pumps. Her necklace was a thin gold chain.

"I'll drive," she said, and entranced by her vision, Keenan stood up and followed her without a second thought. His keys stayed right there on the kitchen table.

"You look beautiful," he said, watching her profile as she drove her foreign car to steak restaurant. *Maxwell's Urban Hang Suite* played softly in the background as she drove. The restaurant had only been open a few months. After the grand opening, people were raving, and it was hard to get a reservation. Keenan prevailed, however, and along with everything else, he was looking forward to a cut of steak cooked over an open hearth of hickory and oak.

"Thank you. Do you know what I like about the restaurant you chose, Keenan?" Veronica spoke while keeping her eyes strictly forward.

"You haven't been there yet?" he suggested.

"No," she said, glancing at him briefly before returning her eyes to the road. "They do more than just steak. I hate getting a steak I couldn't finish in a month. I'm trying to lose weight."

Why? he thought, looking at her perfect silhouette. He let it go, though, not knowing how much her need for weight loss would impact him over time. Here, at the moment when he was still falling for her, all he could think about was her silky skin. He kept his mouth shut and let Maxwell fill the silence.

They parked in the lot of the arts center and walked toward the restaurant.

"Have you ever gone shopping in there?" she asked.

He caught her hand. "No," he said. "Have you?"

"Yes, to get ideas for my apartment."

That made sense to Keenan, as her place was decorated stylishly. He wasn't surprised that she browsed the design showrooms.

Hand in hand, they walked up the tree-lined path toward the restaurant. It was dimly lit and not too noisy, in spite of the crowd. Keenan appreciated how the vibe matched the cuisine: it had the simplicity of a steakhouse with wood dining tables sans tablecloths and a large, open kitchen in the center. Yet, most of the tables were small in the style of an Italian trattoria, and the lighting design was impeccable—made for those who wanted to see and be seen, surely.

True to her intention, Veronica ordered the lightest main entree on the menu: orecchiette with lamb sausage.

"It means little ears," she said, and Keenan couldn't help but think about nuzzling up against her own little ears later. For now, he settled on the spinalis.

"Why the ribeye cap?" Veronica asked, using the more common name.

"The tenderloin is a more tender cut of beef," Keenan said, "but the spinalis is supposed to have more flavor. What do you prefer? Something more tender or more flavorful?"

She paused and batted her eyelashes slowly a few times before answering. "Flavor," she finally said. "I'll take flavor over tenderness any day."

In this setting, Veronica was a jewel. The lines of her face and body already made her so beautiful, and added to that was the veil of unfamiliarity. She glowed in the soft amber light, and Keenan could barely eat his cut of spinalis. Looking at her was enough.

For now.

They talked in soft tones about everyday things—their careers, their sons, how much they liked Atlanta. Their knees bumped up against each other under the table, first accidentally, then intentionally pressing up against each other as they moved in closer together.

They ordered one glass of wine, and it was enough. They were intoxicated with each other.

On the way home, Keenan feasted visually again on her seductive silhouette while the long, slow, sweet saxophone of the last song from *Urban Hang Suite* filled the car.

Veronica silently pulled into her driveway, and they both undid their seatbelts at the same time. It had the erotic effect of taking off clothes. She moved into his arms for a deep and complex kiss, the need for which had been building up in both of them for hours and days. It was the kind of kiss that two people share before they know each other's bodies, with the lips and tongue the first thrilling places to explore.

He wondered if he should ask to come in, or if he should leave it for another night, and the thought of leaving made him automatically put his hand to his pocket where he kept his car keys. They weren't there. The decision had been made without him.

"Baby," he said, his mouth finally on Veronica's tender ear. "I left my car keys on your kitchen table."

"Did you?" Veronica murmured, and turned her face to him for another long, slow kiss. "I guess you better come in and get them," she breathed against his mouth.

He retrieved his keys from the kitchen table and moved to the living room while she paid the babysitter and sent her on her way.

"Matt is sound asleep," she said, closing the door and facing him.

He wrapped her in his arms for a hug. Finally, he could feel her supple body pressed all the way against him from head to toe. It put him in orbit, and his mouth found hers immediately. Again they explored each other's lips, tongue, and throat. He ran his hands up and down her arms, then her sides, then found the zipper at the back of her dress. The soft sound of it going down was music, and she pushed his new sport coat off his shoulders and started unbuttoning his shirt as her own dress fell gently to the floor.

They were both suddenly so hungry for the touch and taste of skin and more skin. He sank to his knees as he kissed down her bare belly to her belly button, then pressed his mouth against the silky texture of her black panties. She put her hands on his shoulders and moaned, then sank to her knees, too, and they kissed again as he unfastened her lacy bra.

He put his hot mouth on her nipple, and suddenly both were lying down on the plush carpet, with Keenan on top of her, sucking and pulling on her nipples gently while she gripped his back and thrashed her head back and forth. Still sucking, he slid his hand in underneath her soaking panties and stroked her swollen clit. It was soft and hard at the same time, and he thrust two fingers inside her, finger-fucking her gently to see if she liked it.

She moaned slightly. "Fuck me," she whispered. "I want you."

That was all Keenan needed to hear. In a flash, his belt was undone and pants were added to the pile of clothing on the floor.

He entered her tender pussy and was engulfed by the hot, tight wetness. She gripped him, wrapping her legs around him and biting him on the shoulder. His mind was erased by his need for her, and his body took over.

At some point, they moved to her bedroom and continued exploring each other's bodies until the first pale hint of dawn struck her windows. Unlike Tanya, there was nothing performative about her style. Veronica was honestly hungry. Passionate. He felt like she needed him, and when she came, over and over, he could feel it.

They cuddled, finally drowsy, and watched the light turn from pale to gold. He traced his hands down her spine and saw a long scar up the middle of her ass.

"Did you have surgery here?" he murmured, tracing it.

"No," she said. "It's from a car accident. Hey, did you leave your keys on purpose?" Veronica asked.

"What? No," Keenan said, chuckling softly, and put his arms around her. "I swear."

"Hm," she said, and he could tell she was still suspicious. It seemed so adorable at the time. But it meant she didn't trust him.

* * *

Keenan had always believed that signs or harbingers of what would come if a person kept traveling down a certain path should never be ignored. He knew that sometimes emotions take over and you miss the signs.

The morning after they made love, the signs slipped out of the closet that they shared with skeletons and danced around the bed as daybreak filtered through Veronica's window.

Veronica had taped a vision board on her wall with cut-out pictures of a husband and wife. The woman held a baby in her arms. On top of the woman's body, she had placed a cut out of her head. On the man's body, she had several cut outs of different men.

Keenan was just waiting for forensic agents to bust into the room. Some type of forensic team needed to evaluate this vision board, because it unnerved him.

The different men represented different scenarios, he guessed. He felt like one of those cartoons where the character rubbed a genie bottle, received the wish, and then wondered why they asked for the wish in the first place. But he believed that once a person becomes intimate with another, he or she ties souls and transfers the good and the bad of their spirits into one another. Making love was more than a physical connection, and he already felt Veronica in his spirit. His feelings had already deepened for her. He lay in bed next to her feeling spiritually and emotionally naked. What she revealed to him about Sam, Pete, and James, along with this vision board, really didn't sit too well with him. The signs screamed for him to go back from whence he came.

But baby girl had him wrapped around her finger.

Something inside of his spirit needed what she offered. Maybe it was that law of attraction she talked about during one of their telephone calls when she mentioned a self-help book. It dealt with the power of positive thinking to generate abundance in wealth, relationships, and health. If he thought that he had enough money to cover every expense and live comfortably, then the financial means would somehow manifest itself in his life. At that moment, his mind envisioned agape love emanating from the angel sleeping beside him with her hair fanned out against the pillows.

It was Sunday, and he was already running a little late to go feed the dog. She stirred as he tiptoed around the plushly decorated room, pulling on yesterday's clothes.

"Where are you off to so early?" she yawned through a stretch.

"Gotta go feed the dog," he replied hastily as he clasped his watch. Maybe it was his hastiness. Maybe it was just her.

"Do you have to go now?" Her tone was a little sharp.

He turned around to face her, completely taken aback that this sounded like it would be an issue.

"Well, just go the fuck on then, if that's what you have to do!"

Wait. What just happened?

He blinked. He swallowed. Maybe he even stopped breathing. "Veronica, sweetie, I just have to go feed the dog and then I'll be right back."

He wasn't sure if she meant for this to be a sexy pout or a temper tantrum, but it was throwing him completely off his game.

"Why can't you get an automatic feeder and then he can just feed himself?"

All right, she was joking. She had to be. He moved toward her side of the bed and she glared at him with suspicion. Those weren't the same eyes that he kissed no more than five hours ago.

He gave a quick peck to her steely jaw and said, "I will be back as soon as I'm done. Promise."

He expected that to melt her a little bit, but the ice queen was not having it. He soon learned that what displeased her would cause him trouble, humiliation, and ultimately money and time.

These were all things that he ignored as he examined what he thought was a perfect catch. He was mesmerized at her shiny color and smooth skin, yet ignored the fact that what he held was more like a hammerhead shark than a delicate koi that swam gently through an inner-city garden.

Section Two

Pretty Wings

Mothers and Sons

The first court day with Veronica—Cross-examination

"DID HE EVER threaten you?" Keenan's lawyer asked.

"No," Veronica replied from the stand.

"Did he ever put his hands on you?"

"No."

"I'm going to read a text message that my client alleges you sent to him: 'You offered to repay me and as of tonight there hasn't been any deposit.' Did you send that message?"

"Yes."

"So, the two of you were arguing over money."

"It was one of the things we disagreed on, yes."

"Without any threats of violence or physical violence."

"No, no threats."

"And no violence?"

"No, no violence."

* * *

He and Veronica were still fairly new when he called his best friend Raj on his lunch break, eager to tell him about the woman who could trump Tanya and Francis, and just about any woman he had met since his divorce. Raj was the kind of old friend who felt comfortable telling Keenan exactly what he thought, even though he was a few years younger. Keenan returned the favor. Both took each other's advice . . . sometimes.

"Why would you talk to someone who just had a child, man? It's only been nine months."

Keenan quickly looked over his shoulder to make sure no one stood by, eavesdropping on their conversation. "Can you think positive for once?" Keenan wasn't in the mood to defend his decisions and convince his friend of anything. *Why couldn't Raj just be happy for him?*

"Man, I'm trying to be. But how do you become a stepfather overnight?" Raj tried to laugh it off. Keenan knew, however, that he wasn't playing.

"She's a single mom, and she needs help," he said. "Who watches a woman struggle through that on her own? Especially when the father isn't anywhere to be found."

Raj paused. Despite his protests, Keenan knew Raj couldn't argue against stepping up to take care of a woman who needed some assistance, especially when a baby was involved. He tried another take. "Have you ever thought that it's a bit strange for this woman, who doesn't even know you, to leave you alone with her nine-month-old son?"

"Nah, you have it all wrong," Keenan said. *Clearly, Raj just didn't believe in true love.*

"Keenan! It's crazy to have you around her kid that early!"

"I think we built a pretty legitimate bond."

"I'm not about to sit here and support crazy on crazy, man. Maybe she's a good person, but you guys are moving way too fast. You can't deny that. Be careful," Raj said, but his words fell onto Keenan's temporarily deaf ears.

Shortly after they met, they discovered that Mathew was missing developmental milestones which he should have been hitting with no problem. He wasn't learning to crawl or feed himself.

They were sitting on her sofa one day and holding hands when Matt decided he wanted a shiny, blue ball across the room next to the fireplace. Keenan was horrified to watch him scoot across the floor on his bottom.

"Your son can't crawl," he blurted out. It sounded more like a statement than a question.

She looked at Keenan with eyebrows raised, possibly trying to figure out how she didn't know that her own son was behind the mark. It was ironic, because Veronica was a pediatric emergency-medicine physician for a hospital who looked for the same developmental missteps in other people's children all day.

Veronica admittedly felt like she didn't have the type of schedule that allowed her to devote time to Matt's development. Keenan soon began to work with him, alleviating Veronica's stress and filling the void of a male figure in the baby's life.

Matt's birthday party in early May 2013 was their first real outing as a unified couple in front of her friends and family. Keenan left his kids at home and picked her up in Johns Creek early that Saturday so that he could drive her to the party. There was no need to overcomplicate the day, and he didn't mind treating her like a lady and letting her focus all of her attention on her son.

When she opened the door, she glowed in a purple, fitted top and dark-blue jeans. He was opening his mouth to compliment her when she glanced off to her left and said out of nowhere, "You know that tree in your backyard? It doesn't look too sturdy, Key."

"Come here, birthday boy," Keenan said as he grabbed Matt from her arms and stepped into her house.

There was an aged oak tree with a heavy trunk and fragile limbs that would scrape the roof of his house every time the wind blew exceptionally hard or rain pelted the area. It was now drizzling, and the ground was soft. This wasn't new information to him; he had been monitoring the tree since the last ice storm shut down Atlanta, but he was impressed that she could discern a natural threat and express concern.

"Yeah, it looks okay for now, but it's been standing for decades," he continued.

"Okay, but all good things eventually fall down. Even the leaves on a tree die once a year," she said with a shrug and a laugh that had a strange echo.

He followed her inside and kicked the door shut with his right foot before handing her a gift.

"For my baby?" she asked, her eyes sincere.

"Yes," he said, putting Matt down on the floor as they entered the living room, "and this is for you." He pulled her toward him and they began to kiss for a considerable amount of time. She was warm and loving in his arms. They were either going to be late to the party or postpone the festivities.

Within minutes, Keenan made the decision to end the romantic moment and travel on to the Bouncy House. This spot is one of those newer pizzeria arcade offshoots that offers space, pizza, and air-filled slides for children to bounce off of and slide down to their hearts' content. It was definitely the Veronica Show, and Keenan was pleased to take the back seat and watch a woman he was beginning to care about enjoy her day with his help. He just didn't know he had to earn his keep.

"Okay, your job is to take pictures!" She quickly shoved a camera into his hands and moved into type-A delegation mode. Keenan fell in step and began looking for the best pictures that Matt would one day hold dear to his heart.

The party was everything a first birthday party could be: kids, friends, family, smash cake, party hats, games, and goody bags. Keenan was actually in the middle of handing out goody bags when Veronica pulled him away from the table and directed him toward a young woman who was taking pictures on her phone of Matt.

"Racine," Veronica said, pulling him behind her, "this is Keenan Green."

"Oh, wow," Racine said as she tucked the phone into her pants pocket and shook his extended hand. "I've heard so much about you already."

This pleased him, because he wondered if she had started the "him" conversations with her family. He knew that he had cleared the friend hurdle, but sometimes you just want to know where you stand.

Veronica turned to him and said, "This is my half-sister through my dad. Not one of my favorite people!" Keenan recalled a story she had told him about how Racine only called her when she needed financial help. Nevertheless, she leaned in and hugged Racine from the side.

Awkward.

He also met four of her teenage, male cousins, whose names blurred together in the whirlwind of the party. Nonetheless, they had great banter until one of them blurted out, "She been mad at you yet?"

That took him by surprise.

"No, we haven't argued. What are you saying?" Keenan crossed his arms defensively as the other three teens all exchanged a look and stifled a smirk.

"I'm just saying, you know, watch out for her when she gets mad, you know," one of the boys named Ricky said. He slid his hands down into his jean pockets.

He found it imprudent to stand there and entertain a monkey court with a gaggle of teenagers. He chalked their words up to them having too much knowledge about her previous relationship. If anything, Keenan thought she was holding up remarkably well to be a young single mom raising a baby in another city away from her tribe.

"Thanks, I'll keep that in mind," he said before excusing himself. He was, after all, still on the clock for his photography services. He watched them weave through the guests to a corner where some other family members stood, talking and laughing as families often do. He wondered if he was the topic of discussion and if they had bribed the kids to be the ones to come over and drop the bomb. One of them sizes him up and another one asks how long he would be around. The whole group laughs, and they wage war over pizza and a soda about how he would respond.

But to be honest, he hadn't seen any of the behavior that would warrant a warning. He held the info close to him and didn't tell Veronica anything about this encounter. But he didn't put their words in a locked vault and tell himself the conversation never happened. He considered it privately.

The rain continued to fall down in sheets over the city, and this created a hum of white noise in the kid's bouncy house and arcade. Keenan was walking to get more refreshments when he saw an older, rounder version of Veronica zipping across the parking lot with a huge, ribboned gift in her hands. He picked up someone's umbrella in the foyer and popped it open as he swung the door open for her to enter the establishment.

"Thank you so much!" she breathed with her chest heaving. They were the only African Americans who were having a party at the time, so he figured she was also there for Veronica and Matt.

"No problem," he said as he took the gift out of her hands.

"This is Keenan, Mom." Veronica was standing behind him, smiling, with her left hand on his shoulder. "This is who I told you about."

His back went ninety degrees against her hand. *He was in there.* He extended his hand, and the older woman smiled back at him with kind eyes.

"Francine Rubio," she said as they walked toward the birthday table and dodged children sprinting from one edge of the room to another. "I'm sorry I'm late, but I got on the road late."

She and Veronica shared a look.

"Mom lives in Charlotte," Veronica said, ignoring her mother's sideways glance.

"Well, that just means you'll have to move here," Keenan quipped. He could have just as easily remained silent, but there was some sort of tension that he was trying to eliminate at the moment. He just wasn't sure why the tension was there.

Ms. Rubio smiled tightly at his suggestion and flexed her eyebrows as if she would keep it in mind. She blended in with the hugs and cheek-pecks from other family members, and the meeting or conversation was over just as quickly as it started.

"She seems sweet," Keenan said to Veronica. Her eyes were focused on Matt, who was currently being passed between some of her cousins as he tried to finish his chunk of cake.

Keenan decided to make himself useful for the next half-hour and clean up some of the trash created by dozens of little fingers, paper napkins, and spilled cups of soda.

He thought it would make a pretty great picture to capture one of the parents asleep in the corner, holding a plate of half-eaten cake. So, he dropped his janitorial duties for the moment and started to make his way over to that side of the room. He was still switching easily between taking pictures and picking up almost one hour later when a harried Veronica approached him, her eyes darting and hard.

"Have you seen my mother?" She wasn't looking at him and kept checking her phone.

"Not since we were introduced. You okay?"

"No! She always does this. I sent her to the grocery store to get more cups, and she's been gone for at least half an hour. It's a simple trip!" Veronica spat out. She checked her text messages and grunted in frustration.

"Calm down," Keenan said. "Maybe she hit traffic."

"No! I'm not calming down. She can't follow basic directions."

"Don't say that," he said, wrapping an arm around her. She felt like a stiff board.

"I'm sick of her shit. I'm sick of it." She curled her upper lip in disgust. Keenan wanted to hide this scene from her teenage cousins in fear that they would point and say, "I told you so!"

"She is the most selfish person," Veronica began as she wrapped her arms around his waist and spoke into his neck. "I pay her cell bill. I pay her mortgage and car note. I told her I need help down here with my baby, but she won't move here and help me, and now I struggle to just stay ahead of everything—"

"Shhh," Keenan whispered and kissed her forehead. "Calm down, baby. Relax yourself."

She shook her head and took Matt from a passing relative. He wrapped his chubby arms around her neck, and she pulled away from Keenan. "I'm selling that house in Charlotte on short sale and her ass is going to move out. In a few weeks, she has to have all her shit out of the house so they can do a walkthrough."

"You're putting your mother out on the street?" He was appalled. She was going to ditch the house just so her mom would have to move to Atlanta.

Veronica was so upset that her voice broke once or twice in the middle of her tirade. "I bet she'll have to help me when she has nowhere else to go," she hissed. "This is always the answer. She does this passive-aggressive bullshit, and I'm supposed to sit here and take it—and I've had it! I have had it! I'm not putting up with her and this slight of respect anymore."

Keenan was speechless. Ms. Rubio was catching hell and had no advocate against being forced out into the street. He figured that this older woman had raised her own children and wanted to enjoy her retirement in Charlotte. He couldn't blame her for being in her sixties and not being ecstatic about raising her grandchild. He got it. But Veronica didn't, and this was the first sneak peek that he had into her cutthroat, calculating nature.

Her mother returned about forty minutes later with no explanation. Veronica snatched the grocery bag from Ms. Rubio's hands and took out the cups on the way to the birthday table.

They kept a respective distance from one another the rest of the evening. No one else seemed to notice, but Keenan did. It was nothing that he liked to witness, to be honest. He thought of his own mother, how much he loved her, and watching how Veronica interacted with hers made him wonder how she would treat his mom if they ever married and the two of them had a disagreement.

On the way home, he got a call from Kelvin, alerting him that his friend Derrick had arrived early to the fight party he was hosting at his own house. Floyd Maywether would be defending his welterweight title against Robert Guerrero, and the boys with their ladies were coming over to cheer him on.

"Oh, and Dad, the tree is down!" he yelled before hanging up.

When Keenan pulled into his driveway that evening, he looked out the driver's-side window and saw that the oak tree had toppled over from the rain at some point during the day. Its heavy trunk was upended across the backyard lawn, and the red Georgia clay around its roots showed its backside to his living-room window. At the time, he appreciated Veronica's insight into predicting this unfortunate event. Later, he would wonder if she'd uttered a witch's curse.

He parked the car and squished around the house before standing silent in front of a snaggled branch. There were twigs and leaves sprinkled across his formerly manicured lawn. His fight party was in a few hours, and he didn't have time to worry about what to do with the behemoth tree.

They all disbanded the tree funeral for a bit while Veronica, Keenan, and the boys cleaned the house. Later that evening, his house swelled to capacity and became exceptionally loud between voices, laughter, and TVs in every room.

He and Veronica were touchy-feely that night, and he continuously squeezed her knee, her hand, her arm, or slow-kissed her on the cheek. He figured the whole room knew that this was the woman who had stolen his heart. She blushed and tried to scoot away once or twice, but for the most part they were *that* couple at the party.

Midway through the fight, he stood to get her another drink from the kitchen. It was empty except for a few greedy people finishing off the snacks. He grabbed a fresh red cup and scooped a few chunks of ice out of the bag in the freezer. When he turned around, her friend Whitney was walking into the kitchen with her own red cup.

"Whatchu drinking?" Keenan asked with his right hand out. He expected her to give him her cup.

"No, I need to say something to you," she responded. She held onto her cup and Keenan slowly dropped his extended arm.

Shit.

He unscrewed the big jug of generic bargain grocery store peach tea and poured it into Veronica's cup, glancing curiously at Whitney. *This was not happening again. How could one woman need so many disclaimers?*

"Don't make her mad, all right?" Whitney said as she sipped from her cup.

"I wouldn't like her when she's angry? Is that it?" He tried to laugh it off, but she only looked at him in a condescending manner that pissed him off.

"You may not know her very well, but she can turn into a monster over the slightest little thing," Whitney said, clearly fed up with his smart-ass response.

Then she turned and left him by the refrigerator.

This could have been an open-and-shut case of jealousy, but Whitney was just as beautiful and just as successful. He didn't feel like this was a jealousy thing, especially coming on the heels of Veronica's teenaged cousins at Matt's birthday party.

He suddenly reflected on a conversation Veronica and he had about a fist fight that she'd had with Whitney. It occurred just two years back at Veronica's home in Grayson, when she had relocated to the Atlanta area from Charlotte. She and Whitney had recently gotten past it and started talking again.

These last two signs were sitting on his shoulder, waiting to be acknowledged. He still didn't feel like it was wise to tell Veronica about the warnings from her friend and family member.

He did feel like it was time to take out the fine-toothed comb, and that's what he did for the next couple of weeks. He never showed up late for a date. He always brought flowers and even sometimes her favorite wine, Pinot Grigio. She would get frustrated with her schedule at work often. She didn't show any anger, just relief that she had a great career. He fell silent on some days, and she never went into panic mode. They enjoyed each other's jokes, talked about their dreams, made love for hours at a time, and spent most weekends either at his house or in her apartment.

He didn't see any horns. He didn't hear any growling. He just saw a woman begin to open up more and more to him.

And he began to open up to her, relaxing as they fell in love. He started to think long-term and ignore the calls from other women. Francis still called from time to time, but it took him longer to call her back. He wasn't picking up numbers from random women. He wanted her, and he wanted there to be an "us."

Raj was still skeptical, and Keenan eventually just stopped bringing her up when they would talk. What was the use when things were going so good, anyway?

He did replay Raj's words of advice one week later on the road to Charlotte with Veronica, Matt, Kelvin, and Cameron. They were traveling to remove furniture from her mother's home, and it was a pleasant nighttime ride in an SUV that Veronica had rented earlier in the day. Everything Raj said made logical sense, but Keenan was a believer of romance and incredible love stories where people connect through kismet.

Raj was going to be wrong. Right?

Keenan looked over at Veronica as she plucked around on her cell phone. They were falling in love. After three and a half months, love was finally here! Or so he thought.

She looked up with the silver glow from her phone on her face and said, "Can I drive?"

"No, I got this," he immediately replied.

"You're an asshole," she said under her breath.

The needle scratched across the record at that point. "Really?" he asked, hurt and disappointed that Raj won the argument and was nowhere in the room. "My kids are in the car and you're going to curse at me?"

She thought better of it and her mouth twisted in self-disappointment. "I'm sorry," she said.

Keenan looked at her for a minute, eager to believe the best. Then he kept driving.

They drove to Charlotte with little to no conversation or no stops. When they arrived within the city limits, Veronica directed them to her mother's three-story brick townhouse. It was a brick rowhouse connected to other homes, and he found the inside was neat and tidy. Veronica walked around the living room with yellow sticky notes, selecting which furniture she wanted to donate to charity and which furniture she wanted to take back to Atlanta.

Keenan complimented Ms. Rubio on her home and she meekly thanked him. "I never expected to live here," she said quietly. She pulled out a chair at the kitchen table and then offered him a chair.

"Just found yourself here, huh?" Keenan said as he sat down and scooted up to the table.

"Well, I was comfortable in New York," Ms. Rubio began, "but Veronica told me that since she was done with her residency, that she was going to establish a practice here in the city . . . and that I could work for her and get paid a salary. So, I moved here and helped her. Then she only paid me once."

Keenan tucked his lips in and listened. There was something irretrievably broken between these two, and it was something that he hoped never reached his sons. They had a solid figure of womanhood in their mother, and he didn't want to introduce anything less into their lives.

"So, what did you do?" he asked Ms. Rubio.

"I went back to school for counseling and established my own self here in Charlotte. I made friends and settled into the city. She told me I couldn't have dogs in this house, and I gave away my babies. Then she up and moves to Atlanta and leaves her dog with me." She sucked her teeth and let some silence sit in the space between them.

Veronica came to the kitchen with the boys hanging from her arms. To anyone peering in the windows, it would seem like they were a loving family worthy to be on one of those warm, fuzzy grocery commercials. Keenan knew, though, that this was clearly an illusion.

Everyone was exhausted when they finally arrived at the nearby hotel, so Keenan's kids were placed in an adjoining room. There were no more glitches between them, until they sat down to eat lunch in the hotel restaurant the following day.

Keenan had called a tree-removal service to dispose of the tree in his backyard, and the guy's now-constant calling pulled his nerves thin. His insurance company was on the hook to pay the tree service, and unfortunately, it was now one week later and the insurance company was taking its sweet time paying the man. This was no reason for him to suddenly start asking Keenan to hurry up and pay him out of his own pocket. It just didn't work like that, especially when he was out of town. The aggrieved man soon began to just send text message after text message, begging for Keenan to call him back. They began a text-messaging diatribe which the boys ignored, but Veronica zeroed in on.

"Key, who are you texting?" she asked with indignation.

Here she goes, he thought. Outdone, he hit send on his text message and shoved the phone across the table toward her. If she thought it was another woman, she could see for herself that he was trying to get this knucklehead off his back.

He meant to shuttle the phone toward her, but the phone skidded across the table with just enough force to knock over her salad dressing. It flipped over and scattered all over her blouse and the table.

"Shit!" he yelled in frustration. "Didn't mean to—"

"You . . . tried to . . . hit me," she said through gasps of air, interrupting his apology. "You tried to hit me!"

"Oh, Veronica, stop the bullshit. It was a mistake," he said, standing to his feet.

Kelvin and Cameron's mouths were open and their bodies were tense as they watched everything unfold. She remained in the same posture that she was in when the salad dressing hit her dress. Keenan tried to touch her and she shirked away.

Now she's scared of me, Keenan thought. *Great.*

She signaled for the waitress to come over and box up the rest of the food. Keenan stayed in the dining room and paid the bill, hoping that the rest of the evening could die down to something manageable, peaceful, and easy.

It felt like he was walking through water as he made his way back to the hotel room. He tried to enter the door but, lo and behold, she had locked the door from the inside. In fact, he could hear her playing with Matt as he giggled and squealed with delight. His knocks went unanswered, and so did his calls. He choked down any bit of anger so he wouldn't unleash on his kids and knocked on their door. Kelvin answered, and he looked embarrassed for him.

"Dad, she put all your stuff over here," Kelvin said, and pointed to a corner that held all of his toiletries, clothes, and luggage. Cameron started to go through the pile and tell him everything he discovered.

"Here's your toothpaste. Here's your brush. Here's your—"

"Okay, okay, okay," Keenan hurriedly said in a tone that signaled "enough."

Cameron returned to his bed and finished watching television. Keenan sat down on Kelvin's bed and thought about how she had the keys to the truck. Despite all the warnings he received from people that knew her best, he moved forward, a soldier of love, and was now wounded on the field in front of his kids. It was very possible that she could leave him and his sons in Charlotte with no way back to Atlanta. He realized this was the same woman who fired and evicted her own mother.

Why should he sit here and play a game with her?

He told the boys to go to the pool, and they obediently changed and were gone in about fifteen minutes. He tried calling Veronica again, but this time the call went straight to voicemail. He opened up his internet browser on his phone and found an affordable rental car on a booking site.

Within twenty minutes he was in the back of a cab and on his way to the airport to prevent a bad situation from becoming worse. When he returned to the hotel, the kids left the pool and they all hunkered down in their room to go to sleep. The plan was to leave first thing the next morning.

Keenan was in the middle of a cozy sleep paralysis when his cell phone rang and jarred him awake.

What the hell was it now?

She wanted to talk. He glanced at the red-numbered clock on the nightstand between the beds and saw that it was close to two a.m. A part of him said to let it go and that this was the confirmation for every warning that he had received since little Matt's birthday party. Another voice told him to go talk, *Because after all, you do miss her*. The voice that told him to stick it out and to go talk things through was the one he listened to as he got out of bed and went to her hotel room.

She was waiting by the door in a robe. He didn't even have to knock this time.

Considering that there was nothing for him to say that he hadn't already said, he resigned to remain silent and hear what she had to say. They both sat down near one another on the sofa. Matt was sleeping in his crib and none the wiser.

"That didn't go well," Veronica said.

"You think?" he tried to fight against the sarcasm, but he wanted her to know how much of a ruse this whole evening had been at his expense.

"I felt like you were trying to just . . . I don't know . . . I just felt like you were trying to abuse me," she said. Her hands were cupped in her lap.

"Veronica, I would never try to hurt you—let alone abuse you over a dumb text message. My sons were there. We were in public. Why would I do that?"

She shook her head and then the tears started. "I'm so sorry, Key. I've been through some things, and I didn't know if I was seeing it again."

"I need you to at least trust me for me and my track record so far," he said. "I mean, I was trying to handle the guy from the tree-removal service and—"

"I know, I know," she said, interrupting him. It was as if she didn't want to hear anymore.

"Can I finish?" he asked. "I want you to know how sorry I am that my actions took you to that place."

She nodded and gave him the floor but kept her eyes downcast, as if she was being yelled at before a beating. He realized then that he had some major work to do before he could even get to the outer corners of her heart. He faithfully believed in love conquering all, and told himself that if he remained patient, loved her enough, and communicated with her enough, that she would eventually drop the iron curtain around her soul and let someone in. Or better yet, just let herself feel the vulnerability that everyone feels when they allow love to have its perfect work.

This was a pivotal moment in their relationship, because this was when he was confronted with the truth of who she was as a person—and he still decided to love her. He decided to not throw in the towel. Some people call it foolish, but he believed that everybody comes to that decision at some point within a relationship. Sometimes the warnings are valid, and you make a conscious decision to stay and work through the behavior that brought on the warnings.

This is what he did, and this is what he believed agape love requires. It's not conditional, nor is it something that you turn on and off when you're angry, rejected, or misunderstood. He felt this in an extra measure because as the man in the relationship, he knew that it was his responsibility to be a role model. He also had to lead two (and hopefully three) young black men by example.

So, giving up and walking away from her never crossed his mind.

At the moment, he had no idea that he was seeking love in return from someone who was preoccupied with someone else. Not that Veronica was preoccupied with another man, but he did recognize that someone had hurt her to the point that she was emotionally unavailable and working to still get past that someone's effect on her heart.

There were so many things going through his head at the

moment, and he couldn't find one reason to end the relationship. In fact, he actually encouraged himself and thought about all of the fifty- and sixty-five-year marriages we all applaud and throw huge galas for all the time. He wondered how much we would celebrate if we knew every petty or immature thing each person had done to the other since the day they met.

Again, he knew that dating in his forties was extremely different from dating in his twenties. He knew there was an added level of care that needed to be taken because of the watchful eyes of their children. He just couldn't fathom Veronica not being in his life. That's where he was at that point, and he was determined to try harder.

All of this went through his mind when he reached out to grab her hand. "Are we good?" he asked.

"We've only been together three and a half months, so there's a lot about me that you can't even fathom."

"That a threat?" He tried to make light of the situation, having worked through everything in his head. He wanted to see where she was, though.

"I just want you to know I have a whole history and life before you, Key."

"I'm aware of that," he said.

"We could get to that point. Anything is possible," Veronica said.

He scrunched his face and pulled back. "Come again?"

"I mean, every couple goes through things," she said before she paused. "Matt's father, Sam, my ex-boyfriend, beat me up, and the guy I dated while in med school locked me in a basement one time while we argued." She said it very quietly, as if she didn't want to hear it herself. Maybe she didn't want him to really hear it.

Either way, he felt like protecting and loving her was something he had to do for her more than him. "I don't want you to ever go through anything like that again," he said, scooting even closer to her. "I shouldn't have tossed the phone like I did, and I'll be more cognizant of those sorts of things."

"I've been raped, beaten, and have had several abortions. I am a pediatrician, Key. I put myself through college and I just—I'm just not perfect."

Damn. The hardest of circumstances had not chiseled her beauty away and what he thought was her kindness. He almost thought that he stood corrected about her vulnerability. Sure, there was some bad history with her mother, but none of that baggage needed to be unpacked right now. She was opening herself up to him and telling him things that troubled her. He wanted to take all of her burdens and hold them, remove them, protect her from them.

"Baby, I'm not going to hurt you," he reassured her. "I'm sorry, and it was an accident." He was growing tired of the drama, to be honest. He told her he had rented a car just in case she thought about leaving him with his boys.

"I would never do that," she said sweetly with a smile.

He figured they were back to where they needed to be. "I'm glad we could talk this through," he said.

She decided that she needed space for the rest of the night, and he gave that to her. It was the least he could do.

The next day they tried to return to normal by taking the kids to an amusement park just outside of the Downtown Charlotte city limits. Kelvin and Cameron forgot the turmoil and uncertainty of the night before as soon as they entered the park gates. Within an hour they were strapped into the thrill rides and screaming their heads off.

Later, they loaded up both cars with the contents of poor Ms. Rubio's house, and their caravan quietly traveled back to Atlanta. The relationship locked back into a steady rhythm that he could count on and look forward to each day. The brouhaha in Charlotte literally stayed in Charlotte and never reared its head in Atlanta.

Kinda.

They were driving to the health food market one Saturday, and he noticed that Veronica was constantly texting on her phone.

"You want me to drive?" he asked with just enough sarcasm to let her know he didn't appreciate the texting.

"I'm texting Pete, Matt's godfather." Despite their dating and romantic history, Veronica thought he would be a good role model for Matt, especially since Pete could not have children of his own. So, she asked him to be Matt's godfather.

"Oh, I didn't know you kept in touch with him," Keenan said, surprised that Matt's godfather was actually someone she could contact at a moment's notice. After all, he was in a relationship and soon to be married.

She had decided that it was best that he not put his name on Matt's birth certificate like they had agreed to do while she was pregnant. This, in turn, made Pete feel betrayed, and he quickly ended the relationship. Sam was the biological father, but he was in New York and had separated himself from Veronica, as well. She had mentioned to Keenan that it was best that Matt not have a father on the birth certificate, as she didn't want any man having equal rights to parent Matt.

"Yes, we're friends. Can you remain friends with an ex?" she responded just as dryly.

"I tend to not keep in touch that much," Keenan said. This was irritating to debate.

They pulled into a parking space at the health food market, and she turned the car off before turning to face him. As he glanced over to her phone, he noticed that she was also texting Ced—the guy she dated just before she met him.

"I don't believe it. Let me see your phone."

He didn't really have anything that he didn't want her to see. He had cut back on dating since they had become exclusive. Francis still called. A few randoms here or there. But nothing like what he could do if he were not in a relationship. He really wanted to give his all to this relationship. So, he passed her his phone and gently put it in her hand.

She smiled big and began to scroll through his text messages.

"Oh. Oh! What's this?" She flipped the phone around and showed him a group selfie that his friend Mia in Texas sent to him. Mia wasn't an ex or even someone he dated; they met and started a friendship that remained a friendship. The picture was harmless, but in her mind, it was a picture of another woman, and that was something that was off limits in the world of Dr. Veronica Rubio.

She gave his phone back and he put his hand on the door handle, certain that the conversation was over.

"Wait," she said. "I want you to call Mia and tell her that you have a girlfriend now and that she can't reach out to you anymore. You know I have the number. I have a way with numbers," she said, reciting Mia's number from memory. Her mind was a computer.

Was she serious? Mia would clown his ass for a couple of months off of this. He felt like a small crunchy French fry at the bottom of the bag. "Veronica, I am not doing that!"

"So, something must be going on," she said defiantly. Her nose lifted into the air.

Just then, her phone rang. He grabbed it before she could answer it and saw that it was Ced.

"You first," he said, holding the phone out of her reach. "You tell him not to reach out to you anymore, and *then* I'll tell Mia."

She wasn't counting on this turn of events. He'd never met Ced, but thanked him silently for turning everything into his favor.

She stopped reaching for her phone and swiped his. He lowered her phone and watched as she sent a text to Mia.

"This is Veronica, Keenan's girlfriend," she spoke each word slowly as she typed. "Do not reach out to Keenan again. He is in a relationship."

Keenan groaned inwardly. This was sure to provide a colorful response from Mia later that evening. He was right—the words she had for him were choice, to say the least. In the meantime, it was his turn.

"Now send one to Ced telling him not to get in touch with you," he said firmly. *Fair is fair.* She did, promptly, and they soon entered the health food market as the smiling, attractive couple that everyone thought they were.

The next morning Keenan got up early at her house to go feed the dog. He knew this was always a point of contention between them, and she had even started to give him suggestions on automatic dog feeders. He was not sure if she thought he had to go check in with another woman, or if she just had deep-rooted abandonment issues. It had become a norm, and it was the same old thing this morning.

Veronica, dressed impeccably in a red lace teddy, was on his heels and fussing about leaving. "I don't know why you can't buy one of those feeders I sent you the links for. I'm about to just buy one and send it to you."

"Oh, okay," he said.

"Then we'll see what your excuse is."

They argued through the living room and the foyer.

"I'll look into it," he said for the millionth time, and then opened the front door while still facing her.

"Oh, my GOD!" she said, the last word a long, shrill scream, followed quickly by another one. And another one.

Keenan watched her face distort in fear as she screamed bloody murder. He turned around to see a snake coiled on the steps in front of the door. He could have stepped on it. He slammed the door shut and just went out the back door instead.

"Keenan, there's a snake on the front doorstep!" Veronica shrieked after him.

"I'll be back to deal with it. Just . . . don't open the front door," he said.

Spiders and snakes didn't give him the shrieks, but as he drove home to feed the dog, he couldn't help but be concerned that this was another sign. So far, he felt that he had beaten the curse of every sign that popped up between them. But this was different. It was ominous. It was blatant and hard to explain.

He sat at his laptop and tapped "snakes" into the Wikipedia search engine while his dog munched contentedly in the background. Before returning to deal with Veronica's problem, he wanted to take a moment to analyze the nature of a snake. Keenan skimmed the information: highly evolved predators that have over 2,900 species. They don't play games with you before they kill, and they don't rip anything out of you to cause pain. They simply get close enough to you in a silent slither before swallowing you whole. The page also said that a snake's nature is often connected to vengefulness and vindictiveness, because they deliver deadly defensive bites without giving prior notice or warning.

Vengefulness and vindictiveness. It did give him pause. Keenan had been in Georgia over fifteen years and had never seen a snake curled up on his doorstep like the morning paper.

He drove back over that afternoon prepared to deal with it using a garden rake or something, but it was gone.

About midway through the week, though, his phone rang. It was a frantic Veronica. The snake had returned yet another time. He drove to the store, bought a box of mothballs, and took care of the matter. In hindsight, he should have just prayed the serpent away *and* bought the mothballs, right?

Veronica's World

The first court day with Veronica—Cross-examination

"DO YOU RECOGNIZE the handwriting on this prescription?" his lawyer asked.

"Yes," she said.

"Whose handwriting is it?"

"Mine."

"And whose name did you sign?"

"Keenan Green."

"And what is the prescription for?"

"Phentermine."

"What is phentermine?"

"A weight-loss drug."

"Did Mr. Green ask you for a weight-loss drug?"

"No."

"Who was it for, then?"

"It was for me," Veronica admitted.

"Just for the record," his lawyer stated, "are you aware that a doctor who writes prescriptions for friends and family is definitely in violation of the Medical Board of Georgia?"

"Yes," Veronica said softly.

* * *

Veronica was getting more and more concerned about losing weight.

"I'm not using this thing enough," she said one night in her bedroom as she removed several now-dry bras and panties from the railing of her stair climber exercise machine. "I like your treadmill. I think I would work out more if I had a treadmill."

"I have an extra one in storage," Keenan said, already naked and lounging in bed, waiting for her to join him.

"Really?"

"Yeah. It's my dad's. He left it here when he moved back to California. I can loan it to you until he wants it back, which could be never."

Not too long after this, he moved the treadmill from storage and set it up in her house. She seemed really happy about it, and Keenan was, as always, delighted to please her. True love, right?

"This is great," she said. "I'm going to use it and get rid of these extra pounds!"

Keenan had begun to notice how intently she spoke about weight loss. But at this point, he was more than happy to help her reach her goal. Later, he would wish that he never even delved into that subject with her.

About a week later, he called Veronica on his lunch break, eating a donut. "We're still on for dinner, right?"

"Sure," Veronica said. "What are you having for lunch?"

"A donut," he said, and laughed.

It didn't seem as funny by midafternoon. *Was something wrong with that donut?* He was queasy and uncomfortable. He felt worse that evening, but he was not going to miss his date with Veronica. As planned, he met her at a little Thai restaurant they both liked, ordered low-spicy beef pad thai, and tried to eat. It wasn't really working, though.

"You're sweating," Veronica said. "Are you okay?"

"Not really," he admitted. "I've been sick to my stomach since this afternoon."

Her sweet face showed the concern of a professional as she signaled for the check and bundled them out of there. Keenan was relieved that she took charge, as he was feeling worse every minute. It felt like he had food poisoning, but he wasn't too sure that that was the case.

Veronica drove as fast as she could safely and stopped at a drugstore across from her apartment. She rushed in and out, and they sped home.

When they arrived at her house, Veronica said, "Here, take this. It will make you feel better."

"What is it?"

"Zofran." Veronica explained how it chemically blocked the triggers in his body that caused nausea and vomiting. He was so grateful for how she took care of him that day, he didn't consider once how he never authorized her to purchase it for him or prescribe it to him. This was the only time that he needed a prescription, but not the only time she would write one in his name.

She wanted to lose weight, but she wasn't for using the exercise machine in her bedroom or his father's treadmill in her living room. Her pick of poison was a prescription for some pills that made her drop weight with little to no effort: phentermine. Surely the side effect of getting an extra boost of energy for her career as a medical doctor and life as a single mother didn't hurt. Whatever she was using them for, she apparently needed more than a single prescription could provide. She began filling out scripts in his name and going to pick them up. Sometimes she even used her mother's name. Half of her family had a file on hand at various drugstores in various cities.

He was just a pawn in Veronica's game at this point. She had a point to prove, and he was the one who had dealt with her long enough to even get this grand prize of a relationship. But the old college try had nothing on Keenan. By now, the little boy in him was sure that he had picked the best koi for his bedroom aquarium back at University Gardens. Sure, the fish wasn't perfect and it had a few scratches and damaged fins here or there. Sure, there were prettier women with less baggage . . . but there was still something in Veronica that made him love her more and more each day.

He loved how she could change her voice to impersonate just about any dialect in the western hemisphere. She worked about five minutes from his job, so he loved that they could meet often for lunch, or he could buy her favorite lunch and bring it to her. This only happened if he was dressed appropriately. If he wasn't dressed in a suit and tie, then he could pretty much forget about stopping by the hospital to see her. Presentation was über important to her, and the last thing she wanted was for him to show up wearing something that made it seem like he stood on a corner.

They decided that they had moved too fast into a relationship, and that they would instead be friends who were dating and ditch the title. They agreed that they just moved a little fast in the beginning of their relationship and wanted to build on the friendship.

He loved how she randomly started calling him Key, just like his mother. No one else had ever done that, not even his ex-wife. Her idiosyncrasies were numerous, and that just made her even more unique in his eyes. She had a stellar memory, especially when it came to numbers. Every night, she made a casserole for dinner, and sex with her made him zone out from time to time at work while his mind was in instant replay. He loved the sexy way she squinted her eyes like she was trying to see when she would listen to him go on and on about something. They did family-oriented activities together which included their kids.

Most of their days were very pleasant, but the disagreements they did have were passionate and heated. Keenan often blew these disagreements off, as they were just something that came with the territory. She, however, kept a running tally of every fault, mistake, and tiff so that it could be presented as proof for whatever she planned to accuse him of in the future.

Some would say that you need to just let things flow and you have to remember the signs when you see them. Maybe that's what Veronica was doing once the honeymoon phase of the relationship ended. The only problem with that philosophy is that you give yourself an easy out and end up taking life like a feather in the wind. Some people want to know what they're getting into, but Keenan was determined to understand what he was getting into. There's a difference.

Keenan believed there is a moment in a man's life when he has to accept who he is and who the person is that he decides to bring along on his life journey. Part of that acceptance is in exhibiting the fruits of the Spirit: love, joy, peace, patience, kindness, goodness, faithfulness, gentleness, and self-control. The Bible says against such, there is no law. There can never be enough of these attributes in a relationship between two people. This doesn't even apply to romantic relationships; it applies to all relationships—

people in your family, on your job, your neighbors, and even the one you call "bae" should be recipients of these attributes at some time. It's hard to do every single day, because we are human and we do have this covering of flesh. But it's so much easier to understand someone when you have taken the time to be kind, be gentle, and execute self-control, among other things.

He thought that he was reaching that point in the relationship and had done everything right by Veronica, in spite of what she did or said to him. He never gave up, and he prayed continually that God would order his footsteps. They started attending church together at an Atlanta mega-church. This was a family effort, since they included the boys early in their relationship and continued weekly.

Francis called one Sunday after church, after Veronica and Matt had gone home. She often called on Sunday afternoons, since she knew that Veronica was less likely to be there. Keenan was glad for a chance to catch up.

"So, guess what," she said. "I'm coming to Atlanta."

"That's great," Keenan said cautiously. "What for?"

She had a friend's bridal shower to attend. She chatted a little about the couple and what she thought their chances were in the long term. It hurt him a little to hear her so excited about someone else's marriage, but he knew better than to dwell on it.

"I was wondering if you might be able to help me be there and support them," she finished.

So, at least he was still good for something. "Let me see what I can do," he said.

He talked it over with Veronica, thinking that he was doing the adult thing in the spirit that both he and Veronica had agreed to be friends at that point and really get to know each other. To his surprise, she agreed that he should help Francis out.

He didn't necessarily make plans to see Francis while she was in town; he just considered her a friend and wanted to help her in any way that he could. So, he reserved a room for her at the JW Hotel in Midtown and forwarded the e-reservation for her plane ticket.

When Saturday came, it was the first sunshine Atlanta had seen in a week. A heavy storm front had just passed through, breaking the humidity and leaving behind a bright, hot day. He was preparing for the strange balance of making sure that Francis was okay while he planned to spend all his time with Veronica. Veronica, however, was missing in action. He called her phone and got nothing. He sent her text messages and they went unanswered. He wasn't sure what sparked this latest hissy fit, but he didn't want it to ruin his weekend.

He was lounging in the living room about to start a movie when his phone finally buzzed. But it wasn't Veronica. It was Francis.

"Welcome to Atlanta," Keenan said.

"Thanks," Francis replied. "What are you up to?"

"About to watch a movie."

"What? No. It's too nice to stay inside. Come to lunch with me," Francis said. "Let's go salsa dancing." This was a Spanish restaurant known for its authentic tapas menu and live music.

Without hearing from Veronica, he accepted his free time and headed out to Buckhead to see his ex. He hadn't been to a salsa club in a while, and was pleased that Francis had chosen their old haunt for lunch. They had spent many fun evenings there ordering new delights from the specials menu, sipping Spanish wine, and dancing. The Latin jazz combos who performed there were always able to get people on the floor, and this place drew a crowd who appreciated the music as much as the food.

The restaurant hadn't changed: festive flags and instruments of all types decorated the ceiling, and couples chatted at tiny tables that filled the restaurant to capacity. Through a stroke of luck, they were able to snag a table on the covered patio, the perfect blend of open-air and indoor dining. They followed their hostess up the two shallow steps to be seated next to one of the floor-to-ceiling sliding-glass doors, wide open in the glorious sunshine. Soon, they were splitting the tomate fresco like old times.

The afternoon was bright and warm, and so was Francis. Her outfit was casual, with a silky, loose-fitting top that flashed a little of her lacy bra, high-heeled sandals, and a skirt that stopped just above the knee.

"You look . . . refreshed," Keenan observed. He recognized, a little ruefully, that the break in time from him had done her well.

"Thank you," Francis replied, smiling cautiously, "I think."

"No, really," Keenan insisted. "You're glowing. You must have a lot of happiness coming in your life."

Now she was undeniably pleased, and smiled in Keenan's favorite remembered way.

They ordered patatas bravas, then the brocheta de chorizo, then an order of mussels, all one at a time, drawing out their conversation and enjoying each other. They laughed together as Keenan shared intimate family stories, appreciating the opportunity to talk about his sons with someone who knew them so well. While he didn't feel necessarily that he wanted her back, he did finally acknowledge that she was still very much a part of his life, and he realized that he was glad that he made time for her. Then Francis brought the final mussel to her lips and finished it off.

"I don't need the hotel anymore," she said. "I'm staying in Alpharetta with a girlfriend. I hope you can get your money back." She lifted her napkin from her lap and folded it loosely on the table, avoiding his eyes.

"Probably not, but it's okay," he replied. He had learned to be patient with this one. Jumping the gun never got him anywhere good when it came to her.

"That's too bad," she said. "It's a shame to let it go to waste." She paused, as if thinking, but Keenan knew her well enough to sense a bit of playfulness rising in her. Then she looked him full in the face. "Why don't I let you give me one last foot rub?"

He had to smile. "Sure," he said agreeably. "Because we wouldn't want the hotel room to go to waste."

They drove their separate cars to the Midtown JW and entered the spacious lobby. Keenan always appreciated how each JW Hotel has its own distinct style. While the Downtown JW was trendy and industrial, the Midtown JW lobby was more traditional and plush.

They entered the lobby, walking past the upholstered armchairs and quilted sofas, and climbed the marble steps with the wrought-iron railing. The line was unexpectedly long, so Francis disappeared into one of the armchairs, and all Keenan could see were her long, sexy legs in those high-heeled sandals. Was this really going to end at just a foot rub?

They rode the elevator to a high floor, chatting amiably, and when Keenan opened the door to the room, both pretended to be engaged in the view. The floor-to-ceiling windows framed Midtown Atlanta to its best advantage, and they could see both the skyline and the city's rich canopy of magnolias, dogwoods, Southern pines, and oaks. After a moment, he began to draw the curtains, but Francis stopped him.

"Why not leave them open?" she said. She perched on the edge of the rose-tinted loveseat and bent down to loosen the tiny gold buckle of one sandal, providing yet another opportunity for Keenan to appreciate her taste in lingerie.

He took the cue to find the small bottle of lotion next to the shampoo and conditioner in the slate bathroom, perfectly stand-ard for a JW Hotel, but nothing spectacular. He regretted not knowing beforehand that he would be using the room; a bath-room upgrade with a tub would have been his first move. He would just have to make do.

The scent of the lotion was perfect for Francis: a subtle combi-nation of peach and musk.

When he returned from the bathroom, she was curled up on the loveseat, her long legs and bare feet tucked up underneath her. He rolled the office chair over to her and sat down.

"No, don't sit there," she said. "Sit next to me." She uncurled herself and placed her feet in his lap, and he skillfully used his thumbs and fingers to apply the lotion to all her favorite pressure points.

"Higher," she said, and his hands traveled up her calves, still so taut and silky. She was both forbidden and familiar. It was heady, and the impersonal atmosphere of the gray walls and thick carpet made them feel as if they were hidden away from the world. Each action seemed like it should follow the next. Why wouldn't he slide his hands up to her thighs? Why wouldn't she moan a little and let him? His hands went higher up her inner thighs until he was stroking her between her legs, feeling her clit swell under her panties. They were all tangled up in each other, and he leaned in for a long, wet kiss as she moved against him, aroused by his stroking hands.

He reluctantly turned his attention away from her pussy and wrapped his hands around her waist, looking for the button and zipper that would slide her skirt down and leave him able to see those sexy panties he had just been caressing. "Don't get lotion on my skirt," she breathed against his mouth, but she didn't stop him, and in a flash he was sliding that skirt over her taut thighs, admiring the tiny scrap of lace that remained.

He quickly pulled off his T-shirt and knelt down in front of her, wrapping her legs around his face as he sucked on her wet clit through her panties, enjoying the sensation of the lace on his tongue. He could smell the peach and musk of the lotion along with her own familiar scent, and as he explored her with his tongue he was reminded of the sweetness and sting of pineapple. It wasn't long until her head was thrown back on the pink loveseat, trying as hard to be quiet as she could, but not really succeeding. He was glad it was still so soon past check-in, so there were likely fewer guests on the floor to hear them.

But he didn't care that much, really.

She kissed him eagerly after she came, and he slid off her soaking panties and filmy top, and pushed the cups of her bra over so the nipples showed. She unbuckled his belt, but he stopped her and pulled off his own pants—he would be so much faster, and he was more than ready for his turn.

Both naked now, they pulled the covers down from the king-size bed and plunged into a long, slow sixty-nine on crisp hotel sheets, the way they had spent so many Sunday afternoons in the past. She sucked his dick in slow, long strokes, relaxed because she had already come, and he licked her clit while keeping his tongue broad and flat, not overstimulating her so she could focus on his dick—which she did beautifully, moving her body after a bit so that she could get more of him into her mouth until he exploded, and, unexpectedly, she gulped it all down. That was not her way.

He wondered if it had been a while for her, because it was clear she hadn't had enough yet. Now he was glad that Veronica had given him the deep freeze, because Francis was demanding his finest work. He licked and sucked her hard nipples until he felt his own erection return, and as soon as she felt it, she wrapped her legs around him and pulled him into her. He appreciated the plush, cushioned headboard that was at least one thing all the JW Hotels had in common. They knew their clientele, he guessed.

The thought vaguely went through his mind that, again, he was glad it was early afternoon, because anyone within a few doors would have a very clear understanding of just how deeply he was tearing this pussy up. Francis grabbed a pillow and clutched it to her own face as she came again and again.

As for Keenan, he was pretty sure he wasn't going to come again, until Francis wanted to jump into the shower and he decided to join her. He started to soap her hot, silky skin, then turned her around and pushed in from behind, bending her over in the steam, exploding one more time into her. They intertwined in the hot spray and made out until their fingers were wrinkled. That was just what he needed after several weeks of the Dr. Rubio treatment.

They didn't stay there long afterward, and she hurried out of the room to get to her friends, smirking a little at their goodbye. He knew she was glad that she could still take him when she wanted. He wasn't sad he let her.

He left the JW and was headed home when Veronica rang his phone. "Where have you been all day?" she asked.

He just wasn't in the mood for the games. Was it because he was getting fed up, or that he was feeling guilty? He didn't care. "Veronica, I've been calling you and my phone hasn't rung at all today," he replied. "Where have you been?"

"I have something to tell you," she said with a pause.

"I'm listening," he said, hoping that this didn't turn into one of those days. Maybe it already had.

"Ced just left my house."

He felt a little slapped in the face. This was the same guy who also received the "Don't reach out to me anymore" text. The same one who never drove to Atlanta and always made her come see him in Warner Robins. This was the same man who never introduced her to his family and claimed that he didn't have any money or savings, even though he was retiring from the US Army.

That guy.

Keenan tried to remain calm and said, "What brings him up here?"

"He interviewed at a job in Alpharetta, and I think he's trying to finally get himself together," she said lightly. Flippantly, almost. It was like she was explaining something trivial that you may have noticed as you drove down the street.

"So, he stopped by to say hello. Okay," he said flatly.

"No, no, no!" she laughed. "He stopped by to pick up one of his shirts. That's all."

Did she really expect him to believe that? He asked if they had sex, and she said that they didn't, and with the same breath she asked him to come out to her house to see her.

He turned his car around to head north and checked his ego. The last thing he wanted was evidence of any kind from this afternoon's romp with Francis. *What kind of games were they playing with each other?*

Veronica was dressed in a form-fitting strapless dress with a waiting babysitter when he arrived. She wanted to go down to a sushi bar for dinner, so he drove down to Lenox and they acted, strangely enough, like there was no Ced who had just spent copious amounts of time over the past twenty-four to forty-eight hours with his "friend." It didn't help that his mind kept drifting back to Francis's moans in his ear as he took her to a very familiar place.

They dined outside and watched the sun set over the city and

Atlanta's young professionals descend on Buckhead. It was a relaxing evening that held possibilities only he could put an end to.

"Let's go dancing," he said as they both fought for who would pay the bill.

She perked up even more at the suggestion, and they had an even better time once they arrived at the JW and danced for the better part of the evening.

Her moves were always so telling. It was her dancing that made him think twice about the story she told while in Charlotte. She later admitted that she was a waitress shortly after graduating high school in the now-closed and still-infamous strip club Nikki's. He watched her move her body like the snake that coiled itself around her welcome mat, and he took in the way she knew how to move her hips close to his body in a taunting manner. This was no former waitress from a strip club. This was a former stripper!

He enjoyed the evening, and it took his mind off all of the things he did that afternoon. He was through making excuses and justifying his actions. He had failed to honor her, and that was that. There was no sense in bemoaning his own actions when she clearly had done far worse with a man who had a long history of treating her like she was still a woman who could be bought with a couple ones and a few twenties.

"I have a surprise for you," he said on the elevator later that evening. She thought they were leaving for the night, but he had other plans. She stood in front of him looking like he was about to bring out the surprise behind door number three.

He hit the button for the top floor and took her to the room that he had just been in with Francis earlier that afternoon. The maids had been by the room and straightened up a bit. He was relieved until Veronica asked, "What is this bottle of lotion? Were you here before?"

Damn.

He didn't answer her. Thinking quickly, he grabbed her, pushed her backward, and they toppled onto the bed together. He made love to her long enough and hard enough to make her forget the bottle of lotion.

They laid there for a while afterward and cuddled before she arose and said that she had to get back to Matt and relieve the babysitter.

He drove her home to Johns Creek and figured this was a day he would put down in his own personal history books. It made him wonder how many times she had cheated, and if he really was sinking his character to the level that she expected. It's hard to gauge when a person you sincerely wanted to marry is involved. He didn't have the same feelings with Veronica. She was a different woman than Francis. He couldn't say that he had a rekindling of feelings with Francis, either. It felt more like it was their own way of saying goodbye to one another.

Cheating when a relationship is bad can often be the chicken move. Other times, it's the first sign that something in the relationship has soured.

He slept with Francis out of opportunity. She's a woman, he's a man, they had history, and they were alone in a hotel room. It just kind of worked out like that. He didn't initially want to see her or plan to see her while she was in town. It was an event he vowed to just keep to himself.

His drive home from Veronica's house allowed him to think some things through, and he realized that something between them was broken. Splintered, maybe, but definitely disjointed.

It was then that the tree falling over, the warnings from her friends and family, the snake on the doorstep, and the stories from her own mother began to echo in his mind. He was heading for something that could only prove itself detrimental.

But when he saw her the next day, they decided to be exclusive again. Maybe seeing Ced was closure for her as well as Francis was for him.

Meanwhile, Keenan began to take even more of an active role in Matt's life. It was nothing for him to babysit or include him in activities with his own sons. He didn't necessarily feel that he and Veronica were at that premarital stage in the relationship, but they were open and shared personal info via their cell phones, emails, and iPads. Many may frown at this, but it worked for them.

What didn't work was the way they communicated to one another. There were still landmines between them that he stepped on or that she detonated without his prior knowledge. Most of the time he was preoccupied with something else, and then *BAM!* The earthquake was upon him in all its glory. By the time he felt the rumble, the building was already swaying and his safest bet was to hide.

Veronica's birthday was in early July and he was trying his best to plan something original and extravagant, just like she wanted. The problem was that her friend Whitney wasn't much help in the way of planning. He suggested that they all meet up at this fusion restaurant in Buckhead. Whitney didn't think Veronica's friends could afford the $15–$20-a-plate meals they offered.

Okay, not a problem. He tossed out some other suggestions that really didn't go anywhere, so he ultimately left Whitney alone on the issue and just neglected to plan something. Of course, Whitney told a sorely disappointed Veronica that Keenan didn't plan anything for her birthday, and he received a major attitude. As a matter of fact, the next day they got into an argument on their way to church.

His boys were heading out to California to visit his mom for the summer, and he wanted to clear all of the logistics with his mom before they left the following morning. Nevermind that he was in the car with Veronica and they were heading to church. Nevermind that it was Sunday and things are supposed to be easy. Nevermind that she knew he was talking to his mother and she decided to turn up the gospel music to drown out his conversation.

He didn't know if she was still angry about no definite plans for her birthday or if she was angry that she didn't have more of a role in the conversation. What he did know is that she pulled the car over onto the side of the road and said, "We're going to sit here until you get off the phone."

He looked at her like she had two heads and put his phone on mute.

"I'm talking to my mother. Can you keep driving?" he said quietly.

"No," she said, and continued to look out the window.

"Veronica, keep—" he cut his words short. There was no need for him to compel someone to drive a car to a destination even though the passenger in the car was on the phone. He drank from a water bottle to try and monitor his anger. He figured that if he had something in his hand, and if he was focused on drinking, he wouldn't yell at her in frustration.

He continued his conversation with his mother and she sat in the driver's seat, pouting more and more by the minute. Once he finished the conversation, he put down his phone and took another sip of water. She didn't start the car. He said, "Well?"

"I'm not interested in attending church this morning," she announced.

"What? Why? What the fuck is wrong with you this morning?"

"Oh, now we're really not going to church! You can't even keep your filthy mouth clean for one fucking morning!"

"My filthy mouth? Veronica, you better drive us to church, because there are two people in this car who need to get right with God."

"I'm not going. And I'm driving. So, you're not going."

"We! Are! Going! To! Church!"

Keenan said, shaking the water bottle for emphasis at each word. Water splashed all over the dash and their clothes.

She immediately turned the car around and unceremoniously kicked him out of the car as soon as they got back to her apartment. He didn't hear from her for at least thirty-six hours. Of course, he apologized for his actions and she did, as well. But they ended up celebrating her birthday on the fourth of July instead of the actual day. She later explained that she stopped the car because she was frustrated that he didn't plan anything for her birthday, but he was on the phone planning his son's birthday.

Please.

Then Keenan had to endure another awkward moment with one of Veronica's exes. This time it was Pete—Matt's so-called godfather.

"Pete wants to come over and see Matt," Veronica announced one day as they were at her house, watching a movie.

"Okay," Keenan said.

"He's engaged," Veronica said, and her mouth made a sad little moue. "I want to see if she's good enough for him."

"Wait, his fiancée is coming too?"

"Yes, I told him to bring her. You'll be here too," she said.

Thanks for asking, he thought, but said nothing. He knew he would give in and be there. The next weekend, Pete came over with his fiancée, a leggy woman with warm, tawny skin and tight, reddish curls. She seemed to have a gentle and quiet nature, but maybe she was just intimidated by the situation. Pete played with Matt and bounced him on his knee a few times while they all made uncomfortable small talk and sipped coffee. Keenan breathed a sigh of relief when it was over, but Veronica's energy stayed aggressive. "I can't believe he got engaged before I did," she said through gritted teeth when they left, like it was a competition.

Keenan caught his friend Derrick up on the latest drama between Veronica and him, and he suggested a relationship counselor. So Keenan did some research and subsequently reached out to his ex-sister-in-law for a referral. She immediately recommended Dr. Harper Jones of Decatur, Georgia, who gave him a wealth of insight. Keenan checked out his website and saw that Dr. Jones was a Christian psychologist who had shared his relationship expertise on National TV, all over the internet, and several magazines. He was expensive, with rates at $150 per session, but he was definitely worth it. As a matter of fact, Keenan went alone to his sessions, bought his book, and even began to implement some of the book's suggested communication techniques and pointers.

The one particular lesson that stuck with him was to demand that his current love interest pay full value for his love. He had never considered that being too nice to Veronica would devalue himself in her eyes. He believed in giving and offering his very best to a woman. His self-esteem probably wouldn't allow him to expect for the woman to do as much as he could offer in a relationship. But after analyzing himself and the short history of the Veronica and Keenan Chronicles, he came to realize that he was giving a level of transparency and respect that Veronica clearly skipped out on most weeks—days, even.

What was most indicative of this "short sale" on transparency and respect was how Veronica and he argued. If you could create their arguments into a visual art, you would eventually have a fight scene from *300*, the moment when Sophia hit Miss Milly in *The Color Purple*, or any part of *Predator*. He began to reflect and see that there was strategy, calculation, a moment of silence, and then an attack that would come from seemingly nowhere.

He soon began to listen to Dr. Jones's advice more and more, and ask the right questions. He was looking for ways to fortify himself, learn from and improve his weaknesses, and yes, find out exactly how much he was playing into the rocky nature of his current relationship.

His responses could have been better. Tossing the cell phone, cheating out of opportunity, and shaking water from a bottle in a small, enclosed space are not actions he would want to see replaying on a billboard outside of his house.

Cracking through his ego was the hardest part. Allowing his ego to heal with the new information wasn't a walk in the park, either. He had to accept certain things about himself.

He also had to accept certain things about Veronica and the union they had built. Whether God was in this relationship or not, he had to accept it because Veronica didn't build the relationship. He helped her to build it, so what they created also had his DNA, and it was pointless to try and figure out who had the stronger genes. Liken it to having a child if that makes explaining it easier. Sometimes it is evident to see whose genes contributed the most, and sometimes you don't see one person's genes until the child is more mature.

He wasn't sure if their relationship was mature, had run its course, was tied together only by a soul tie, or if it was still in its infancy and in need of nurturing and growth. Later, he would consider his confusion as a part of not understanding the relationship pyramid. Keenan had come up with a relationship theory based on the model of a pyramid on his own, and a quick internet search revealed that many therapists and psychologists used a similar model to explain the transition of relationships from acquaintances to friends to lovers. What he had conceptualized as his own theory was an educated guess, and he was interested enough to continue his research and further develop his idea.

When there's unconditional love involved, there's high tolerance levels for the unexpected or the undesirable from people. For example, if someone you love sneezes in front of you, it's much less disgusting than if the sneeze came from a stranger. Up the relationship pyramid, there's millions of people at the bottom and only one at the top. Keenan reasoned that if you ignore a lot of your preferences and ignore their preferences, and date for convenience, sex, or money, you might move too fast to the top of the pyramid. At each level, there's a certain amount of increased tolerance for the other

Further, two people navigate to the top together. If you skip a bunch of steps, then it's like taking a final before taking the class. Some people pass, but most people don't. You can't skip the levels. You can move through them fast, but if you skip the levels, you will fail. And fast, he thought, is relative. If both people are moving at 180 miles an hour, they're still moving at the same pace. Keenan understood that he needed to pace himself to understand where he was in that pyramid and identify whether or not he was skipping steps.

The only thing he knew at that day and time was that he loved Veronica, and not the temperamental love that one would see in a movie or on a reality show. She made him want to be a better man so he could only love her in a more perfect way. He wanted to give her everything that her heart desired, protect her from anything she deemed a threat, and provide a safe space for her that kept her happy. He was also vested in the task of providing for and protecting her son.

One Saturday Veronica had to do rounds at a hospital, so Keenan spent the day babysitting little Matt. He loved the way Matt would wrap his chubby arms around his neck and cling to him before they crashed on the carpet and played games or tried to match his blocks into the corresponding-shaped holes. He loved the little duck-waddle run that Matt would do when Keenan turned into a hulking high-yellow bear and chased him, roaring, through Veronica's living room.

It began to bother Keenan that if he broke up with Veronica, Matt would miss out on having a father figure, and he would simply miss the joy that he felt filling that role.

He had no immediate plans to leave, but he wanted to know exactly why Matt's father, Sam, was willingly giving up this part of his life. In his opinion, these were the golden years for any father to enjoy. Who would willingly miss out on a first birthday, first haircut, first words, first steps, eating solid food for the first time, and the heart-aching first day of kindergarten?

His mind wandered to where Matt would be and who he would be when he entered middle school. He wondered if Matt would know at that time that it is okay to be smart. Who would guide him through his choices of peers and first romantic partners? How would he know what it means to be a man of integrity with a focused mind?

The savior complex isn't something Keenan subscribed to in his interpersonal relationships, but he liked to understand those who were around him the most. He knew that he couldn't understand Veronica, and what Matt would ultimately need, until he understood the one who sired him. Since he had access to Sam's number, he reached out to him and really didn't know what to expect. The conversation could either end with him giving Keenan a stern rebuke to mind his business, or a telling insider's look to who Veronica really is, or he could just end up being a slack-jawed waste of human flesh that she decided to procreate with during an especially lonely period.

Keenan quickly changed Matt and put him down for a nap in

his bedroom. It would have been especially problematic for Matt to let out one of his squeals in the middle of his conversation with an absentee dad. Once he could see that Matt was well into some quality REM sleep, he shut the bedroom door and sat down at the dining room table with Veronica's iPad. He scrolled through her contact list and found Sam's name and phone number within seconds.

He answered just before Keenan disconnected the call.

"Sam?" Keenan was cautious. He had heard of women saving the wrong name for different guys in their phone to prevent moments like this.

"Yeah, this him. Who is this?"

"My name is Keenan and I live in Atlanta. I'm dating Veronica Rubio," he replied. He wanted to give him enough info to know that he had a right to call.

He paused before speaking again. "She okay?" He sounded concerned.

"Oh, yeah, yeah!" Keenan tried to assuage his fears. "She's fine and Matt is fine. I'm calling about Matt, actually. But it has nothing to do with him. He's fine."

Sam paused again and simply said, "Okay." He gave a slight exhale of laughter and patiently waited for him to say something else.

He wanted to spit it all out before he wore the man's patience thin. "Veronica doesn't know that I'm doing this, but I wanted to know why you don't come around more. I mean, I love your son. He's smart and just a real beautiful kid."

"Why I don't come around more, huh?" Sam asked. "Let me ask you something, man. How long you been around my son and dating Veronica?"

Keenan started to lie, but figured it didn't matter at this point. "Almost five months," he said.

"Is that right? Okay, well let me explain something to you. I love Matt, too. I get the pictures that she sends to me. I just don't get the time that I deserve, and want, and ask for."

The conversation was going toward an insider's look. Keenan took a deep breath. He already knew what was coming. "She's keeping you from him?"

"Aw, man. Lemme tell you a few things about that woman you holding in your arms at night," Sam said. "She's a piece of work. Don't get me wrong—nicest person in the world. But she can be crazy!"

He was finding great pleasure in finally being able to tell his story. They both shared a chuckle, and that opened him up even more. "You understand where I'm coming from, and let me tell you that I appreciate you being man enough to call me and figure out what's going on. Okay? A lot of dudes wouldn't have done that shit, so you got some heart," Sam said, his voice becoming more animated.

"It's okay, no need to thank me. I taught him how to walk and really moved him forward in development when he needed it. He's a happy baby, and I just thought that since I connected with him so well, that I would . . . you know . . . " Keenan felt like he was rambling and began to trail off at that point.

"Yeah, yeah, yeah, yeah. That's no problem, man. Look here," Sam began, getting comfortable. "She ain't always in her right head, you know? I'm sure you doing all you can do, but she is nuts! Whatchu say your name was? Kevin?"

"Keenan," he replied. He was listening intently to whatever Sam would say next.

"She used to give herself insulin shots because she thought she had diabetes. Never been diagnosed, right? Just giving herself shots for no reason whatsoever," he said. "And get this—I try to put money in her account. She won't give me the routing number. I send clothes to her down there, and she sends them joints back talkin' about the clothes too big!" He blew a raspberry through his lips, and Keenan instinctively knew he was waiting for a response.

"I didn't know any of this. She always says that she never hears from you." He didn't want to offer anything that would give him more gasoline for the fire.

"And you ain't gonna hear none of this, you got me? You ain't gonna!"

"Wow," he replied.

"Man, listen, you seen Matt's godfather?"

Keenan remembered her telling him about Pete. He was the ex-boyfriend who met her while she was pregnant and wanted to stay with her and help her to raise Matt as his adopted son. Then she refused to put his name on the birth certificate.

"Yeah, I remember her telling me something about a godfather," he lied, not wanting to go into detail about Pete and his awkward visit.

"So she met that dude at the airport when she was dropping me off after my visit down there. Okay, get this: She met him then they start dating. In no time, this stranger is considered my un-born kid's father. What the fuck? Then they break up after Matt was born and now he's the godfather?" Sam finally guffawed.

Clearly, Veronica had fallen into the "crazy baby mama" category in his life. Keenan wondered how Sam viewed him and considered that he probably saw him as a small field mouse who kept overlooking the viper by his nest. Instead of the fisherman, he imagined himself as one of the koi fish in that garden pond that chomped down on a hook of meat as he swam by without a care in the world.

Duped.

Entrapped.

Suckered.

Gullible.

Sam shared story after story about Veronica's antics, her lack of compassion. He explained Veronica lied on him and shunned his every attempt to be a father to Matt. Even though he claimed that she called the police on him for no reason, Keenan already knew that she had experienced domestic violence in a relationship. He assumed without any doubts that this had come at the hands of Sam.

"Listen, man," Sam said finally when he had run out of gas, "I appreciate you. So, I'm going to tell you something you need to hear." He paused for dramatic effect. "Run," he said. "Don't walk. Run. Run while you still can."

If only life was that easy. If only he had the stealthy nature to slip away and disappear into the crowd of Atlanta singles. It would be nice to just detangle himself from every attachment and throw up deuces as he drove back to the southside of Atlanta. It didn't work out that way because he cared so much. Too much.

Or maybe he was really trapped in a relationship with a crazy woman.

Seven

Keenan Keeps Trying

WHEN KEENAN LOOKED back, he realized that the perfect transition out of Veronica's life could have occurred when he neglected to plan anything for her birthday. They didn't do anything together that day, and he could have moved on. He wished later that he had recognized the calm before the storm.

The tornado was unleashed in August 2013 when he took her to see R&B singer Maxwell perform at Chastain Park Amphitheatre. Veronica had originally purchased tickets for them as a surprise, but when they seemed shaky in early July, she gave them to her friend Whitney. Keenan thought it would be a good concert and a plus for the relationship, so he repurchased $400 tickets for the second row in front of the stage at Chastain Park Amphitheatre.

Los Angeles has the Hollywood Bowl; Washington, DC, has the Carter Barron; and Atlanta has Chastain, an outdoor amphitheater which is secluded in the woods and has become a summer favorite for those who want to enjoy warm, easy-going evenings with live music and a crowd that will enthusiastically sing along to every song and dance in the aisles. You can bring in food, candles, tablecloths, and wine to your reserved table, and it's common to see neighbors, coworkers, friends, and family members at some point during the evening for an especially popular show.

This was an event he had been looking forward to for a while, and he hoped that it would spark something again between them. Maxwell's music lends itself to romantic summer evenings, so he was hoping for the best and had purchased a table in the pit section of the amphitheater. They were close to the stage and had walked down what seemed like a million steps to get to their special seats.

They both unfurled the tablecloth and set up the table with picnic fare. As fellow concert-goers squeezed by, they unpacked a rotisserie chicken, pasta, and wine from a nearby health food market. Veronica knew that he liked a sweeter wine, and she had purchased plum wine for him while he gathered some other items in another part of the store.

He had just placed the bottle of plum wine on the table when she snatched it away and placed it back in the cooler.

He stood up with his mouth open as other concert-goers laughed and set up their own tables for the evening. Veronica sat perched on the edge of the green metal seat, her legs crossed and her elbows digging into the white concrete table.

He glanced in the cooler and put the wine back onto the table. He then turned and started unpacking the petit fours she selected for their dessert. He saw a flurry of movement out of the corner of his eye and turned around to see an empty table.

"What are you doing?" he asked. That seemed to be the question he asked her weekly now. He was beginning to feel like

Veronica was his own living, breathing crystal ball. Remember those? You shake them, and a die inside the toy reveals a definitive answer of "Yes," "No," "Maybe," "Of course," or "Absolutely not" in the little window.

He never knew what he would get on any given day.

"We don't have to put everything out now. Sit down," she hastily said.

"No," he responded with a plastic container of napkins and cutlery in his hand. He shook his head in confusion.

"Key, please sit down," she said again as she moved the cooler closer to her legs.

Incredulous, he dropped the container on the table and sat down next to her. This was once again one of those crazy moments where he couldn't tell what started the drama.

He tried to reach for the cooler and she kicked it out of his reach.

God, he just did not have room in himself for one more "What's wrong, baby?" She'd used them all up.

"Bitch?" he said under his breath. It came out before he could stop it. He wasn't proud of it, and he couldn't even make an excuse for himself. He was well aware that love doesn't do that sort of thing, and until that point, he had never used that word with her.

It was too late to apologize and take it back, though. Veronica grabbed her purse and stood up. He instinctively anticipated some sort of ugly confrontation, and that made him stand, as well. He grabbed his keys, and without another word, he walked up the numerous steps toward the top of the amphitheater.

This was all preconcert, and their spat didn't draw any extraordinary attention. As hundreds of people piled in and made their way to their seats, he stood at the entrance of the venue with his eyes square on Veronica's back. She was still sitting prim and proper at their table. Anyone would have thought that he left to retrieve something from the car!

He reflected on the amount of money he paid for the concert tickets and quickly deduced that they were going to stay and they were going to enjoy Maxwell if it was the last damn thing that they did.

He slowly meandered back down the steps, casual and cool, and sat down next to Veronica. She looked up and smiled tightly, but then kept her eyes straight ahead. For the rest of the night, they sat there like two stone lions in front of the New York Public Library. They never turned to look at one another, and they never spoke to one another for the entire show.

The couples around them were scarfing down vegetable medleys and all manner of BBQ or roast meat. They had champagne at one table and Malbec and Riesling at another. There was a sea of people coupled up and hugging, swaying to classic songs from his early albums like *Maxwell's Urban Hang Suite*, *Now*, and *BLACKsummers'night*. It was a magical evening—for everyone but Keenan and Veronica.

Eventually, the crowd stood to their feet and slow danced to Maxwell's music in the aisles or by their tables. Keenan had to move his feet more than once to make sure that no one stumbled as they spun the love of their life (or the evening) in a circle during Maxwell's crooning rendition of "Whenever, Wherever, Whatever."

He had no appetite, and she didn't, either, because neither one of them made a move to open any of the food or drink any of the wine.

Did he want to reach for her hand?

No.

Did he feel like apologizing and asking her to dance with him?

No.

It was just the epitome of a bad date, and calling a woman out of her name is one of those things that he knew he could not explain away. They were both adults, and very few adults utter or say something that wasn't already in their heart or in their mind.

They began to pull the remnants of a promising evening together and stuff it in the cooler. They gathered everything as everyone around them cheered and sang along. The crowd sang as if they were just reacting to the music and the lyrics and the way Maxwell would squall out a note.

As they packed up and began to climb the steps to leave the amphitheater, they heard the soft chimes that introduce "Pretty Wings," Maxwell's last song of the evening. Through the song, he seemed to speak a prophecy over them that created an even greater tension.

Veronica walked in front of him, and he believed that they left a major part of the sweetness in the relationship down there in the pit that night. Maxwell continued to belt out lyrics from "Pretty Wings" which made him cringe:

By the time Maxwell started to declare that "someone better is going to love you," he knew that he had to let her go at some point. He also knew that she was thinking the same thing.

It can be a long walk to the car from the amphitheater in Chastain Park, and usually, the band will play for a while to provide added music as people make their way through the dark streets to their parked vehicles. This was usually when couples make plans for the next move that evening. They, however, were walking in silence, as if they were strangers.

Keenan still opened her car door and helped her into his car, but they sat in silence as they left the park and made the long forty-five-minute drive back to her home in Alpharetta.

When they arrived at her apartment, he rushed in and dropped off the cooler while she took her time climbing out of the car. Her teenage babysitter was eager to find out how the evening went and met him in the kitchen with wide, hopeful eyes. "How was it?" she asked. "I have always loved Maxwell and his music!"

"Horrible. I called her a bitch," he muttered as he breezed by and left the house to return to his car. The babysitter froze in place, and Keenan was sure she and Veronica had a great conversation about him that evening.

He didn't talk to Veronica for two days, so he was actually surprised to hear from her and thought that she may have been calling to just give him a piece of her mind. She actually wanted to talk, and he couldn't apologize enough for saying something so stupid and ruining the evening.

"Thank you. I was shocked that you would call me that," Veronica said after his mea culpa.

He still felt like he couldn't apologize enough, but his curiosity about what started her strange reaction took him into another direction.

"I was embarrassed," she said in a whiny tone. "We were at this gorgeous locale for a concert, and all we had was plum wine."

"Huh?" he blurted out. He was truly lost.

"Everyone around us had champagne," she said.

"But you bought the plum wine, not me," he responded. He still missed the point.

"We looked like we were so low budget and everyone else was balling. Then you called me a bitch, and I—I mean, there was nothing else to say."

So, that was it. The attitude, snatching of the wine bottle (which they never opened), the uneaten food, and the horrible evening from hell were a direct result of her perception that they didn't have a more expensive brand of wine.

He tried at that point to not throw the phone on the floor and stomp on it. He fought against unleashing a tirade against her to tell her that that was the most stupid, shallow, idiotic crap he had ever heard in his life. He wanted to make sense out of what he was hearing, but the only reasoning for her train of thought pointed directly back to foolishness. He just couldn't understand pure foolishness.

Later, he would remember this moment as one where he accepted that he had fallen for a woman who didn't seem to be his ideal from Proverbs 31. Proverbs 31 captures the words of King Samuel's mother as she directs him toward the type of woman he should search for and plan to marry. Keenan was keenly aware that Veronica made some of the attributes on this list of the Proverbs 31 woman, but there were some very important characteristics of the Proverbs 31 woman that she sorely lacked.

Up until then, Veronica had brought a fair share of anger, confusion, and deception to him in the last six months! Keenan also had to admit to himself that he couldn't stay on his high horse and act like his responses were something he could be proud of if his sons heard about it.

"Okay, sweetie," he said. "I'm sorry you were embarrassed. I really don't think the other couples were paying attention to us."

"I felt like they were. I think I saw some of the women look over to see what I had on and what type of food we took out of the cooler," she explained.

"I didn't see any of that, but that doesn't mean that I don't believe you," he said, feeling like he was mentoring a high school student. "I wish you would have said something to me before responding the way you did."

"Is that why you called me a bitch?"

Her question sucker-punched him in the gut. He had gone out

of his way, for so many years, to treat women with respect, even when he felt disrespected. After everything he had done in the relationship, none of it mattered because he had committed a cardinal sin in the dating community and been demoted to some thug with gold fronts who grabs his crotch. But he took it because he said it.

"I was frustrated, and I can't fathom why that was the first thing to leave my mouth," he said. "I didn't know why we were having so many disagreements, and I felt like I didn't understand, and—"

"Have you always considered me a bitch?" she asked, interrupting him.

"No, sweetie. No," he wanted to reassure her.

She seemed satisfied that he understood, and apologized.

But things were in no way easier. Things were actually rockier than usual after the conflict at the concert. He felt as if he was trying to move in step with something and found that the rhythm was off. No matter how much he tried to fix it, there was a misstep that was keeping him one beat behind. She brought out the worst in him, and he brought out the worst in her.

Yet, he loved being around her. He began to remember the lessons he learned from his time with Francis:

- Holding on to dead things leaves you depleted
- Watch actions before you listen to words
- You can't force anyone to love you, but you can force yourself to move on

The first two lessons were at the forefront of his mind. It was that last lesson that made him struggle. He could never force her to love him the way he wanted to be loved. But he could force himself to move on and find someone who would love him without all of the bipolar tendencies. He just didn't know how to do it at the moment.

That's the tricky thing about love. Once you submit to it, love will rule your actions and mind, bringing truth to the scripture that says, "The heart is deceitful above all things and beyond cure. Who can understand it?"

Keenan couldn't understand his actions, and neither could his friends. He and Raj started talking about everything other than his relationship just to stay on neutral ground with each other. He didn't want to divulge the tension and the drama that he was going through with Veronica, and he knew Raj understood. Especially as August moved into September and Veronica began to bring him around her family, and he had to deal with not only her drama, but the drama of relations.

It didn't help that he wasn't briefed on her unspoken "meet the family" rules. Some may say that you keep your feelings about your love interest's family to yourself until you are married. Others may say that you should have the type of relationship where you can speak openly and without restraint. Keenan subscribed to the latter train of thought and openly spoke his mind about one of her cousins.

Wrong move.

Veronica was looking for a new TV stand at the time, and they decided to strike out one Saturday and go to a discount furniture store. They made a pitstop first to pick up her little cousin Ricky at her Aunt Olivia's house in Norcross. Both of them were anxious to get the day's errands out of the way before the midmorning summer heat fell over the city and baked everything in sight.

She rang the doorbell of a red-brick rambler, and they waited in silence before a tall, dark-skinned kid answered the door. He was dressed in black skinny jeans and a gray Future concert T-shirt.

"Hey, Noah!" Veronica said with her arms open wide. They embraced, and she introduced Keenan to him briefly as they stepped inside the house and stood in the foyer. When he turned the corner to go get his mother and little brother, Ricky, Veronica nudged over to him and said, "Can you believe that he's eighteen with four kids?"

He was startled. "Four!" he exclaimed. Veronica patted him on his shoulder and brought her index finger up to his mouth, telling him to shush.

"Veronica, how does he afford four kids at eighteen?" he was trying to keep his voice low. He had a feeling he already knew the answer, though, due to the long pinky nails on both of his hands.

She shrugged as her Aunt Olivia walked toward them. "He works in construction," Veronica said quickly and quietly before she stepped in front of him to give a warm hug to Ms. Olivia in the kitchen.

Ricky, who was about fourteen, followed after her, and they all were briefly acquainted before striking out to start the great search. Ricky had a soft baby face and was quiet, but tall and solidly built. Keenan's mind, however, was still on Noah.

Four kids, construction worker, long pinky nail on both hands, several tattoos, and long hair. To most people, that was a conglomeration of life-hindering patterns. For him to be eighteen and already on that type of path was concerning. Keenan felt like someone he had a strong relationship with should talk with him about some of his life choices. He brought it up to Ricky when they stopped at breakfast diner for lunch an hour later.

"What's up with your brother and his long pinky nails?" he asked Ricky. The boy looked surprised that Keenan had inquired about his brother, but he didn't seem offended. Keenan could also tell that his question wouldn't be answered because Ricky thought the world of his big brother.

He shrugged and said, "Oh, he's cool. I don't—I mean, I wouldn't put anything into that. A lot of people got nails like that."

Veronica remained silent and Keenan let the conversation shift to another topic. But that evening, after they dropped Ricky off at his house and found themselves trying to put together the TV stand, Veronica brought up the conversation again.

"I want to talk about something that happened earlier," she said. He halfway heard her because he was trying to count the number of bolts in the small, sealed plastic bag next to the TV-stand pieces.

"M'kay," he responded, reading the instructions.

"I don't want you to talk down about my family," she snapped.

The needle scratched again on the record.

"Are you talking about earlier when I said something to your cousin?" Keenan asked as he put the instruction on the carpet. She was standing near her bedroom door with a hammer in her hand.

"Yes! Why would you say something like that? Who the fuck do you think you are, anyway?" She dropped the hammer and crossed her arms.

He breathed a sigh of relief. "I wasn't talking about your family. But I'm telling you that someone should speak with your cousin about his choices and the life direction he is choosing," he quickly said.

"Who are you to talk about anyone in my family?" Veronica said as she pulled her head back and slid her eyes to razor-thin slits.

"Veronica, this really isn't about me. I'm a man, and I can see when another young black man, in your family, which could one day be my family, is making choices that will hinder him later in life. You are a doctor, Veronica, and I just think you have a responsibility to mentor your family, if possible."

"What makes you so sure that one day he will be hindered in life? Who the fuck are you to judge?" she spat back at him.

Keenan tensed up, but he was ready to stand his ground. He couldn't understand how someone as successful as Veronica could be so nonchalant about a young black man exhibiting behaviors that represent him as a "thug life" member. Keenan felt like Noah, as a black father, needed to be mentored to be an intelligent and responsible provider . . . not to mention the cultural implications of his long pinky fingernails, which most people consider a "coke nail."

"Judging would be to say that he will never be anything. Right now, I find him to be making some misguided decisions, and I know he can prepare to do more," Keenan said as he returned his attention to the instruction and TV-stand pieces which were spread out around him.

"Oh, really?" She took a step toward him and now stood over him.

"Yes!" he began. "Long pinky nails really only point to one thing, and I don't think either one of us need to ask what that is."

"So, now my cousin is on drugs. Okay, Keenan."

"If you thought that, how do you think an employer would think any different?" He asked this with a sincere tone. This woke her up, because Veronica was a major supporter of proper perception and appearances. "I don't know what a long pinky nail means in your mind, but from where I'm from and from what I've seen, a long pinky nail is considered a coke nail," Keenan calmly said as he stood to his feet.

"I know what you're implying, but he is not into that!" Veronica said, her head bobbing.

"You don't know what he's into because you aren't around him enough," Keenan snapped back. "The evidence is right in front of you."

She looked at him as if he was filth. Before she could open her mouth to say something else, he continued to try and reach her. "Veronica," he said, "he doesn't know that he is communicating the wrong thing, and you have to speak truth to him. I would do it, but he doesn't know me that well. He can look at you and say that my cousin is a doctor and she had to keep herself away from certain habits and decisions in order to get where she is."

He paused, expecting her to say something, but was only met with silence and a look of disdain. Not to be outdone, he continued to express himself.

"You know how you said that you didn't want me to stop by your job in casual clothes because you wanted to prevent a certain perception?"

"Get the fuck out of my house. Now!" she roared at him.

He dropped everything in his hands and willingly left. He knew she had rounds at the hospital that evening and that he probably wouldn't see or speak to her until the next day, if that. His suspicions were correct until around five thirty a.m., when a chime roused him from sleep.

He rolled over in bed and lifted his head off of the pillow. *Was that the doorbell?*

It rang again and he sat up in bed. His feet hit the floor, and he immediately realized that he could very well be walking into another Veronica-spun drama moment. He swung his feet back into the bed and nestled down into the covers again.

The doorbell continued to ring, and then it suddenly stopped.

He was relieved that he could finally return to his sleep, but within minutes a car horn began to honk, honk, *hoooonk*. Now, that made him get up out of bed.

He ran to the window and inconspicuously lifted the blinds to see Veronica sitting in her car, driver's door open, and left foot on the driveway. She looked straight ahead at the house as if she expected someone to lift a window and start an argument.

This went on for another three minutes before she slid her left leg back in the car and slammed the driver's side door. Her reasoning was inconceivable to him, because she had worked all night and then apparently driven straight to his house. She called numerous times throughout the evening, but he wasn't ready to speak with her. All of her calls went directly to his voicemail. Most people would just wait for their call to be returned—but not Veronica. She drove to his house and demanded his attention.

The interesting thing was that her demands no longer moved him.

He carried himself back to bed and tried to get some sleep for the rest of the morning. It was now Sunday, and he wanted to take some of the drama from the last few months and pick through it. He now knew that this type of relationship wasn't what he wanted, and he wasn't entirely sure that counseling or a meeting of the minds would work. It was time to do some more dirty work that day and pick through everything that was stinking.

Keenan was not one to bounce a lot of problems off of someone until he was ready. He knew when he officially rose later that morning that he would be in need of some alone time. That indeed was the case, so he took his dog to Grant Park to walk him and enjoy some of the nice weather. It just happened to be House in the Park Day, so the park was filled with people and there were couples everywhere.

Unfortunately, he took his dad's truck, a ten-year-old XL SUV that he seldom drove, and it conked out on him and wouldn't start once he was ready to return home. He and Veronica had been texting back and forth from the morning until the early afternoon. She had been calling him all day, and he finally picked up once the truck refused to turn over.

"Can you come pick me up in Grant Park?" he asked.

"You only picked up because you need help and you know that I'll help," Veronica said dryly. She was out with her mom, but she came by the park and picked him up. The three of them ended up at the zoo parking lot, and Ms. Rubio watched the dog while Veronica, Matt, and Keenan drove to an auto-parts store to get some supplies to start the broken-down vehicle.

He reached for her hand at the same time she reached for his, and in spite of themselves, they began to sync up on the same rhythm.

"I felt like you were looking down on me," she said. "My family was there for me when I had nothing."

"I know that about your family," he said, "but I wasn't talking about your family. I was talking specifically about your cousin. He was probably no more than six when you entered college, so I know he couldn't do anything to help you," he said. He glanced at her while he proved his point. He knew she couldn't possibly expect him to believe that her eighteen-year-old cousin held her down and kept her head up when she was at her worst.

She smiled and squeezed his hand as families squeezed by them on their way to the Gorilla House.

"I know, Key. My family isn't perfect, and it was just embarrassing for you to point it out the way you did."

The pattern was hard to ignore. Every time she felt embarrassed, there was a sharp change in her behavior and Keenan ended up getting his head swiped off. He couldn't imagine life with a woman who was so insecure that other people's perceptions could manipulate her attitude, how she felt about herself, and how she felt about him. He was peeling back layers on Veronica like an onion, and there were more bruises behind those layers than he knew about. If she wasn't so mean-spirited, then he would have tried to hang in there.

But he couldn't. It wasn't worth it, and he knew that he was being dragged lower and lower to a bottom-feeder level.

That's when he began to pray for help.

"At some point, you're going to have to stop judging me by the things that other guys did in your life," he said.

"There is so much that I wanted to say to you," she said, wiping away what he thought were tears. "That's why I came to your house this morning. I thought it would be a better time to talk."

"As opposed to just calling?"

"Key, I called but you wouldn't pick up," she said, looking at him like he had just said something uniquely ignorant.

"Why would you put yourself in harm's way by driving that early in your morning from North Atlanta to Metropolitan Ave. after working a midnight shift?"

"It's only an hour," she said, shaking her head, "and I really wanted to talk."

"Veronica, you were honking the horn . . . I'm just surprised at how you acted."

She seemed to accept that her behavior was not striking a soft spot in his heart. So, she switched up her tactic. "I was so upset this afternoon that you wouldn't pick up my calls, so I went to your house and just sat in the driveway," Veronica said. She was still going to drive home a point that she was the victim.

"I was at Grant Park with my dog, Cane, at the House Music Festival," he said quickly.

She let go of his hand and wiped sweat from her face. "I know that now, but at the time I was so upset. You wouldn't pick up the phone or open the door, and I just cried and cried. I didn't have anyone to talk to, so I called Ced."

"Ced," he dryly repeated. *This clown's name kept coming up.*

"Don't be like that," Veronica said as she patted his hand. "He really gave me something to think about and I never considered it before."

"What did he give you to consider?" He was waiting for the stupidest observation since Cookie Monster rejected crackers.

"Ced said that I should leave your house and leave you because what I was experiencing was not love," she said between sniffles. "Love wouldn't have let me sit outside. He was so patient with me, and he listened to me."

It seemed she was echoing those familiar words about love found in the Bible: "Love is patient and kind; love does not envy or boast; it is not arrogant or rude. It does not insist on its own way; it is not irritable or resentful; it does not rejoice at wrongdoing, but rejoices with the truth. Love bears all things, believes all things, hopes all things, endures all things. Love never ends."

Keenan held his relationship up to this light and discovered that they both had been missing the mark. He hadn't always been able to endure without envy or boast. But he had definitely had his share of trying to ensure that love never ends.

On the other hand, Proverbs spoke to hatred stirring up strife, and that the Lord hates someone with a lying tongue and one who sows discord. Keenan wondered if Ced could talk her through those scriptures without throwing him under the bus or being duped by Veronica's one-sided stories.

So, this quickly turned into the Ced Show, starring Ced. He knew the angle, and he saw through the tears which were supposed to make him feel like there was another man out there who could love her better. The reaction was supposed to make him stand up and prove them all wrong.

But, no. He wanted to hear just how low and grimy this woman would get when she felt like she wasn't getting her way.

"Interesting," he said as he withheld any more emotion. "What else did he say?"

"Oh, you don't want to know," Veronica said as she continued to drive. "Let's start to head back to my mom."

He didn't budge. Deep down he felt like he needed this to snip some of the remaining heart strings. "No, I think this is important for us to work through," he lied.

"I confide in him often," Veronica said. "So, he asked me to come visit him."

Okay, now he was ready to go. He was ready to get back to his house, find a way to fix the truck, and enjoy the rest of his day.

"And what did you say?" he asked her as they began to walk in the opposite direction.

"You know I told him no," she said quietly. "You're the only one I want to be with. The only one."

And just like that, she pulled him back into her grasp.

NEW
YORK

New York City

THE RELATIONSHIP CONTINUED its descent into uncertainty, attitude, and misplaced anger. Keenan couldn't stay away, and he
didn't even try to negotiate with himself. He knew that he would
break every promise. If someone didn't stop him, he would probably stumble like an entranced zombie into the nearest jewelry
store for an engagement ring.

These were the feelings he was grappling with when his son
Kelvin secured a show at the historic Webster Hall in New York
City. His music career was blossoming, and Keenan was so proud
of his tenacity and talent to make music. He was also excited that
he could accompany him to the Big Apple and cheer him on.

He asked Veronica to go as soon as he found out that the venue
was booked and told her that he thought it would be a great opportunity for Matt to meet his biological father, Sam. She agreed
and mentioned she also wanted to catch up with some old friends

and to see her aunt. He had never been to New York, and as a native of California, was looking forward to his first experience in the Big Apple.

He rented a burgundy minivan from the rental car center at the airport near his house and picked Veronica and Matt up on the way up the road. Kelvin and his dancers were already in tow, so they all started and made the fourteen-hour drive through the night to New York from Atlanta. Veronica drove for the last two hours, but Keenan handled the brunt of the drive. It's one thing to be trapped in the car for fourteen hours with a baby and three preteens. Adding hunger, back cramps, and fatigue to the mix didn't sweeten the pot.

They made some stops along the way, but it's impossible to really rest the body after a five- to ten-minute stretch at a Denny's or an interstate rest stop.

In spite of the driving fatigue, Keenan was immediately charged and ready to have a memorable weekend as soon as they exited the Lincoln Tunnel. The energy of the city was something he had never experienced, and he loved the clash of cultures, the lights, the people rushing to get somewhere by foot or vehicle. It had snowed a few days before they arrived, and the city was cast in a gray, cold atmosphere before dusk fell.

They pulled up at the JW Hotel near Times Square around five p.m. and climbed out of the van with stiff legs while taking in the sea of people. They all limped inside the lobby to check in, and Keenan was sure they looked just as exhausted as they felt. He initially missed the front-desk attendant trying to get his attention until she leaned over the counter to speak to him about the credit card he handed her for incidentals.

"Mr. Green, your card was declined." This grabbed his attention, as he felt like another stone of torture was tossed on top of his head.

Veronica whipped her head to the left and moved forward a couple steps.

"Did you run it again? Wait, it may be a security hold," he said as he took out his wallet and prepared to give her another card.

"We ran it twice thinking that it was the machine, but . . . do you have another card?" the attendant asked.

Before he had a chance to say anything, Veronica plunked a credit card down on the counter and said, "You can use mine."

When the front-desk attendant asked for her ID, she began to look around and realized that she couldn't find it.

"When was the last time you had it?" Keenan asked as she tore through her purse and wallet. "The rest stop or when we stopped in Philly?"

"I don't—I don't know," Veronica stammered.

They both glanced at the front-desk attendant, who now had a twisted mouth. This was uncomfortable for everyone, and the line behind them was starting to grow further into the lobby with other weary travelers. They were given the rooms anyway, but the comedy of errors didn't stop there.

They made their way upstairs and got the kids settled into their room. When they attempted to enter their own room, they found that their key cards didn't work. The JW Hotel had to redo the entire lock, and that took an extraordinary amount of time, which resulted in them being given a $200 credit to their account. By the time they got into the room, everyone's focus was different from Keenan's. He wanted to track down what happened with his credit card. There was no way that he could stay in NYC all weekend with no cash and no access to his funds.

"Can we do that later? I really want to feed Matt," Veronica said as she watched him dial his bank. "I'll just cover dinner until I find my ID."

He thought better of his desperate quest to find an answer, and they all hit the streets and headed toward Times Square, searching for a place that could quickly feed them. They were barely fifty feet from the JW before Veronica took off in front of him and the boys as she pushed Matt in his stroller. They couldn't catch up to her as she weaved in and around the sidewalk traffic and darted across busy intersections. He actually had to jog a few steps ahead of the boys and walk next to her so he could get eye contact and retrieve her attention.

"Veronica, can you slow down? You're walking pretty fast. The boys and I can't keep up with you!"

She turned slightly and paused just enough to make sure that someone wasn't in front of her before she started walking again. Kelvin, Lucas, and James were literally running to keep in step with him as he tried to keep in step with her.

"This is New York, Key. You need to walk faster like New Yorkers. If you can't keep up, go back to the room." She brushed him off and took off again.

This time he knew what was coming, and in his eyes, it wasn't worth the squabble, so he let her go and sent the boys with her. They fell in step with her and rounded a corner before they disappeared into the crowd. He had noticed a Bank of America ATM machine and was eager to see if his card would work there, so he made his way in that direction.

After speaking with his bank's customer service department, he soon found himself in the middle of one of those flukes that can't be explained. There was no hold, and despite the $9,000 available, he could only withdraw $40 at a time. Just as he was making another call to the bank, he simultaneously received a phone call and text message from Veronica.

"Keenan, you have my credit card. Where are you? We can't eat without the card."

He told her he didn't know where he was and that she would have to direct him. This was his first time in New York, and he had no idea how to navigate around that city. He told her to meet him at the corner where they left off. His heart dropped into his socks when they met up in the middle of Times Square and it was just her and Matt.

"Where's Kelvin, Seth, and James? Where are the boys?" he asked as his eyes darted behind her. He wanted to believe that she was walking fast and the boys would be approaching soon.

But, nah.

"They're a couple blocks back," she said nonchalantly.

"Couple blocks as in walking this way?" He was now in a mild panic. "Why the heck would you leave a fifteen-year-old and two seventeen-year-olds from Atlanta, a much slower city, in the middle of New York City?"

"If you would let me finish, then I could tell you that the boys are a couple blocks back shopping," Veronica said as they began to walk in the opposite direction to go get the boys. People shoulder-bumped them as they strolled at a much slower pace and walked past flashing neon signs on shady storefronts and packed-to-capacity fast-food restaurants.

"Like that's any better," he responded.

"Can I finish?" she said with an attitude. *Like she had a reason to have an attitude.* "Let's go get them and then go get something to eat. Also, I'm leaving tomorrow with Matt, and my mother is going to overnight an old ID she found for me at her house in Charlotte."

He stopped in his tracks right at the intersection of West 46th and Broadway. "You're leaving?" His eyes were wide and creating a look on his face that he was sure she had never seen before. He was responsible for three teenagers, and they were all about to be homeless, hungry, and stranded in New York City.

"Yes, so—" she began.

The signal changed in the crosswalk and a herd of people moved forward. He joined them, leaving her standing on the corner and trying to explain an asinine decision. She quickly fell in step with him and pulled his arm to make a right. He followed her direction and they walked in silence until they reached the department store.

He entered the massive department store and squeezed by other shoppers until he saw his son. His heart was able to return to a normal pace and he no longer had visions of calling his ex-wife and stumbling over words as he explained how the boys were kidnapped and sold in the black market.

"Hey, son," he said as he walked up to him picking through a pile of sweaters. "How much money do you have? Veronica is leaving, and we have to put our money together."

He put the sweater back and started to rummage through his pockets.

"Come on. Let's go eat and we can figure it out," he said as he waved to Seth and James to come along. The four of them made their way back to the entrance of the store and found that Veronica and Matt were gone. He only had forty dollars, so they headed back to the JW to find Veronica.

The boys went to the room and ordered room service thanks to the $200 credit on the rooms. Keenan stopped in the lobby and bought a glass of Pinot Grigio, Veronica's favorite. By the time he made it to the room, he saw that Matt was asleep and that she had already eaten. No, there was nothing left or ordered for him. She was also acting very distant. So distant, in fact, that if a stranger walked in the room, they would think that Keenan and Veronica were cousins who were stuck in a hotel room for the duration of the trip.

The room was narrow and true to JW Hotel style with simple, clean color schemes. There was a desk, a bed, a dresser, TV—the essentials for any hotel room. The room just wasn't big enough to not be on speaking terms. She sipped on the glass of wine and said, "How much was the total for the kids' room service?"

Keenan stepped out of his shoes and told her that he didn't know and would call the front desk to find out. She laid across the bed and said, "Can you just go back to the boys' room and check on the cost of the food they ordered?"

He wasn't doing that. He was beyond tired and fed up. Plus, he was busy eying her for clues as to why her behavior changed so suddenly. His thoughts were interrupted when her cell phone chirped to announce a text message. He looked down at the phone on the desk, and saw that Sam was asking for the location of the JW Hotel where she was staying.

"You meeting up with Sam, huh?" he asked as he picked up the landline to call the boys' room. She jumped up out of the bed and smacked the phone out of his left hand, scratching him with her nails.

The room stood still. *Did she just . . . ?*

He picked up the receiver off of the floor, and she snatched it out of his hand and slammed it back into its cradle. Without skipping a beat, he grabbed the glass of wine and tossed what was left of it into her face. Now the room really did stand still.

He shouted, "Don't you ever put your hands on me! Keep your hands to your fucking self, and don't put your damn hands on me!"

She threatened to call security on him, and he stepped aside as she reached for the phone and called security.

Great.

Within five minutes, two hulking men in black suits arrived from security and escorted him out of the room. Veronica stayed behind, screaming that she paid for the rooms and that he and the boys should be kicked out with just the clothes on their backs. He remained silent and followed the lead of the hotel security as they walked down the long, gray-carpeted hallway.

The security guards were in the middle of a "good cop, bad cop" routine, so he played along. Minutes later, he found himself sitting on a lobby sofa next to a brooding monster of a hotel cop who said very little. He watched Keenan every time he shifted or blinked. Within five minutes, he saw the kinder security guard walk off of the nearby elevator and approach them. He stood to his feet, ready to hear whatever he had to say (via Veronica).

"Okay," he said with an inhale, "she doesn't want to press charges, and she doesn't want to have you all kicked out. I've moved all of your stuff into the other room, and you gotta stay away from her for the rest of the weekend, you feel me?"

He agreed to these terms and felt like he was slammed back into time to their trip to Charlotte: bunking with the boys again and his personal effects in a neat little pile on the bed.

The kids wanted to hang out in Times Square, but Keenan told them to rehearse. To calm his nerves, he called Raj and asked to borrow some money since he was already in town to film a music video.

This was not how he expected his evening to go after a fourteen-hour drive. He soon went to bed and just thanked God that he had circumvented a homeless weekend in the greatest city on earth.

* * *

Late Friday evening, Sam sent Keenan a text message saying that he wanted him to be present when he met Veronica. Keenan received the message the next morning as he was traveling with

Kelvin, Seth, and James to the historic Webster Hall for a sound-check. He spoke with Veronica, and they all agreed to meet at a clothing store because Sam wanted to buy Matt a hat.

Keenan arrived a bit before them and tried to process how the afternoon would go. He definitely didn't know what to expect.

Fifteen minutes later, a silver convertible coupe pulled in front of the store. A large group of people passed in front of him, and by the time he made it to the curb, Veronica, her aunt, and Sam were standing on the curb, waiting to greet him. Baby Matt was limp with sleep in Veronica's arms. Keenan shook Sam's hand and immediately put Matt into his stroller. It felt so awkward to Keenan to care for the baby, considering that his biological father was standing right there. It seemed, however, that this wasn't something Sam dwelled on; he was focused on spending money on his son.

The store didn't have baby clothes, so they traveled next door to a high-end department store and searched through the clothes together as a blended family unit—but a unit with conditions. He and Veronica broke off for a while so she could go to the ATM and get money for her aunt. While they were at the ATM, she passed along $400 to him since he was still struggling with access to his own money. They then returned to the department store, and everything got real.

Sam looked at a pair of yellow child-size pants for Matt and turned to Veronica. "What do you think about these?"

She curled her lip in disgust and said, "Uh, that would be a no."

Sam laughed and put the pants back on the display table. "Kinda had that feeling, you know?"

He began to look for other clothes, and Keenan surveyed the situation from where he stood. "Yellow pants are fine," he said.

Veronica turned around and looked at him like he just cursed out her mother. "No, that's not the way to go," she said.

"Kelvin has some yellow pants," he replied. Sam glanced up, looked at Veronica, and went to another part of the floor.

"You can leave now, Keenan," Veronica said firmly and just loud enough for him to hear.

At first, he balked at the idea, but then he thought better of it, just gave her the $400, and hailed a cab. He made a stop in a drugstore and was able to get cash back from the cashier. So, he bought eight packs of gum and selected the $100 cash-back option each time. Within minutes, he had $800 cash and was set for the rest of the trip.

He went back to Webster Hall, supported his son, met up with Raj, and enjoyed the early evening without Veronica and the stipulation that he function as a puppet that doesn't speak unless spoken to.

Later that evening, he was in the kids' room thinking about how much of a sorry trip this had turned out to be. He was in New York for the first time in his life, and there was enough drama, betrayal, and arguing to shoot a sitcom. His room phone rang not too long after this thought, and Veronica invited him down to her room—the one he had been kicked out of by security.

Against his better judgment, he walked in to find Veronica sitting with a short, brown-skinned guy who smirked like his hand was caught in the cookie jar. He sized Keenan up with insincere eyes as he walked intently toward him to find out just what in the hell was going on. Veronica stood and moved between them as the man also stood to his feet.

"Key, this is my friend Will Da God," she said with a smile. He stuck out his hand, and Keenan shook it firmly in what was the first instance of him feeling like he was locking ram horns for

Veronica. Prior to them coming to New York, in one of their many conversations, she had explained that Will was one of New York's producing hitmen.

He asked Keenan some investment questions, some relationship questions, and left shortly thereafter. He also explained that he was thinking about getting engaged, but his girlfriend wanted to move to a bigger place. Should he save for a ring or get her a bigger place?

The whole meeting made no sense to Keenan whatsoever. *What was the point?*

"I envy his girlfriend," Veronica said after he left. "They are in a good place, and we aren't."

By the end of the weekend it was clear that he and Veronica were not put together on this earth to grow from their past experiences into a new unit. He wanted them to get along and to understand each other, but there was too much negativity between them. There was anger and a very loose interpretation of what it meant to be in a relationship. If the shoe was on the other foot, and he brought a woman to the hotel room without Veronica's knowledge and told her that she was his friend, Keenan was sure that he would have made the top spot on a list of the nation's sorriest men. A meme would have gone viral, and his name would have been synonymous with infidelity and disrespect much the way Ike Turner's name is now synonymous with domestic violence and irrational anger.

The ride home to Georgia turned horribly dramatic before they even made it through New Jersey. It started quietly enough. The boys sat in the backseat with their headphones, dozing. Veronica was also using headphones to listen to her own MP3. To Keenan, the car felt like an isolation chamber.

"Veronica, will you run the MP3 into the car speakers? I need music."

"No," she said. "I want to listen in my headphones."

Not one thing would she do to make his life just a little easier while he took on this massive drive. An exit sign for a rest stop emerged from the distance, and he took it.

"What are you doing?" she said. "We've only been on the road an hour."

"You will do your part and help me drive by putting the MP3 through the speakers!" Keenan said with a voice loud enough to wake up the kids.

"Fine," Veronica said, and they were soon on the road again.

Wouldn't you know she unplugged the MP3 and put the music into her personal headset? *Again.*

Amidst his own yelling, Veronica began to scream that she was not one of his kids and to pull over at the next stop. She actually asked him to pull over more than once before he decided to stop. He figured that if they kept going, the whole issue would blow over and they'd be able to get to Georgia in one piece.

Not so.

The boys and Keenan watched in amazement as she grabbed her things out of the trunk and disappeared with Matt to a hotel across the street. He climbed out of the car, teared up, and begged for her to get back in. The kids were upset, he was upset, and this was turning into a TV movie of the week as people began to stop and stare. He entered the hotel and asked her again to return to the car.

"Just go away! Get away from me. You're a monster!" Veronica screamed as she held Matt protectively in her arms.

He could have heard a pin drop. A matronly brunette in an overstretched hotel attendant uniform moved carefully in short little steps toward them, as if she expected him to be armed and dangerous.

"Ma'am, do you need help? I can call the police," she said with a shaky voice.

Keenan retreated and went back to his car, choking back emotion so he wouldn't further upset Kelvin and his friends. The confusion and the fear in the car was palpable, as they fell silent once he slid in the car. They sat there for about two hours. He called her, her mother, Sam, his mother, Raj, and Derrick, and then prayed like his life depended on it.

The kids were tired. He could feel their eyes on the back of his neck, so he told them that they were going to move on down the road without Veronica. Without protest, they put their headsets back on, turned up the music, and tuned out the ordeal between Veronica and him.

He took this moment of semiprivacy to speak with Raj, his stepfather, and even Sam for advice before pulling back onto the highway.

"Leave her."

"You're on your own. I told you what was up!"

"Get out of there before something worse happens."

The advice was all the same, and he had experienced enough surprises and inconvenience to last him a lifetime. He pulled the van onto 95-South and headed back to Atlanta, wondering how Veronica was doing, how he got into this situation, and if anything else needed to be written on the wall for him to finally gather his nerve and ditch this bad relationship.

She didn't call, and neither did he. His advisors had told him to leave well enough alone, and this time he listened. He did, however, try to reach Veronica's mother, but she wouldn't pick up the phone.

He finally got in touch with Veronica's mother two hours after he left Raleigh. He was passing through Charlotte and figured that Ms. Rubio wasn't picking up her phone because she didn't want to speak to him. He wanted her to help him figure out how Veronica was going to get back to Atlanta with no ID and for her to hear him out, in spite of whatever preconceived notion she had about him or the situation at hand.

So, he pulled into a gas station off the 85-South exit ramp and found an older gentleman with kind eyes. He was pumping gas into an old European family sedan and almost denied Keenan the privilege of using his personal cell phone until one of the boys extracted himself from the car and stretched next to the car. He shook the pump's drizzle into the gas tank and replaced the pump before reaching into his car and handing Keenan an antiquated flip phone.

"I appreciate it," Keenan said with a sheepish smile. "My phone died and the charger won't work."

He knew the man didn't believe him. It was nighttime, they were on the side of an interstate, and there were three teenage boys moving around his car now and complaining of hunger. Simply put: the gentleman understood.

He dialed Ms. Rubio's number, and this time she picked up and was definitely not in a pleasant mood. "You left my daughter and grandson! A baby, you left a baby on the side of the road."

"Ms. Rubio, you know I wouldn't—"

"She's fine, no thanks to you," she snapped, interrupting him. He let her attitude continue, though. What else could he say or do? Whose side would she take in the first place?

"Veronica is fine and riding the train from New Jersey to Charlotte. I'll pick her up and drive her the rest of the way to Atlanta," she said. She paused, and then spoke carefully as if she wanted him to hear every syllable when she said, "I'm going to get to the bottom of this."

"Yes, ma'am, I'm sure you will," Keenan said before ending the call. The old gentleman had heard everything and only smiled politely when he passed the phone back to him. Satisfied that Veronica was indeed all right, Keenan ignored her mother's threats and headed back towards I-85. That is when Seth passed Keenan his phone. Veronica had been texting him this whole time and he had been offering his condolences about how the trip turned out. Keenan had no idea she had bonded with the kid to that limit, that they had exchanged telephone numbers. The level of craziness in his life was now at a destructive level. As soon as he hit Atlanta's city limits, he dropped off Kelvin's friends and pulled into a gas station to clean out the minivan so he could turn it in at the rental company. When everything was clean, he dropped it off and watched impassively as the agent gave the car a once over. The guy was pretty thorough, and even glanced far under the seats as part of the check-in.

"What's that?" he said, as he reached under the seat and brought out a small, flat card with a very familiar face on the front. "Do you know"—he read the name carefully—"Veronica Rubio?"

Keenan swallowed hard. "Yes," was all he could choke out. He hadn't even bothered to look for it when he cleaned out the car. That damn ID. He wondered how much drama from the weekend would have been missed if they had thought to just check the vehicle one more time.

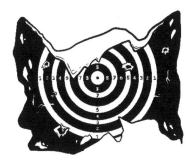

The Final Breakup

The first court day with Veronica—Cross-examination

"AND DID YOU threaten in a text message to get my client fired?"

"I did," said Veronica, looking progressively more uncomfortable and helpless.

"Since Mr. Green was let go within a few days of this text, did you have anything to do with that?"

"No, I did not," Veronica said, but she said it softly, and Keenan could tell that the judge was not convinced.

* * *

Only one good thing came out of this nightmare of a trip: When he was at his lowest, Keenan received unconditional love from a woman who had no interest in marrying him. That woman was Francis.

Before finally getting in touch with Veronica's mother, they had stopped in Raleigh, and out of desperate need he called and asked Francis to meet him at the restaurant in Southland Mall. The boys were shuttled to one booth while she and Keenan sat in another booth nearby, and she watched him cry and sob over another woman.

"Did you put your hands on her?" she initially asked with her eyes quizzical.

The waitress placed their drinks down, and he remained silent until she left.

"I can't believe I'm confiding in you," he said. "But no, I didn't touch her. After six years with you, did I ever put my hands on you?"

Francis nodded and looked as if she was thinking some things through. "It's going to work out," she said, finally raising her eyes to look at him. "I'm really sorry, but it's going to be okay."

Surprisingly, she continued to comfort him and told him that Veronica wasn't the right one. She also encouraged him to keep looking until he found what he wanted.

Was this a twist of fate, or just a model of unconditional love?

He marked this moment as one that changed the way he thought about love.

The love he was searching for in a woman wasn't necessarily a love that developed quickly over sex, trips, and common interest. The love he yearned for was indeed unconditional, and it was something that would only develop when there is full transparency, reciprocity, and commitment between two people. It was rare, surprising, and not exactly attached to a time limit.

It had been exactly a year for Francis and him to be apart. He never considered in all of his brokenness that it would have hurt her to see him crying over another woman. Whether it hurt her or not is a question that he never found the answer to. The one answer he did have is that Francis showed him unconditional love because she saw him hurt and gave him the truth, even when he didn't want to hear it.

Now, he was very aware that love was much more than a pat on the back and a firm "You will be okay." Love is an action that you work to perform every day. You choose to love somebody, and that love is what prevents you from consciously causing your partner hurt, creating lies, seeking your own way, and holding onto unforgiveness.

He realized that he finally had some clarity. He was free and ready to move forward with his life and with his pursuit of love and happiness. He would let it all go.

But not quite yet.

The afternoon he arrived in Atlanta, he drove by Veronica's house to check on her, but she wasn't there. As he pulled out, though, her car was pulling in. Both rolled down their windows to talk from their respective safe spaces. He passed her ID through the window.

"It was in the van all along," he said, and shrugged, as if her lost ID had been a minor inconvenience of their trip.

She took it from his hand. "We should talk later," she said. "I'll call you."

She didn't actually call, but that night she texted him to come over. She was wearing her usual sexy lingerie—this time her matching bra and panties were hot pink and lacy, barely covered by a silky black robe that only went to her thighs.

So, that's what this was about. Without talking, she led him to her bedroom.

"Take off your clothes," she said.

He wasn't even sure he wanted to fuck her, but then his dick was hard. This crazy woman and her moods! Horny and frustrated at the same time, he plunged his dick into her from behind, with his pants still around one leg. Impulsively, he slid his belt out of his pants and began to whack the shit out of her while he fucked her. She screamed but didn't tell him to stop. He was blind with lust and anger. She slithered away after a moment, laid on her back, and opened her legs wide. "Eat my pussy," she said.

He wrapped her legs around his face, the belt still in his hand. She grabbed it from him, then gave as good as she got, smacking him over and over with the belt while he ate her pussy. It was a rage-fuck of the highest order.

When it was over, they both lied there, breathing heavily.

"Just because I let you eat my pussy doesn't mean you're out of the dog house," she said.

He didn't sleep over, and he didn't see much of her for a few days after that. But it was getting near Halloween, and he wanted to walk Matt around the apartment complex. This offer was accepted and then mysteriously rejected as he was driving to her place.

He came anyway.

But he stopped beforehand at the drugstore down the street from her place to buy Matt a toy: a pushing lawn mower with the loud bubbles that popped as you moved the lawnmower forward. He also got her a bottle of Pinot Grigio and some flowers.

While at the register pulling out his wallet, the automatic glass doors opened and a familiar face rushed in out of the cold. It was Angela, Tanya's mother. They caught eye contact, gave each other the nod, and went about their business. He hadn't thought about Tanya all year, but he quickly wondered how she was doing, paid for his things, and left.

When he made it to Veronica's place, he saw her sitting outside in a chair and passing out candy to a bunch of neighborhood kids.

Matt had on a green dinosaur costume and was having the time of his life. She watched him exit the car, and he walked up to the chair as all of the other children scattered. Her hair was pulled back in a ponytail. Effortlessly beautiful.

"I was already down the street when you sent me a text telling me not to come," he told her. The box containing the pushing lawn-mower toy was in his left hand, and he offered it to her.

She glanced at the toy, uncrossed her arms, and said, "Thanks. You can put the toy together, but then you have to go."

He put together the toy, took Matt trick-or-treating, and left as requested. He was barely twenty minutes down the road when she asked him to come back to the house. He turned the car around.

That night, he sucked on her nipples while she pleasured herself with a little silver bullet, then fucked her juicy pussy. He was so far deep into crazy.

This last-ditch effort was not something that he broadcasted to his friends, but his chief voice of reason had seen just enough to question him in full length. Raj was no slouch, and he specifically had a point to drive home when they met up to play pool one night.

"You mean to tell me that there was something left to make up between the two of you?" he asked as he stalked his next shot.

Keenan held his hands out as if to say, "What do you want from me?"

"We're learning how to communicate," he said out loud as Raj moved out of the way for Keenan's next move.

"Learning to communicate?" Raj scoffed. "Then what type of communication did you perceive it to be when she brought ol' boy in your hotel room? Or wait, what were you communicating when you splashed a drink in her face?"

He always knew which rhetorical question to throw out there.

"Come on, man," Keenan said, shaking his head.

"Keenan, Seth was upset and said you were yelling at her the way his dad used to yell at his mom. You gave the boy issues for the weekend. You come on, dude," Raj shot back.

Ouch.

Having this play out in front of his sons was not something he wanted to continue. He didn't want their memories of him to be ones of running through New York behind some batshit woman or watching their friend cry as he flashed back to a domestic conflict in his own family. That was never his intent.

The lessons kept rolling in, and he now included his sons and how a woman would interact with them to the list of what he was looking for. He wasn't sure if he was so busy looking for a woman who took care of her family and herself like the woman in Proverbs 31 that he forgot to look for a woman who just had some common decency. He forgot to ask God to allow him to see decency when it crossed his path.

Dr. Jones's classes were long over by now, but these introspective moments and conversations with Raj made him ponder on what he could have done differently that weekend in New York. That reflection led him to think about what he could have done differently the entire year. Of course, once he was through with the entire year, he moved on to what he could have done differently with Francis and, eventually, his marriage.

He was trying to grow through all of this and learn more about himself and his reactions to others in situations of adversity. To show Veronica that he was serious about their relationship growing, he registered for an anger-management course in Atlanta and looked forward to exploring. He wanted to be better at communicating and have healthier and more positive yet assertive responses to adverse situations that may happen to him at any time.

He completed four to five sessions and learned how disgruntled feelings grow from frustration, to anger, and then to a potential all-out rage. He was able to see the subtleties of angry moments in certain situations in his life. One of the key questions that stuck with him was this: *Have you ever been disappointed that someone doesn't react the way you do in a moment where you receive surprising information that may change your whole day?*

It was all a part of anger management, and he was determined to make sure that he was able to respond in the best way possible. This had nothing to do with Veronica at this point, although he did ask her to attend a couple's session. She respectfully declined. Regardless of her participation, he was on a course to be a better Keenan, and if this didn't work out between them, then he knew he would be prepared for a better caliber of a woman.

The next few weeks were a dance of rubber-band intimacy that was mostly at his expense. He and Veronica went to the movies one evening to see *the newest Black rom-com*, and he got sick again. She took care of him when he became sick during mid-November with the same nausea and constipation that he experienced earlier in the year. This time Veronica didn't dispense any pills, but she did stand by his side and help him to feel better until he actually recovered.

Within days, though, they were back at odds, and he was caught in the middle of her bipolar approach to love and relationships. She'd call him there, and then tell him not to come while he was en route. *How much can one man take of this?* He was through and ready to move on after this last instance.

A few days later, Veronica sent a text message to him in reference to being repaid for the room in New York:

> "At least be decent in the end. I helped you when you needed it. You offered to repay me and as of tonight there hasn't

been any deposit. I helped put food on
your families (sic) table, please do not
take from mine. I'm sure it was an over-
sight on your part and you will remember
to make the deposit tomorrow. I truly
appreciate it with all my heart. Be
blessed."

*How could she send a shady text message like that and then end it
with "Be blessed"?* He thought it over and surmised that it made
no sense to pay for a hotel room that he was kicked out of and
never stayed in while he struggled to even find money at the time.

It was the principle of the thing, okay?

So, he didn't immediately respond to her text, and he let the
silence speak for him. That Friday morning he responded with:

"Veronica, I am out of town on a family
emergency. I don't feel comfortable paying for your hotel bill. Please consider
removing $450 from my payment schedule,
as I did not use your room in NYC nor
did I have a key. I refuse to be taken
advantage of by anyone anymore just because I have feelings. Lastly, I will
take care of the remaining balance $550
upon receiving my fax machine and my father's treadmill at my address, valued
at over $700. I work from home on Mondays
and Fridays. Please alert me of delivery
in advance.

God bless,
Keenan"

She got pissed and threatened to serve him with papers at his
job.

"I only want what you promised to repay.
I will have the papers delivered to you
at work. Sorry about this, but I'm a
single mom and you owe a debt. See you
in court."

It was Friday, November 22, and he was on his way to Washington, DC, so his son Kelvin could do another show on his tour. He took her threats with a chuckle and a smile. While he was in DC, he received another text and then a call from Veronica late that evening.

"Listen," she said, "I need your help. I need money."

"What are you talking about?" he said.

"I don't even have money for gas right now," she said. "I'm stuck at home. Some fucking collection agency decided to play catch-up with me and took six monthly payments at once. My account balance is actually negative right now."

"Oh, come on, Veronica," Keenan said. "You're a fucking doctor. You make like $165K a year!"

"Do you know how expensive it is to have a baby?" she said. "I didn't have insurance when Matt was born. The hospital sent me to collections."

Her plea for help came at a very inconvenient time. It was now Saturday morning, the banks were closing at noon, and he was in a hotel in DC with five kids twelve hours away from Atlanta— and nowhere near her bank.

Despite the extreme inconvenience, he managed to find one, and still drove thirty minutes to the nearest bank in Downtown DC, withdrew $400 from his own account, and deposited it into her account at the bank. As he turned on his heel, he thought better of his blind faith in Veronica's words and asked the bank teller to give him an account summary.

Without responding, she tapped on the keyboard and began to write on a slip of paper.

$8,506?

Veronica had a balance of over $8,000 in her account. Were they at this level of deception and pettiness?

He barely made it back to Georgia that weekend thanks to the snowfall in DC and along the way home while driving through Virginia in the middle of the night in a snowstorm. Driving in almost zero visibility with the heater blasting, he mentally checked off each mile, knowing that he had very low funds for handling any emergency. By the grace of God, nothing happened which would have required him to spend exorbitant amounts of money.

Picking up the treadmill and the fax machine from her house became his first priority once he dropped off his boys and the dancers that Sunday morning. He contacted her, got permission, and drove out to her apartment in Johns Creek.

She was relaxing in a robe when he arrived. After she handed him the hammer and screwdriver, he took the doors off their hinges and removed the exercise equipment. She sat in the kitchen and sipped tea while he lugged the treadmill outside. The treadmill was kind of a monster to move around. He grazed his finger on one of its sharper edges.

"Do you have a bandage?" he asked.

She put down her mug and crossed her legs. "No," she said flatly. "All out."

So, he kept working. If she was okay with him bleeding all over her precious designer furniture, he was, too. As he dragged the cumbersome machine toward the door, he heard her approach from behind him.

"You know, I hung out with Whitney yesterday."

He glanced over his shoulder and heaved the treadmill out of the front door. "Oh?" he said without a hint of emotion. He wasn't sure where she was going.

"Yes, we went target shooting."

As he walked out the door, he saw her make a point to unfold the dark-gray, bullet-riddled sheet of paper and wave it at him. He didn't know what to make of her veiled threats. They seemed extreme, but he was beginning to see her as someone who was mostly all talk.

He took his family to church that day, and he felt that God led him there to prepare him for what was to come. The Bishop preached from a series that day, and everything he said spoke directly to Keenan and the storm he had been going through which was trying to deplete, destroy, and hinder his process. He fought tears from his eyes and really felt like he was in tune to God's presence in his life.

He reached out to Veronica via text and was quickly swatted away by her response that she was watching the same service as him, so he didn't need to recap it.

Her verbal swat was brought to fruition later that week. The next day at five thirty a.m., he woke up to his contracting company texting him and telling him to not report to work at the CDC. He thought he was doing his job well. He never had any negative performance feedback.

She threatened him on Friday, then he lost his job that Monday. She was always using her credentials to get away with things.

Reeling in shock, he reached out to Veronica to confide in her. Her response via text was simply that "karma did it." He then reflected on the threatening text message she had sent him that prior Friday. He couldn't help but to ponder what part did she have in his being fired? Then he was contacted by his ex-wife via text message who stated that Veronica was sending text messages to his ex-wife inquiring about Keenan's mental status and expressing concern for Kelvin and Cameron's safety.

In the texts, Veronica had asked his ex-wife to call her, but she refused because she was worried it would cause problems. Veronica ignored this broad hint and told his ex-wife that Keenan had been calling from strange numbers, accusing her of getting him fired, calling her son's father, and sending strange emails. She, in turn, accused him of mental instability and suggested someone from his family come pick him up.

Thankfully, his ex-wife graciously declined to become involved and alerted him to the alarming series of text messages. It was as if Veronica was doing a calculating roll-out of sabotage and defamation to rip everything out from underneath him. This was a new low. Attempting to jeopardize his connection with his kids?

Okay, he saddled up and prepared himself to handle it, but he refused to let this impede on the upcoming Thanksgiving holiday. He suddenly had no plans for Thanksgiving, which was in three days, so he needed to act quickly. Maybe he could visit an out-of-town friend.

He remembered how Veronica had made him send that ridiculous text to his friend Mia in Dallas and wondered what she was doing for Thanksgiving. His main goal was to clear his mind; he desperately needed to get away.

Mia initially agreed to let him come celebrate the holiday with her in Dallas, but after he bought his plane ticket, she flaked and told him that she had decided to make plans to go visit her brother in California. So, he reached out to his sister instead and made plans to fly into Dallas and drive to Houston. Since he needed some time alone, the drive would give him an opportunity to think and reflect.

The Tuesday evening before he left, more of Veronica's

"karma" found him. He woke up at three a.m. to his dog barking. *What the fuck?* Then he heard the sound of loud knocking on his front door. Suddenly wide awake, he slipped on a robe and went into his walk-in closet. His small gun safe was on a top shelf, and he keyed in the passcode quickly, hearing the incessant and violent knocking continue. He pulled out his .45 caliber, loaded it quickly, and moved downstairs, adrenaline pumping through his body. Was this a home invasion? Once downstairs, he went immediately to his security cameras and looked out. It was a police officer at the door. The gun in his hand, so necessary a split-second before, became a potential death sentence. As a black man, this was the worst situation he could be in. He had every legitimate and legal right to defend his home from being robbed or attacked with a gun in his hand, but suddenly the officer on the other side of the door had the right to kill him. And there's no afterward. There's no coming back from that "accident." You're just another dead black man at the hands of the police. Keenan had fought all his life not to be a statistic, and he wasn't about to stop now. He tossed the gun on the couch like it was radioactive, and opened the door to the grim-faced officer on the threshold.

"Keenan Green?" he said sternly.

"That's me," he said.

"You have been served, stay away from her," he added intensely.

He was served with a temporary restraining order and a court date set for December 9. He skimmed through the charges—they were ridiculous. Among other accusations, she wrote that he yelled at her in front of her son. He read the charges carefully once more and then slipped the papers in the pocket of his robe before going back to bed.

Hours later, he rushed out to the airport, eager to escape the madness with a visit to his sister Aesha. The next day was Thanksgiving, and he had nothing to really rejoice over in his mind. The last couple of months had served him more annoyance and embarrassment than he ever thought he would have to bear as an adult.

He boarded the flight to Dallas, settled in an aisle seat about midway through the plane, and closed his eyes to the flat chime of the fasten-seatbelt notification. Breathing in the stale, recycled air, he felt the slight g-force of takeoff. It did nothing to alleviate the stress and drama in his body, and he could not stop himself from wondering again why he didn't heed his intuition to just leave this woman alone.

Section Three

Three-Ring Circus

Winning and Losing

THE NEXT FEW weeks were a bleak combination of survival and sleepwalking. Keenan hired a personal trainer, Britney who came to his house every day, and that helped immensely with the stress of losing his job, girlfriend, and this crazy upcoming court case. Looking back, he later laughed at himself that he had hired the personal trainer before he even found a lawyer. Priorities. She was a true godsend, though, and working out helped his mental health immensely during this time. Every day, she came over at five a.m.—this tight-bodied, twenty-three-year-old who was dating a famous producer in town. He never tried to hit on her—he respected her professionalism and matched it, but it sure was easy to get up early in the morning and work out with her. She drove him like a drill sergeant, too. He'd gotten a bit of a gut with Veronica, but by the end of December, he was all cut up and muscled. It felt great, both physically and emotionally.

And he didn't ignore his other legal issues. It was only a few days after his first at-home workout that he called his friend Monica, a lawyer, mover, and shaker in Atlanta who knew everyone. "I can't take your case," she said, "but maybe my uncle can."

Uncle John Smith, Esquire, had an office in a building where Keenan used to work, and they recognized each other immediately. Mr. Smith was tall with a high forehead due to his receding hairline. Keenan guessed he was probably in his late forties, early fifties. His navy-blue pinstriped suit fit him perfectly, and he pumped Keenan's hand in a manner both friendly and assertive. Keenan felt comforted.

"Hm," Mr. Smith said as he paged through the documents Keenan had brought. "I know the judge on this. Our sons go to the same school." He paused, reading. "I'll take your case," he said finally. "I'll be in touch if I have any questions. We'll want to do a run-through of your cross-examination. What date is good for you?"

At home after the meeting with his lawyer, his tentative good mood was blown by a sudden phone call from his brother Benjamin, who was a career US Army officer.

"Just wanted to let you know that I'm about to start sending over some of my stuff. Are you ready for me?"

"What?" Keenan said, then suddenly remembered. Benjamin was moving to Atlanta after his retirement from the US Army. His brother had called him earlier in the year, but he forgot about it due to his rollercoaster relationship. Now, Benjamin's retirement was coming near and all of his things were scheduled to arrive at Keenan's house within the week.

Just one more thing to deal with.

He reassured his brother that he was ready for him, hung up, and brooded. He knew what he needed. A woman. Yes, despite everything that he was going through, he was still addicted to the smell, touch, and the chase of a woman.

So, after he met with his lawyer one more time, and after he made room in his house for his brother, he also sat down again in front of the computer and updated his profile on the online dating site. Once again he began to peruse the profiles and met a few women, went on several dates at an upscale restaurant, and developed a sex partner or two.

He even made an attempt to look for a real partner by reaching out to matchmaker Layla Hazel. In a response email, she asked him to describe his current situation, now that he and Veronica were finally through. He tapped out his answer while sitting up in bed one night alone.

"I feel that I've given my all to different women during my journey for love," he wrote. "I still yearn to find a special lady to share my life with and partner with as the years fold into the final bittersweet stages of life. On dating sites, I have found so many women who were focused on what they wanted, while I was focused on what we could want and build together. I need to seek fulfillment in people who can appreciate the type of love that I am willing to give."

Layla responded, "Keenan, thank you for your thoughtful words. I have a couple of clients who I think are as serious-minded as you."

The first date stood him up.

Nice job, Layla, he thought.

Embarrassed, the matchmaker quickly set him up with a second date. At first, this woman seemed to be everything that Layla had promised. Violet was originally from Philadelphia, and Keenan was immediately struck by some differences in her attitude as compared to the women he was used to dating in Atlanta.

For example, she was really down on the quality of education offered by HBCUs, which in Atlanta was a scandalous opinion. She had been educated in the Northeast and was currently a physician at the CDC.

Their first date was at a restaurant and video arcade, and he was pleasantly surprised at how enthusiastic she was about the chance to hang out at the bar, play some vintage video games, and shoot pool.

"Most guys are boring," she said. "You're really fun."

He was beyond charmed that he had brought this brown-skinned goddess a positive experience and a nice memory. That and her hypnotic hazel eyes encouraged him to ask her out again.

She was crazy about the Eagles, so they watched a couple of football games together. Then he bought tickets for the single-ring African-American circus, and she agreed to go. While they were going up the stairs to their seats, he took her hand. It was, he thought, a natural gesture.

"Can you stop trying to touch me?" she asked in the stands.

"What do you mean?"

"I'm not a touchy-feely-type person"

Okay. At the end of the date, he gave her a farewell hug with her consent and they went their separate ways.

Even though he wanted to move on with his life and find a bride who would complement him, his heart was jagged thanks to Veronica's games, getting him fired, and crying wolf to the court system. To top it off, his brother was in the middle of moving into his house, and it felt like the walls were moving in closer every single day.

How was he supposed to survive? How was he supposed to work again in his field with something that pointed to mental instability hanging over his head?

He thought back on the many times he let Francis, Tanya, and Veronica dictate their wants and desires without any of his input. He thought about how he waited for them to tell him the rules of the game and then adjusted his life, appearance, and expectations without offering his opinion. As a matter of fact, he remembered offering his opinion in New York—the smallest opinion about a pair of yellow pants—and being told to leave the store.

He had been complacent and reactive for far too long, and look what it had gotten him: a temporary restraining order from a woman who only wanted to one-up him. If she wanted a fight, he had enough of one boiling deep within him to give her one hell of a battle.

Maybe it was that battle energy that made him irresistible to the job market. Within a week, he had interviewed, been hired, and started to work at OnlineMD for more money than he had been making before. This victory gave him the energy to fight for his name. It also gave him a source of funds so that he could afford to spend more time with his lawyer in preparation for the case.

By the end, he was relieved but not surprised that the court dismissed Veronica's temporary restraining-order case. The judge found no cause for what his lawyer called the "exaggerated rash action" Veronica took by filing. Keenan knew he had Mr. Smith's skills as a lawyer to thank, along with the fact that he was making enough at his new position to afford him.

They celebrated at a popular restaurant.

"You did great on the stand," Mr. Smith said. "You sounded reasonable, and you didn't lose your cool. Impressive."

"I couldn't have done it without you," Keenan replied. They felt a friendliness toward each other like a coach and quarterback after a big win. Still, his gratitude was genuine.

"Let me give you some advice," Mr. Smith added, like a good

coach would, as they waited for the check. "You had a solid case, but also, we were lucky. Take this win and leave that crazy woman alone."

It was worthy advice, and Keenan knew it. Filled with coffee, dessert, and victory, he even thought he was going to follow it.

Then he got the final lawyer bill: $2,500 he spent to retain an attorney for this nonsense. And even though he was pleased with his new job, it didn't change the fact that Veronica had sabotaged his finances—first by probably getting him fired, and second by knocking a hole in his wallet with lawyer fees for his "win." Then, he had to reapply for insurance due to switching jobs.

During the application process, he was asked if he had any recent prescriptions. He couldn't remember off the top of his head, so he retrieved his prescription history from the drugstore chain. That's when he saw that Veronica had illegally used his name to fill prescriptions for herself more often than he had thought. This was not just a one- or two-time thing.

Based on these events, he began to brood in spite of himself. He would try to change the subject in his mind and focus on work, but eight months with Veronica had filled him with negative energy, and one bright winter morning at his new desk, he gave in to the wicked temptation: he would fight back.

First, he collected a dossier of her forged prescriptions in which she had signed his name in her handwriting over and over again. Then he contacted the Atlanta Police Department, calling for justice to unfurl at his feet. Instead of justice, however, his call was answered by Officer Phil Cantone.

"I want to report a forgery in my name," Keenan said.

"Go ahead," the officer replied, his voice calm and professional.

Encouraged, Keenan began to explain how Veronica had written prescriptions in his name for her favorite weight-loss drug, phentermine. "And she was never my medical doctor," he finished.

Officer Cantone thanked him for calling. "We'll investigate and provide you with an update as soon as possible," he said.

When he got back in touch, Keenan noticed immediately how his tone had changed. "Hello, Mr. Green," he drawled. "This is Officer Cantone."

"Hello," Keenan said cautiously.

"So, I had a nice long chat with your ex-girlfriend Dr. Veronica Rubio. It seems the two of you have quite a history."

"Yeah. And?" Keenan's tone changed, too.

"First, these charges are not in my jurisdiction. You would need to file in Johns Creek. Second, are you sure you want to move forward with this? Why don't you just leave her alone and move on?"

What?

Yes, Veronica had turned on the charm, and Officer Cantone had taken a side. Keenan was the unstable ex-boyfriend now.

Undeterred, he soldiered on. He could no longer tell himself that he was doing anything but seeking sweet revenge. He and Veronica had developed a habit of torturing each other, and that habit was hard to break.

"I became aware of the first use," he wrote on the police report that he was finally able to file in Johns Creek, "and sent several emails to the doctor asking her not to write and sign prescriptions in my name." The ball was rolling, and even though he knew that revenge might leave him vulnerable to something larger, it was a risk that he was willing to take.

In addition to the prescription-drug charges, he decided to file a civil suit to be financially compensated for the nightmare that was Veronica. That was a much simpler process. With no Officer

Cantone to doubt his word, he was able to fill out his statement of claim and submit it, no questions asked.

In his civil suit, he put Veronica on the hook for over $15,000 due to the following claims: (1) Defendant contacted Plaintiff's place of employment resulting in loss of employment; (2) Defendant led a frivolous petition for stalking/domestic violence costing Plaintiff attorney fees, loss of wages, undue stress, and defamation of the Plaintiff's character; and (3) Defendant coerced Plaintiff into allowing prescriptions to be written in his name for use by Defendant and Defendant's mother.

As he submitted the claim, he felt something that was too wild and reckless to be satisfaction and too premature to be triumph. *Let the games begin*, he thought.

Meanwhile, Keenan tried to get on with his romantic life. It wasn't too difficult, in spite of the roller coaster he had just experienced, and he met many beautiful women with good heads on their shoulders. He just didn't want to get serious with any of them, for many reasons.

He saw Stacy's profile still on the dating site and gave her a call, wanting to catch her up with his latest drama. She had her own news update.

"I got a job offer in St. Croix," she said. "You should come visit me. I'm just having my baby and then moving." He promised he would—an easy promise given the beauty and peacefulness of the island. In the meantime, he continued his search.

Ada was thirty-eight and a former Miss Botswana beauty queen. At least that's what she told Keenan, and he believed it. She had the face of a model, dark-skinned with long, dark hair and a fit but curvy body. He wasn't ecstatic about her weaves and the fact that she wasn't a US citizen, but she was nice and seemed to have a relationship with God. Many evenings she would come over to his house and they would cuddle or watch television. Unfortunately that also led to sex, which complicated things a bit.

"I want to do more than come over and have sex and watch movies," she said one evening as they pulled themselves apart on the sofa. He wondered if this was what she had been thinking about the entire time he was screwing her brains out.

"I thought you wanted to have sex," he said as he pulled up his boxers and sat back down next to her, confused. He hoped the conversation wasn't going where he thought it was going.

"I did want to have sex, but I also want us to be together," she said. "Let's be a couple and date now. Okay?"

What in the pushy hell was this? He had never told her his intentions, and he never assumed they had to talk about it. Sex was one thing, in his opinion, and a relationship was another.

"I like you, Ada, and I'm open to relationships, but I want to continue to get to know you."

She nodded as if she understood and said, "Okay, you need more time to think. I will give you that time. Can we talk about it again on Friday?"

He was in the middle of rubbing her calf when she said this. His mouth dropped open a bit and he paused in mid-rub. She noticed that he was silent and turned away from the TV screen.

"Okay, Sunday. I'll make it an entire seven days," she said before refocusing on the movie and nestling down into the throw pillows.

He realized then that she wanted a lot more than he was ready to give at that moment, and she was really a nice girl. He told her that they should remain friends so that she could spend her energy looking for what she wanted. It was an option that she didn't see coming, but respected nonetheless.

During the season where he was dating Ada, he also met a

woman named Ellen who was another that he considered the right woman at the wrong time. Ellen was a prominent entertainment attorney, his age in years but much older in wisdom. She was the type of woman whose hair, nails, and accessories were always on point. With her large, expressive eyes and confident smile, she was the whole package: witty, grounded, and professional.

She worked tirelessly to ensure that anything with her name on it was flawless. So, he was secretly a little flattered that she asked him to make T-shirts for a charity event which was the pet project of a famous R&B singer. That went off so well, she asked him to build a website for her. It was good timing, because it happened when he was still between the CDC and his next position, so he quickly built one for her without any problems.

He and Ellen were definitely attracted to one another, but often they seemed more like flirting coworkers than a possible romance. Still, it was exactly what he was looking for at this moment. His plate was full with dates and new women, and he had made every effort possible to move on in pursuit of what he knew he deserved.

He met some women online, like Ruby, and he met some women as referrals from friends, like Asliyah, but he also met some women just from his own ability to connect.

One Saturday afternoon Keenan found himself looking for a techie book while in the local book store. He couldn't find the book and approached the customer-service desk for their assistance. A woman with short, androgynous, blonde hair led him to the correct section that contained all of the titles and subject matter pertaining to building apps and the proper software to use and not use. He thanked her and began to search the shelves for his particular book. He found it after crouching near the floor and looking on the next-to-last shelf. When he stood up, she was standing in front of him.

Her hair was long, straight, dark, and pulled into a messy ponytail. She wore jeans, a sweater, and strappy heels. She was holding books called *Sushi That Impresses* and *How to Build Drones For Dummies*. He stood and looked at her clear, light-brown skin and stuck his hand out before his brain could even process what he was doing.

"Hello, I'm Keenan," he said with his hazel eyes fixed on her beautiful hazel eyes and long Bambi eyelashes.

She smiled and placed her hand in his. "Hi, I'm Rose."

Rose came and went in his life, but another woman from this time of casual relationships became something almost like a steady thing. It was at the beginning of the year when he and Ellen started seeing each other more. He was getting into the rhythm of his new job at a web-based medical resource, which was located in Colony Square. It just so happened to be the same building where Ellen had her office.

While eating sushi at lunch one day, he saw this beautiful woman pacing back and forth on the phone as if she was trying to locate someone.

This is how he met Summer, another lawyer who was intelligent and fun. She had a classic hourglass figure and a joie de vivre that Keenan found very attractive. However, as a lawyer, he found that she sometimes had trouble turning off her debate skills, and little conversations would turn into arguments. He valued her sense of self and independence, but sometimes she could be pretty rude.

A couple of months after they met, he saw her at a steak house one night on his way to a salsa club. When he said that he was going, she asked if she could come along, so he took her to a club for salsa night. It was his favorite place to dance, with two stories, multiple bars, a giant sign that spelled out *ATLANTA* in brilliant yellow lights on the ceiling under the wide, industrial-style stair-case, and a state-of-the-art array of strobes, track lights, spotlights, and disco balls. The place was designed to create high energy.

They entered under the black awning and were immersed in the sound of classic salsa playing on a well-balanced sound system, loud but never muffled. Even though it was early, people were already dancing, and Keenan took Summer out onto the floor immediately. He liked how the main bar was at the center of the dancefloor, almost forcing you to dance your way up to the bar.

They worked up a sweat, got a drink, and went upstairs to sit down on one of the tiny, pink couches that overlooked the main floor. That's when Keenan noticed that he didn't have Summer's full attention. She was visibly staring at some dude at the upstairs bar.

"Do you want to dance a couple more and get out of here? I have to work early," Keenan lied. He figured he'd rather come back next week than sit next to a date with a wandering eye. She agreed easily, and they danced for another few songs. Then Keenan waited for her outside while she got her coat.

She walked out talking to that same guy . . . while he was stand-ing outside waiting for her so he could drive them home. Then Keenan saw this guy pull out his phone and take her number.

"What the fuck was that?" he asked when she walked up as if nothing had happened. "That was some disrespectful shit."

"We're not together," she replied casually.

"*You* asked *me* if you could come along," he pointed out.

The evening ended with more toxic words and Summer order-ing a rideshare service.

A few weeks later, Keenan and his brother went out to a res-taurant, and they were seated at a table right next to Summer next to the same "friend" who had introduced himself at the salsa club.

They seemed uncomfortable, but Keenan and Benjamin found themselves having a really great time. After that, he wouldn't see much of Summer for a while. But she would pop back up for years after. Dating her was like having a one-night stand with the same person every six months.

In late January for the Super Bowl, Keenan booked a trip to New York to really see the city. Ellen was hosting a party at the Super Bowl for some of the athletes that she represented. The online medical resource site had an office there, and it was a free trip to the Super Bowl hype, since NYC was hosting it that year.

On the way to New York while at the airport, he saw a woman who looked slightly familiar. She was tall and slender, almost as tall as he was, with long hair and a graceful demeanor. Her eyes were large, and she had a pronounced bone structure and strong features. He watched her answer her ringing cell phone and admired the way her perfectly shaped lips spread into a wide smile. He couldn't help himself but to approach her as soon as she ended the call.

"Pardon me," he said as she put her phone back into her purse. "I was watching you from over there, and I think we may know each other."

"Really?" she asked, clearly open to the idea. "Where do you work? I work at NBS."

"No, I don't, but I used to work at NBS!" Keenan said quickly as her face brightened. He left after grabbing his food and returned to her. "I remember you, and I always wanted to say hello. May I give you a call sometime?"

"Okay," she said. "I'm Faith."

They exchanged numbers, and Keenan thought that it was a good omen for the trip. It turned out he was right.

This journey to New York City was 360 degrees from that life-draining episode with Veronica. He settled into the Kerry Hotel in Times Square, yet another sparkling glass tower in a city full of them. Ellen had suggested the hotel, and she was right—it was perfect for what he wanted, and the high floor gave him the stunning view of brightly lit signs, two-story screens, and masses of people with much less noise.

Without all the drama from last time, the city seemed exciting and fun instead of a negative hassle.

Ellen's energy was completely taken up with the event, so he knew he wouldn't see her until it was over. Held at a tony event space next to the Hudson River, the evening was a success, and Keenan found himself posing for photos like a celebrity. He looked across the room and saw Ellen laughing and enjoying herself. She had already promised to meet him for a wind-down drink at the lobby bar later, and the knowledge made him feel almost smug. Like he had inside information.

Hours later when they met, the bar was quiet and they had a chance to bask in the glory of the night. Ellen was still on a high from the success of the evening, but finally, she seemed to relax. She sipped her martini slowly and batted her perfect eyelashes at him. "Let's finish these in my room," she said, and Keenan was happy to comply.

He took care of her sexy body until she made him stop, begging for sleep. The whole weekend had been just what he wanted, but Keenan couldn't stop thinking about Faith.

He and Faith had already started texting while they both were in New York, and once he arrived back in Atlanta he gave her a ring. It turned out that they knew some of the same people, and she was down to earth and into IT like him. She had a degree from Howard University in IT and worked at the NBS TV station as a hardware-implementation specialist.

He was attracted to her: she was slender, elegant, and smart with deep-set, almond-shaped eyes that looked right into him. She was into fitness, like him, and her long legs were tight and sexy. Her high cheekbones made her look like a model. Beyond being amazed by her sexy body and gorgeous face, he wanted to respect her feelings and was very open with her. He explained everything that had gone on, so she knew the story about his civil case against Veronica.

Their relationship turned intimate almost immediately. She loved to speak to him on video chat, and even more to turn around and show off some new lingerie on her tight frame. She constantly wore a gold snake bracelet that coiled twice around her wrist, ending in an ornate and curving tail.

They had only been on a couple of dates when she left for a trip to New Orleans. It was after midnight when she called him, and when he turned on FaceTime, he saw that she was in her hotel room, alone, and wearing nothing but a sheet. "I need you to help me go to sleep," she said.

"How can I do that?" he asked, teasing.

"Just tell me what you want to do with me," she said, and Keenan told her that it was his hands stroking her pussy, his tongue licking at her hard nipples. He spent the night on FaceTime with her, as exhausted the next day as if he'd spent the night with her in person.

The night that she returned from New Orleans, she didn't even go to her house, but went straight over to him. They put on a late-night movie, and she said, "Let's have sex."

Sex with Faith was wide open. She was down for any adventure and loved going down on him. This was totally unlike Veronica, who not only did not enjoy giving head, she would scrape him with her teeth like the hammerhead shark that she was. If that was the kind of head Veronica was offering, he was more than happy that she wasn't into it.

Faith, though, had her technique down. She had very small breasts, but nice long legs and a tight ass. The first time she guided his hand to her ass, he wondered if it was really what she wanted, but he slipped his thumb into her lean shape and could tell that she was getting off on it. From then on, he knew what to do. Keenan was delighted that he found someone passionate and erotic with a sex drive that matched his.

Besides sharing their passion in bed, Faith was his confidante, and at first, he was amazed by how well they got along. They jogged together, went to concerts, enjoyed nature, and had a blast in each other's company. They were always doing something fun, unlike with him and Veronica.

And besides that, the sex was crazy. Besides constantly having sex at each other's houses, she had a thing for sex in his car. They fucked in parking lots, or sometimes even on their way out.

Keenan had picked up Faith to go see a late-night showing of the *Robocop* remake. It was playing at a movie theatre, which was all the way over in Edgewood. Traffic from roadwork on the interstate forced them to take side streets through random residential neighborhoods. As Keenan drove, Faith put her hand in his lap. He shifted slightly as she unzipped his pants, then took his growing dick in her hand.

"That's right, baby," he murmured as he drove slowly down yet another tree-lined street glowing from the street lamps. The next block was darker, and Keenan pulled over. Before he could undo his seatbelt, Faith had slipped out the passenger-door window like a racecar driver and gracefully pulled herself onto the roof of his car!

"Come up here," he heard her say.

He looked around. No one seemed to be anywhere near. *Okay.* He pulled himself up so he was sitting next to her, and she attacked his mouth with hers, her tongue pushing against his wildly. He slid his hand under her skirt and up her inner thigh to her panties and found that she was soaking wet. Pushing her panties aside, he rolled over on top of her and fucked the shit out of her on the top of his car, keeping one hand over her mouth to keep her from crying out. She bit his hand hard when she came.

They missed the opening credits.

He pulled together the sum total of their relationship as they left brunch one Sunday afternoon. It was cold, and she huddled close to him after a particularly nasty snow day. Ice still covered certain parts of the sidewalk, and cars crept by on the streets in the Inman Park neighborhood. Parking was a problem for the city which wasn't accustomed to northern weather, so they had to walk to get back to his car. He chose this as the perfect opportunity to bring up the only challenge he could see between them at the moment.

"Faith, where do you see us in a couple of months or years?"

She had her arm linked in with his and was walking in step with him, but she slowed her gait after he asked the question.

"I don't know," she said, sounding lost and harried. "I can't even think that far. I actually have a boyfriend in London, remember?"

"Of course I remember," he said. She had never deceived him about this other man.

He seemed to be pulling her along at this point, she was walking so slow. "I also seem to remember you saying that he had no plans to move to the US, and you had no plans to move to the United Kingdom. Am I wrong?"

"No, you're not wrong. You're very right," she said with an exhale. "I know it's cliche, but this is very complicated."

"I don't understand what's so complicated about a dead-end relationship," he said. "You know what's complicated? To spend a lot of time with you, and to make love to you, just to hear that you aren't sure that you want to be with me."

"Oh, Keenan," she sighed. Like this was such a hard thing to deal with.

"You're wishy-washy, you know that?" he said with a forced chuckle as they approached his car. He opened the passenger-side door for her, closed it after her, and hoped for the best as he entered the car on the driver's side.

"Okay," she said as she turned to face him, "let me just say that I really love being around you even when you act like this."

He turned to look at her as he pulled into traffic. In that brief moment of connection, they both burst out into laughter. He loved her sense of humor, even though he knew she was just trying to keep it light.

"When I act like what? When I express my feelings?" he said as she playfully tugged on his right arm and laughed.

"I know it's not right, but I'm with Oliver. He's in London and I'm here, and we do see each other. I know it's not a traditional relationship, but it works for me and it works for him. I just don't see a future with you now because Oliver is still very much in the picture. I hope you can accept that."

"I'm not sure that I can, but I can deal with it while I continue to date other people," he responded.

Her smile faded a bit and she repositioned herself back into the passenger seat. He realized that that wasn't what she wanted to hear, but she really laid the law down to him and he felt like this was the best way to comply. *Hey*, he thought, *at least I said something.*

The rest of the ride was shockingly quieter, but sometimes truth brings about a silence.

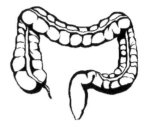

The Meaning of Life

TO THE UNASSUMING, what developed over the next eight months was kismet. But he still continued to date and see other women. Faith was a constant, but she would often disappear for days at a time. Sometimes he couldn't catch her, or talk to her, and he wondered how she could connect with him and then back away and retreat into a self-imposed solitary confinement. Yes, there were signs that probably wouldn't register with the average person. But to Keenan, he took notice of some similarities that he kept in mind.

For example, Faith loved to wear snake necklaces in addition to her snake bracelet. His mind went back to the snake that routinely slithered across Veronica's front step. Also, in February 2014, he was burning leaves in his backyard, when the fire somehow skipped from a couple hundred yards away and began to spark another fire. At first, he saw the smoke and Faith pointed it out to him. By the time they moved into action, the fire was burning in a small pocket of trees, and they put it out in just the nick of time.

It was during this time that Tanya reappeared into his life. They decided to give it another go as friends, and for a season that's what they were. She was in a new relationship, and it was Keenan's pleasure to celebrate this new relationship with her.

Around Mother's Day of that year, they went to dinner at a restaurant on the river and he thought this would be a new beginning for them to be good friends. They barely gave their drink orders before she began to deviate from a positive energy to sludge-level energy. It was as if the conversation picked right up from where it left off that day when she was lambasting him for not being a good dad.

"One of the things I loved about Bobby immediately was how dedicated and proactive he was about spending time with his kids," she said as she smeared butter on a piece of bread. Crumbs flew all over her side of the table, but she was oblivious.

He felt something uneasy between them, but tapped his fingers on the white-linen tablecloth and waited for it to either show itself or hide.

She was dressed beautifully in a blue wrap dress with her hair in a chignon. He had pulled out a conservatively tailored gray suit, and there was no need to make a scene. Not on Mother's Day. Not at this expensive-ass restaurant.

"Well, he sounds like a great guy, and I'm happy for you," Keenan replied as she chewed.

"Enough about me! How is Faith?" she said with a wave of her hand. He told her the truth about the relationship between Faith and him. She looked at him with a deadpan face and just flexed her eyebrows.

"Do you really like her?" she asked as she glanced at the menu.

"I mean, you do see that this isn't someone you need to be with on a serious, permanent level."

"Why do you say that?" he answered. He was interested in her perspective.

"Keenan, she is emotionally unavailable and she seems to only use you for outings while her boyfriend is out of town or away on business," Tanya said. "Get a grip! This isn't the one."

He nodded his head, stroked his goatee. "Hmm," he said after a few beats. "You may be right. But have you considered that she really just came to grips that her relationship may not end up the way she thought it would?"

Tanya laughed, and they were momentarily interrupted by the waiter. He ordered salmon and she ordered the grouper. As soon as the waiter retrieved their menus, Tanya went in full steam ahead.

"She may know exactly where the relationship isn't going, but since she is so vocal about wanting to be with you and not wanting to be with you, it would seem like she is a dangerous option. Another Veronica you should look out for, in my opinion."

Then she laughed. She laughed as if she enjoyed whatever confusion she perceived him to be in at the moment. "See, that's why . . . " she said before pausing to take a sip of water, "I am so glad that I'm with Bobby. I mean, he actually thinks things through, and he is a man who I would never have to worry about this with. I can't believe you're even telling me all this."

Keenan shrugged, careful to take the humble route. *No one is perfect—especially no one sitting at the table with him at the moment.*

"I'm sure we all have an opinion about the way things should go. I choose to be optimistic," he said.

She scoffed and replied, "Optimistic, huh? Well, Bobby is optimistic, and he really seems to have his life together—unlike you. I know you're sitting there wondering if I'm putting on airs, but I'm not. You just aren't capable of seeing a good thing when it's right in front of you. Did you know that? For example, after we stopped talking last year, I had a revelation about who I was, and who I am going to be, and what I can do, and it didn't make sense to me that I spent so much time trying to get you to see . . . "

Tanya droned on and on without so much of a break to breathe. She was still talking when the waiter returned with their meals. He let her spew out everything in her heart because he was genuinely curious about how she really felt about him.

Of course, his appetite was gone by then, and he knew that it was a bad decision to pick her up and take her to dinner. He waited for her to stuff some food in her mouth and then reached for his wallet. As he threw $200 on the table, he stood to his feet and her bottom lip dropped.

"I'm going to excuse myself now, Tanya. It was good to see you, and there's enough money here to cover dinner and a cab ride home. I'll see you around." He dabbed at his mouth with the black-linen napkin and walked quickly away from the table without looking back to see her reaction. He just didn't care, and he hoped to never again in his life experience that type of dinner.

Tanya did make it home. She actually called and left him a voicemail saying that her boyfriend and father were aware of how he left her at the restaurant, and that they were going to kill him when they found him. He didn't respond, but he did save the voicemail in case anything questionable happened in his life.

This was the last time that he heard from Tanya for a while. He really wanted to be friends with her, but for whatever reason, it wasn't the right time for them. He didn't want to be friends with her to the point that he disrespected himself and his own self-worth.

* * *

Keenan Takes Veronica to Court

Meanwhile, the wheels of justice were grinding on for the civil and criminal cases he was plotting against Veronica. For the civil case, Veronica was served on December 31, 2013, at her job, and Keenan requested a default judgment in mid-February 2014.

Four weeks later, Veronica's lawyer backdated a counterclaim, and a criminal-warrant hearing was scheduled for April 2014. Veronica didn't show up for this court date, and the judge issued a warrant for her arrest. Keenan let the arresting officer know this bit of information in an email and CC'd Veronica. She forwarded the email to her lawyer, and the warrant was never executed. He couldn't help but to think that if he had just kept his mouth shut that justice would have had its opportunity.

On April 24, Keenan entered the courtroom again, only this time as a plaintiff seeking his revenge. For these court sessions, he chose a lighter gray suit in harmony with the season and with his role not as a defendant, but as an avenging angel.

The civil case against Veronica was set for eight a.m. and the criminal case for one p.m. He had scheduled lunch with Faith at a sports bar near the courthouse a neighborhood grille.

His lawyer for this case was not the expensive Mr. Smith, but some third-stringer he'd found after a brief internet search. In his quest for vengeance, he didn't think he necessarily needed great counsel; he believed too much in his case. But then he listened in disbelief as the civil case was postponed once again. *Another day taken off work for nothing.*

His new lawyer, Mr. Laughlin, conferred briefly with Veronica's lawyer, an intimidating woman named Karen Kennedy. At 5'11", Ms. Kennedy was a blonde bombshell with long, straight hair and really well-defined arms. Keenan hated her at first sight. Later, he would wonder if his reaction was yet another sign. For now, she was civilized enough, and before Keenan met Faith for lunch, his lawyer told him the plan they had cooked up to end this thing forever.

"We think that if the both of you just sign this agreement, you can both walk away, no damage done. I mean, think about it. This is Matt's mother. Do you really want to put her in danger? And how much time do you want to waste on this?"

The proposal was simply for both of them to sign a no-contact agreement that Ms. Kennedy had already drawn up.

"Let me think about it," Keenan said. "I'll tell you after lunch."

He headed over to Hudson Grille, where Faith waited at the bar. He sat next to her, and they both ordered burgers while Keenan told her about the proposal.

"So, both Ms. Kennedy and my own lawyer think I should sign. What do you think?"

Faith took a deep breath. "I think you should sign it," she finally said.

"Really?" Keenan was a little surprised.

"Sure," Faith said. "Your lawyer is right. Think of the baby. Think of your own precious time spent fighting a toxic ex. This is a chance for both of you to move on."

"Maybe you're right," he said. After all, Veronica had a child to raise. He didn't want to take Matt's only active parent away from him.

He walked back to the courthouse, and at one p.m. was signing an agreement that contained a no-contact clause. Out of everyone surrounding him, the one dissenting voice was actually the judge.

"Are you sure you want to do this?" he said. From the tone of his voice, it was pretty clear the actual judge did not think it was the greatest idea.

But the pressure put on Keenan from his lawyer, from Faith,

and from his own weaknesses when it came to Veronica was too much for Keenan. His drive for vengeance ended not with a bang, but a whimper.

"You did the right thing," Faith reassured him. But those words would ring pretty hollow for Keenan in the very near future.

Keenan still had an online dating profile, so he still met many women online and even around the city. There were also very sweet women who he crossed paths with and couldn't seem to keep in touch with due to his ongoing relationship with Faith. They were not exclusive, but she thrived off of knowing that he put her first, and she used it to her advantage. For the most part, it was all fun and games, but he could never really get over the way Faith sabotaged his chances with Crissy.

He met Crissy online, and she just took his breath away. She reminded him a little of Tanya, but younger and less authoritative. Like Tanya, she had two children, a boy and a girl, and from her conversation, it was clear that she was a caring and loving mother to them. She had a good relationship with their father. Besides her sweet personality and good character, she was beautiful. Crissy had long legs and a spotlight smile. Her almond eyes were hazel like Keenan's, with spiral curls when her hair dried naturally and these pretty, tan-colored freckles all over her nose. He looked at her and his heart melted.

Her beauty, her sweetness, and her character, though, were no match for Faith and her wicked games.

Keenan glanced down at his phone one afternoon and read that Bee and Jay were scheduled to perform at Philips Arena. He immediately thought of Faith. Would she like to go? Then, a better angel whispered in his ear. *Why not take Crissy?* She loved music, and she didn't cause him any grief or worry. Wasn't it time to move on?

"That sounds like fun," she said when he called to invite her.

He spent the rest of the week looking forward to spending time with her. This would be a chance to get to know her better. He even thought of future dates and considered the idea of introducing their children in the near future.

Crissy arrived at his house dressed in tight jeans and a black, sparkly blouse that fit her frame perfectly. *The night was going to be perfect,* he thought. Then his cell phone vibrated in his hand.

"You look beautiful," he said, and glanced down at the phone. *Faith. Uh-oh.* "Let me pour you a drink while I finish getting ready," he added, stalling for time. He mixed her a vodka soda, settled her on the couch, and escaped to the solitude of his bedroom to return Faith's call.

"Hey," he said hastily as he pulled out some shoes and reached for his cologne.

"Hey yourself," she responded. "What are you getting into?"

"I'm on my way out," he said. He was being careful to just give her enough info to let her know that he wasn't available. He hadn't talked to her in four days, and this was the most inconvenient time to have a "How have you been?" discussion. Besides, he had made his choice for the evening: Crissy. The nice one without a boyfriend overseas.

"Out where?" she demanded to know. "I know you aren't taking some random girl out on a date!"

"Can I call you later?" he asked as he grabbed his car keys off the nightstand.

"Keenan! Where are you going? Are you going to the Jay-Bee concert?"

There. She called it out. It was eerily as if she had already been told where they were going. This woman was clearly dedicated to being the dog in his manger.

"Yes, I'm on my way to that concert, and I—"

"You're actually going to take some random chick to the concert? Are you kidding me? If you don't get rid of her, I'm going to beat her ass when I pull up. You're going to take me to the concert."

"Faith, would you stop the madness? I'm about to walk out the door," he replied.

"I was on my way over to your house and I just thought I'd call, but I had no idea you would take some chick who doesn't know you and care about you, as opposed to me. Dang . . . "

Yeah, she poured it on thick.

"I'm around the corner from your house. You better get rid of her!" Faith continued.

Keenan then realized that she was serious. He wondered with a sinking feeling, Was Faith dangerous to other women? Was he doing the wrong thing by bringing sweet Crissy into some random confrontation that she didn't deserve?

Ugh, he was being pulled into drama without his consent, but it wasn't hard to realize that it might be best to get Crissy out of harm's way. Faith had never exhibited aggressive behavior before, but after dealing with Veronica, he didn't want to take any chances, and in spite of his best intentions, he would rather temporarily deceive Crissy than bring her into a bad scene from an Atlanta housewife show.

He flew out of his bedroom and almost jogged into the living room. Breathing heavily, he reached for an excuse. At least he didn't have to pretend to be upset.

"I am so sorry," he said, "but I just got a call from my brother. I have to deal with a family emergency and I can't make the concert. I'll call you later," he said, "but I've got to get out of here, so you'll have to go."

He didn't know if his demeanor or his words alarmed her more, but she was visibly upset. "Are you serious? I was so amped to see Jay and Bee," she said with a long face. "Whatever it is sounds awful! Will you be okay?"

He assured her he would be fine, opened the door, and was walking her outside to her car when he looked up and saw Faith's foreign coupe drive slowly by his driveway. Crissy was in a daze and kept asking if there was anything that she could do to help. Keenan continually told her no.

"I've just got to get on the road and go across town to check on some things," he said. The whole time he was actually eyeing Faith's car and making sure that she didn't pop out of that driver's seat and start a row in front of his house.

Crissy finally got into her car and drove away. He breathed a deep sigh of relief as Faith walked up the street toward his house. *Faith*. She didn't walk, actually. Rather, she strutted like a super-model down that suburban sidewalk, clearly delighted that she had won this round. Her victory and attitude were undeniably sexy, and instead of being angry, he could tell that she was having a great time.

His relief at the fact that she was not coming down on him like an avenging demon of fury put a dumb, relieved grin on his face. And that was enough. She looked at him and they both started laughing, like two teenagers who had pulled a prank.

"I can't believe you!" she said in between giggles.

"Me? I can't believe . . . " He stopped himself. The game was over, and she had won. He was on her ride now, so he pushed away his conscience, laughing also before putting an arm around her and escorting her to his car. They went to the show that night, and the guilty pleasure made it so much fun that they were like teenagers. It didn't hurt that the whole *On the Run* concert series was built around the concept of Jay and Bee getting away with a life of crime, Bonnie and Clyde style. That night, Keenan and Faith were their own Bonnie and Clyde.

Keenan's high spirits were further boosted by the fact that he saw in the crowd one of the women he'd been matched with by Layla Hazel. They had a good time, but somehow had never gone beyond a first date. When she saw him in the crowd as they were making their way through to the exit, she deliberately steered herself in his direction, then as she brushed against him, she murmured, "Call me," in his ear. Faith didn't even notice.

The emotional peak lasted for days.

But it wore off eventually. In the back of his mind, he knew that he owed Crissy something special. She didn't deserve to be treated like that, and he knew he was complicit even though Faith was the instigator. She had manipulated him with the skill of someone who knew him well, and he felt trapped by his attraction to her.

That night, intoxicated by the energy of the concert, at least, she had told him that she thought she wanted to be his girl. But Keenan knew well enough that this was not an epiphany for Faith—she loved to get caught up in the moment and make all sorts of wild remarks. Then later, she would change her mind and wonder why he was upset. So, he didn't get upset anymore.

But somehow, she still had a hold on him.

He wasn't done trying to break free, though, and he couldn't help but wonder if a kind and beautiful woman like Crissy couldn't help him move on. So, he waited a few days, and called Crissy with a peace offering that he hoped she would accept.

"Hey," he said gently.

"Hi, how are you?" Crissy responded flatly. It was a little discouraging, but Keenan pushed on.

"So, I thought we could go see Jay and Bee in New Orleans. What do you think?"

She paused. It was a long one. Her skepticism was wordless but unmistakable. "I don't know," she said, and fell silent again.

Keenan pushed on. "Listen," he said, "I'll do the driving and get the hotel. I just want you to come and to have a good time. Promise. It's the least I can do."

He heard her sigh. "Okay," she said slowly.

They journeyed to New Orleans to enjoy the show. Bee and Jay seemed as fired up to be in New Orleans as they had been in Atlanta, and he appreciated that he had the chance to see them perform to two separate audiences.

After the concert, they each slept in their own separate double bed at the hotel. Still, even without sex, it was all Keenan had hoped for—no drama, no wickedness. Just two adults enjoying each other's company and experiencing a great concert together. Crissy's smile was all Keenan could have hoped for, and he felt some of his bad conscience ease. He allowed himself to hope that he had actually made it up to Crissy, and she seemed to relax in his company, too.

After the concert, they strolled Bourbon Street, then walked down St. Peter's and caught another set in Jackson Square by some performers who called themselves Tuba Skinny. Just another night in New Orleans, but for Keenan and Crissy, it was special. There's something about the cobblestone streets of the French Quarter that make you feel like you're in a different world.

So, Keenan felt great on the drive home, at least at first. Then he couldn't help but notice that Crissy's demeanor had taken a drastic change. She was so quiet, and she had been really animated and fun through their whole journey. They had even held hands walking down Bourbon Street, and her smile had lit up the night. In the car, there was no smile. She said little to nothing until they were in the middle of Alabama.

"Who is Faith?" Crissy asked.

His hands reactively gripped the wheel and he nervously licked his lips. *Shit.*

"Faith is a friend of mine. Why?" he responded, never taking his eyes off the road.

"Because I saw that you took her to the Jay-Bee concert in Atlanta. That's why," she said. She was very still and her voice was calm.

"What makes you say that?" he asked, never ready to put all his cards on the table.

"I went through your phone last night while you were in the shower. I saw the pictures and the text messages," Crissy said before turning to look out the window. She rested her elbow on the passenger-side door, and she stayed in that position for the next hour.

Keenan didn't respond. What was there left to say? He just nodded his head as if he had heard a new formula for a trigonometry problem. He wasn't sure if her silence reflected his lack of response, or if she was just getting things off her chest.

They made a stop at Tuskegee so she could see her alma mater, and seeing the red bricks and white pillars of the historical campus seemed to cheer her up. They continued home to Atlanta in a more companionable silence.

"Thanks," she said halfheartedly as she climbed into her car where it was parked in front of his house.

Though he tried to call her a few times, they never got back on track. Eventually, they just didn't keep in close communication. Keenan was disappointed, but mostly in himself.

It was just that he found himself turning Faith's declarations of love over and over in his mind. *Were they sincere?* His confusion meant that he couldn't give his all to someone like Crissy, even though it was a little heartbreaking to see her drift away. One thing he knew for sure was that Faith was systematically blocking him from moving on, and he was allowing her to mess up some pretty great budding relationships with some pretty great women. Once again, he was in over his head.

As if he needed more of a lesson, the same storyline played itself over again when he met Amy. She reminded him of Veronica with her long hair and thin frame, dark-brown skin, and large, expressive eyes. She had a successful career as an RN. Amy had a sweet demeanor, but could be verbally aggressive at times with all sorts of surprising words coming out of those sweet coral lips. He loved that she was so relaxed in bed, and she had a playful sexiness that captivated him.

He wanted to get to know her better, so he bought tickets for them to go enjoy John Legend in concert. Like clockwork, some evil fairy whispered into Faith's ear that he was going out with another woman. He picked up the phone (again), and this time he heard Faith declare how much she loved him and didn't want him to go out with anyone else.

"You are not gonna just take a random chick to see John Legend," she declared. At least this time she had the courtesy to call a whole three hours before the concert started.

Yes, really.

Was he hypnotized? He pushed Amy off and went to the John Legend concert with Faith. Unlike Crissy, Amy had some choice words about being pushed off. She didn't need proof from text messages to know that he had taken another woman to the concert at the last minute.

She did accept a make-up trip to Boston to see John Legend live in concert there. Even though the trip was pleasurable, it was undeniable that they started out on the wrong foot, and he could tell that their relationship was going to drift into the friend zone as a best-case scenario.

They continued to date and even attended church together on Sundays for another year. Ironically, the church they attended was the same church Faith introduced him to when they started dating. Amy was already a member, and Keenan continued to worship there because it was within walking distance to his home and he admired their kind approach to ministry. He felt lucky that he was able to create a friendship with Amy, but once again Faith had prevented him from finding someone who could give him her whole heart.

One Sunday morning before church in the parking lot, he found himself walking behind a familiar head of tight, reddish curls next to the tall and unmistakable figure of Pete—Veronica's ex and Matt's godfather. They gave each other the nod and went into services. After church, some undeniable impulse caused him to get Pete's phone number.

"I'd just—really like to know what happened between the two of you," Keenan said. "I think it would help me get some closure."

Pete agreed to a meeting, and the following week they met at a local fast food restaurant. "So you want to know why we broke up," Pete said, with very little small talk.

"Yeah," Keenan replied. "I mean, you were an important part of her life."

"I thought so," Pete replied. "I don't know that she ever did. So, look," he continued. "We were supposed to get married, but then my mom got sick. She moved in with us, and Veronica didn't like that one bit."

"That sounds typical," Keenan responded.

"Yeah. So then she's pregnant, and I leave Mom and go to live with her. She starts talking about whether or not she's going to put my name on the birth certificate, like she's holding it against me. One day she's going to do it, then next day, no way."

"Go on," Keenan said.

"Thing is," Pete said, picking up a french fry, "I wasn't sure I really wanted to be on that birth certificate anymore anyway. So when I wasn't, that was okay with me. After the baby was born, I told her we needed to back up and move more slowly. And I moved out."

"Did you see Matt at all during that time?" Keenan asked.

"I tried to," he said. "I came around a few times. But she started dating Ced, and I met my fiancée. That's about the time I came over to the house."

"I remember," Keenan said.

"I don't know if this helps you, man," Pete finished.

"Me neither," Keenan admitted. "But I appreciate your time."

"Hey, we both survived her," he said. "I consider that a win." The wins and losses were a roller coaster during that time period, but he couldn't push all of the stress onto the court system. One morning in June he woke up sick to his stomach, like he'd felt a couple of times while he was with Veronica. Thinking it was a mild case of food poisoning again, he continued to dress and go to work as always. When he didn't improve, he left his desk around noon and went home. He walked unsteadily into the house, stripped, tried to drink water but couldn't keep it down, and collapsed on the steps on the way to his bedroom.

His brother Benjamin found him a few moments later when he arrived home. He roused Keenan, who was finally realizing how sick he was. They called Faith, and she rushed over.

Benjamin and Faith took a barely conscious Keenan to the

hospital. At the hospital, he didn't spend much time in the waiting room. They saw how sick he was and gave him a bed a lot faster than other people who had been sitting there waiting when he arrived. As relieved as he was to be seen right away, Keenan knew that wasn't a great sign.

Not yet attached to any IV, he lay there with his street clothes still on while Faith and Benjamin sat with him.

"They're just going to give me some medicine," he said to Benjamin. "Maybe I'll have to stay overnight."

"Let's see what the doctor says," Faith responded.

One wasn't long in arriving. A young woman who looked like a slightly younger Veronica came over just a few minutes later, checked him over, pushed on his stomach, and called for an MRI. After he returned from his scan, the three of them waited some more, trying to make small conversation but mostly scanning their phones. Keenan, still reeling with nausea, dropped his own phone and closed his eyes.

When the doctor returned, she had not-great news.

"Your appendix has ruptured," she said flatly. "We're going to immediately prepare you for emergency surgery. We need to stop the toxins from getting into your bloodstream."

At her words, both Faith and Benjamin seemed to melt away, and he didn't have much time at that moment to think about anything other than his kids and the importance of life. Nurses and anesthesiologists circled around him with wires, needles, and beeping machines. Someone placed oxygen in his nostrils as another found a vein in his left arm. Within minutes he had surrendered to a senseless void.

It felt like he only blinked for a second before he opened his eyes. His first vision was of a matronly, redheaded nurse with wide hips and thin lips standing over him. It was dusk and the sun was beginning to set, so golden rays were striped over the harsh-white wall and the industrial-style sink.

Keenan hated hospitals. Hated them.

"You're awake!" the nurse said in a comforting voice. "And what pretty eyes."

They all love me, thought Keenan groggily as she pushed buttons behind him and adjusted the bed.

"Let me go get the doctor," she said.

As she left, he blinked again and tried to take stock of everything around him. Suddenly, his brother Benjamin and Faith were following the doctor into the hospital room. They took positions at both sides of his bed while the doctor came in closer to him.

"We thought it would only take one hour," the doctor said, "but you had a lot of scar tissue around the appendix. You've been sick before?"

Keenan cleared his throat and barely said, "Yes."

"He said he was sick last November with nausea and vomiting," Faith said, looking at his brother for confirmation.

Benjamin nodded and said, "Yeah, I remember that. I believe there was a time before that, also."

The doctor scribbled something in the file that she held in her hand and said, "Sounds like your appendix started rupturing a while ago, and the scar tissue that formed kept you alive." She patted Keenan on the shoulder. "You're a lucky man," she said.

That was new. Maybe he was. Life looked different from this hospital bed.

"You'll be fine now. We're going to monitor you overnight, and I'll get some prescriptions for you. You'll need to come back in two weeks once you're released."

It was hard to talk, but he felt like he had to.

"Thank you," he managed. He looked at his dream team of

doctors, Faith, and Benjamin, and just thanked God that they were there to help him. Benjamin followed the doctor out to talk further.

"You're my dream—" he started, but Faith grabbed his hand.

"Shh," she said, and smiled. "Don't talk right now."

He smiled back and closed his eyes. When he woke up again, he was alone except for the nurses and the machines. Inevitably, his mind went back to what the doctor said.

So, it had been his appendix, after all. He had been in more danger than he thought, and he was lucky, he realized, that Veronica had been there with him both times. He could see that she played a part in preserving his life. It occurred to him how wrong he had been to keep any anger or revenge in his heart. Whether they had bad blood or not, he wished he could let her know how much he appreciated her kindness. He felt like he owed her an apology.

A Vicious Cycle

In Court Again - Veronica's Revenge

"WELL, EVERYTHING HE'S done since we've ended the relationship has been threatening, from intimidating me at my job, jeopardizing my job—my career, not just my job—my safety with my son, and then showing up at my house after signing an agreement," Veronica said on the stand.

"Let me ask you about that," his lawyer said. "The medical board opened an examination regarding some prescriptions you had written."

She bristled and said, "Some medication that I had refilled for Mr. Green."

"And that investigation is still open?" He was leading her to a specific point.

"It's still ongoing," she said. "Actually, the investigation has closed. I just spoke to the investigator on Friday. The investigation is closed, but the board has to meet to go over to see what the next step would be . . . all of this because Mr. Green, during the time that I dated him, had no insurance. He'd ask me for a medication refill, and I gave him that refill. After I ended the relationship with Mr. Green, he then went on this rampage of trying to harass, and intimidate, and scare me any way that he could. And this was one avenue that he took."

"Now, just for clarification, it's your testimony that the diet pills and the skin cream were not for you?" his lawyer asked firmly.

"Mr. Green asked for the prescription," she said quickly.

"Please answer me yes or no."

"Yes, sir," Veronica replied.

"Your testimony?"

"Yes, sir," she repeated.

"And those were the only times you've physically seen Mr. Green since April? The day he honked and waved at you, and the day he left the note on your door, correct?"

"Yes, sir," she said again.

"And you said that in court today he was doing something else?"

Keenan sat there thinking about how in a guilt-free world he could get up and walk away from this bullshit without having to ever face it again.

"On June 26, 2014, at about six o'clock p.m., I was driving home with my mother and my son from work down State Bridge," Veronica said with her hands clasped over her lap. The judge peered at her over her glasses, and she sat with her back straight against the witness-stand chair.

Keenan rested his elbow on the edge of his own defense-table seat and wondered what spin she would put on something harmless. *Poor little princess caught in a big bad lie.* And Keenan, the hapless knight in shining armor who never saw the army coming that the princess had raised against him.

"We were stopped in traffic, and all of a sudden there was beeping, someone was beeping alongside of me," she continued. The princess was literally and expertly holding court.

Keenan glanced around the room and saw looks of concern on almost every face. He guessed it wasn't a good time to jump up and exclaim that he only honked once as he drove by her damn car, and that they worked within five minutes of one another, so passing one another on the route home was bound to happen. It actually did happen more than once while they were dating.

"I looked over, my mom and I both, and it was Mr. Green waving and beeping, and he made a big thing about us seeing him, I guess, and he kept going. And then on July 8, when he came to my house . . . "

* * *

Keenan's recovery from appendicitis was not as fast as he wanted, but he soon felt better enough to go to work. The prior weekend before returning to work, Faith, Benjaman, Kalvin, and Keenan participated in the annual HBCU 5K, of course, they walked the 3.5 miles together. Prior to Kalvin heading out from the park he pulled Keenan aside. "Dad", Kalvin said. "Can you please stop introducing me to the women you date, there are a lot of them and I don't want to meet them anymore." Keenan agreed. Prior to that conversation, Keenan had never considered how his dating life was affecting his children. The next morning, Keenan was not too surprised to see Veronica driving with her mother a few car lengths over. He remembered, of course, how close Veronica's hospital office was to his. In his new, forgiving mood, he honked and waved, but their expressions stayed frozen. He didn't think too much more about it, and a few weeks later, he picked his truck up from a mechanic who was completing a transmission replacement.

The mechanic was near Veronica's house. He had a sudden impulse to stop by to apologize to Veronica for all that he put her through. He knew in advance that this could go sideways, so before he got to her house he pulled over to call his friend Joe.

"Go with your gut," Joe advised, so he proceeded. He drove up to Veronica's building, got out of the truck with good intentions, then knocked on her door but no one answered. So he went back to his truck to write a quick note.

"I come in peace," he wrote. "I'm sorry. You saved my life. Thank you."

Keenan left the note on the door. The windows were screened, but open. As he was walking away, he heard Veronica say, "It's Keenan."

Then he heard Veronica's mother say, "What is he doing here?"

Then he heard little Matt's voice say, "Yay!"

It was a punch in the gut. He kept it moving, though, and was back at his truck when the front door popped open and Veronica stood in the doorway, full of rage.

"We have a no contact clause," she said with a look of disgust.

He paused before sliding his left leg into the SUV. "I'm not doing anything illegal," he said. "The agreement was not a TPO."

Probably not the best thing to say under the circumstances. He'd just left a note saying he'd come in peace, and here he was arguing his right to be on her property on a technicality. He realized—with that sickening "too late" feeling—that he'd made the wrong move. She hadn't just been through some life-changing event, and of course, she didn't know that he'd been through something serious. He had just shown up at her door.

"I've already called the police!" Veronica screamed at the top of her lungs as she snapped a picture of him on her phone. She took the note off of the door and slammed it behind her.

He didn't waste any more time and left quickly, with a sinking heart and Matt's happy little voice in his ears. He reminded himself that what they had between them was more of a civil agreement and couldn't be upheld in court without a great effort. But regardless of what was on file at the courthouse, a sheriff showed up at his door about three weeks later, notifying him of a court date for Veronica's second attempt at a temporary restraining order, to be held on Monday, August 4, 2014.

Things weren't so great with Faith, either. By late summer, they were on rocky terms in spite of the concerts, nights out, amazing sex, and even the surprise party he had thrown for her birthday. She wouldn't commit, so he went out with other women, and then she got jealous, and they went round and round.

Besides, as he got to know Faith, he realized that she was not beyond bending the rules when it pleased her. For example, NBS was lax about keeping track of their equipment, so Faith always had an extra laptop or two lying around, and she was not above selling them to friends and family. She even loaned one to Keenan for a while. At this point, he had left online medical resource to go work for a telecom company on a side project.

"Do you like what you do?" Faith asked him one evening not long after she loaned him the laptop.

"Building mobile applications? Yeah, it's interesting work. Why?" Keenan asked.

"I'm just tired of my work with NBS. How hard is it to get into what you're doing?"

"Not that hard," Keenan said. "I'll help you get started if you want."

Faith liked the idea, so he funneled a portion of his job assignment to her and wrote her a check for $600 to build the apps. But as their relationship soured and the work didn't get done, he wondered why he had decided to mix business with pleasure.

She wasn't very sympathetic to his upcoming court date, either.

"I'm going to be in Thailand," she said when he called her and told her about Veronica's latest scheme to ruin his name.

"Oh," he said. "Well, have a great time. I'll be in court."

At least she won't be around to give me bad advice, he thought, and when he hung up with her, he scrolled through his contact list.

Hm. Summer. It had been about six months, so she was due. He decided to text her. To his delight, she texted right back. "Come over," he finally texted, and she showed up about a half hour later for a movie that quickly turned into Keenan's head buried into her large, bouncy breasts while she sat on his dick. Summer rode him so hard, she ripped the condom to shreds. He didn't really get too worried until he got a text from Summer a few days later that simply said, "You should get checked."

Shit, Summer, he thought. But after a quick trip to the clinic, he found out he was clean. *What kind of dudes was that girl fucking?*

The night before Faith left for Thailand, she came over, to Keenan's house as a surprise. She was just all keyed up for her trip so she wanted to talk to someone about it he thought. She jabbered on about where she was going, what beaches she was going to visit, how long it would take to get there. He finally kissed her just to stop the pre-vacation monologue. She flicked her tongue against his seductively, then he took her upstairs to his room where he pushed her onto the bed. Wordlessly, she pulled off her clothes and got on all fours. Keenan grabbed her by the hips, ragefucking her, thinking of Summer's round booty as compared to Faith's more lanky frame. When he withdrew from her pussy, he placed the head of his cock at the entrance to her tiny asshole, she didn't resist. He eased his way in, feeling the tightness of her ass against his dick, then exploded into her, muttering, "You filthy bitch." She loved it. But when he texted her the next day to see if she had arrived safely in Thailand, it went unanswered. How much could he worry about it, though? Faith would do whatever she wanted—he'd learned that lesson.

He had one bright spot to look forward to before his court date—a concert at Aaron's Lakewood Amphitheater. Once again, Layla Hazel had set him up with a potential match, and after they had a nice chat over the phone, he asked her to go to ONE Musicfest with him. She agreed, he bought tickets, and then she flaked. Having dealt with Layla's ladies before, though, he wasn't super surprised. He shrugged it off and went by himself with the extra ticket in his pocket. The lineup was exciting—three stages with some super talented acts, then Method Man and Redman in the late afternoon on the main stage, then Kendrick Lamar and Nas as the headliners. It was a mild September day and the vibe was relaxed and loving, the way all the ONE Musicfests tended to be. It was easy to meet people and get reacquainted, and as soon as Keenan was waiting in line at the gate, he saw his old friend Dan, who saw him at the same time. They fell into an easy chat.

"Who you here with?" Dan asked.

"No one," Keenan admitted. "My date stood me up."

"Her loss," Dan said. "I'm meeting my girl—she's already inside—come hang out with us."

"All right," Keenan said easily. That's always how it was at this festival. Keenan thought again about how much he loved Atlanta and the people he knew here. In his good mood, he looked around at what almost felt like an extended family and saw someone else that he knew. Regina, an old friend from work, was standing in line to buy a ticket. She was a thick, fun-loving girl and Keenan knew she'd be great to hang out with for the night.

"Hold up," he told Dan. "I see someone who might need a ticket."

He strolled over to the ticket line and tapped Regina on the shoulder.

"Oh, hey," she said, all smiles, when she saw it was Keenan. "How are you? How's your new job?"

"It's working out pretty good," he said. "I miss you fools, though."

"We miss you too," she said. "Seems like you're in a better place."

He shrugged. "I think so," he said. "Listen, I've got an extra ticket. Why don't you come and hang out with us?"

Her smile got wider. "All right," she said, and joined Keenan and Dan. Now it was a party. The music washed over them as they moved through the crowd, and they joined Dan's girlfriend in the audience for the main stage. Method Man and Redman were performing as the sun set over Atlanta, and Keenan felt himself relax. When Dan saw his cousins in the crowd, they all gladly joined together. *The more the merrier*, he thought, enjoying the music and the slow increase in energy as day turned to night and people started to get hyped for Kendrick Lamar.

One of Dan's cousins was best friends with Francis. So it was perfectly natural of him to ask her how Francis was doing.

"She's great," his cousin said. "She's married with a baby now, did you know?"

"No," he said, feeling his smile go stiff on his lips. "That's . . . great."

To his relief, Kendrick Lamar took the stage and he didn't have to talk about it. But the evening deflated like a broken balloon. Damn. What a way to find out. How's Francine? How's that lady who wasn't ready for marriage or commitment? Turns out she's married with a baby! Turns out she just wasn't ready for a commitment *with him*. He forced himself to enjoy the rest of the show and thought, *at least she never took me to court*.

When his court date finally came, he sat through a character assassination that continued all the way to the closing arguments. Keenan's lawyer meticulously took notes as he dryly watched Veronica make him out to be Mark David Chapman. He'd been called many things in his life, but a "stalker" with "threatening intentions" had never been one of them. Dr. Veronica Rubio was trying to make this a grand show that would go down in the annals of Fulton County Superior Court.

"He knocked on the door, came to the window waving, trying to get us to come in. I told my mom to call 911 . . . "

He had actually stopped by to bury the hatchet. Waving and trying to come in? Nah. That didn't happen.

"So after the initial TPO back in November that I filed that was dismissed, he started to send me letters threatening me, threatening that he was going to report me to the medical board, threatening that he was going to go to the Atlanta PD, threatening all kinds of things, which he ultimately did . . . "

Keenan exhaled and looked at his watch.

Finally, her lawyer, Karen Kennedy, stood from the heavy oak table, ready to pounce on what was left of his character in her closing argument. "I just think that the evidence is clear in this case that Mr. Green needs to be given a strong message that you cannot conduct yourself in this way in today's society," attorney Karen Kennedy said as she stepped backward toward the plaintiff's table. "Thank you, Your Honor."

The judge nodded her head in acknowledgement, and Keenan began to tap his foot against the floor in anxiety. She was exactly like the description of a snake that he read about on Wikipedia. The only difference is that she knew how to speak English and had two feet to walk around.

Keenan's lawyer approached the bench and said, "Your Honor, essentially what we've seen is someone putting an apologetic note on someone's door, and honking and waving at them when they ran across them in traffic. This is not harassing or intimidating conduct. And as I know Your Honor knows, the statute does not address no contact. It does not say that there cannot be any contact. It says there cannot be any harassing or intimidating contact."

Keenan felt like jumping up and yelling, "Yes! In the face!" like Prince Akeem in the beloved movie *Coming to America*. Finally, someone had made the point that his actions were not harassing or intimidating. But because he was a black man in a Georgia court of law, this very fact would have been debated, cross-examined, and ruled on before it was accepted.

"Should Mr. Green have gone by and left the note? Probably not," his lawyer continued. "There was an agreement in place that said they're not going to contact each other. However, Your Honor, going by and leaving that note there is not something that rises to the level of stalking. It's not harassing. It's not intimidating as you saw—or as you heard when Ms. Rubio testified—that the note said, 'I'm sorry. You saved my life. Thank you.' He got in his car and left after leaving it on the door. This testimony does not show reasonable fear. No reasonable fear is taking place."

Keenan never took the stand that August day, which baffled the judge. And the lawyer he had hired, though he was trying, just didn't have the same commanding aura as the legendary Mr. Smith, the lawyer who helped him get Veronica's first case thrown out. There was a different energy to everything, because he wasn't exactly sure that this lawyer was working for him. He was working; it just didn't seem to be enough for Keenan.

But then, he himself had been too demoralized to even take the stand. He felt like an overmatched prizefighter in the fifteenth round. He just wanted it to be over so he could slink away and nurse his wounds.

With Ms. Kennedy's help, Veronica successfully presented him as a monster when all he did was apologize and go on about his life. He had sat for hours in the courtroom listening to his name get tossed around as a danger to society. As he listened, he realized that of all the lost opportunities to leave, the one that pained him the most for missing was the moment at the zoo when, even at that late moment in the relationship, he had a whole drama-free life ahead of him. He should have apologized for any part he played in her angst and then escaped to his car so he could ride off into the sunset.

This addiction to women, or certain types of women, was pulling him forward by his throat. He was like a horse with a bridle that couldn't help but to get dragged into the next level of doom and disaster.

Veronica's restraining order was granted that day in August. This time, there would be no celebratory lunch. Instead, he shook hands with his lawyer and drove home alone.

Even his work with a telecom company, usually a great distraction, was of less comfort to him because it reminded him of the breach of contract with Faith. The deadline for completing these apps was looming, and he was already working on them on his own, just in case.

At his home office a couple of weeks after the court date, he called Faith to try one more time to nail down a deadline. Of course, she didn't pick up. He paused for a moment, then called her roommate Kahdijah.

"Hey, it's Keenan," he said. "I don't want to get you into this, but I've got a serious deadline with work and I need to know if Faith is going to do this work. She's not picking up my calls."

Kahdijah laughed. "As far as I know, she's not working on anything of yours right now," she said. "But she sure did cash your check. You helped pay for her trip to Thailand, I think. Anyway, you're not going to hear from her while Oliver's around."

"Oh, Oliver's there," Keenan said, feeling the muscles in his jaw get tight.

"Yeah, he's staying at the house."

Keenan hung up with Kahdijah and felt a quiet rage burn in his belly. Before he could stop himself, he typed out a heated email to Faith. In it, he demanded that she repay the $600 and threatened to tell NBS about her lifting laptops and selling them to people outside the company. He had already given the laptop back to her sister by then, but he still voiced the threat. He was so pissed at her for reneging on her end of the bargain for the mobile app, her lifting of $600, all of the time wasted, and the budding relationships she shipwrecked in an effort to protect her fragile ego.

Faith's TPO Attempt

Faith didn't appreciate being threatened or exposed, but she did appreciate knowing every detail of his previous cases with Veronica. Within days of his September email, she reached out to his nemesis: attorney Karen Kennedy.

"Hi, is this Karen Kennedy?" It was Faith's voice on the line. "I have some questions for you about pursuing a TPO case against Keenan Green. You, um, recently were able to secure a TPO against him for Veronica Rubio?"

"Hi," Karen the snake said. "Yes, I was able to successfully secure a TPO against Mr. Green after about a year of his antics. Are you interested in pursuing a case?"

"I am," Faith said. "I was just wondering, would it be possible for you to put me in touch with Veronica Rubio?"

"I'll be happy to send her an email with your phone number," the lawyer replied.

"Great," Faith said. The wheels were turning. "And what is your fee?"

"It's $7,500."

"Let me get back to you," Faith said, and hung up.

Ha. Faith would never pay $7,500 for some hotshot lawyer. She went ahead and filed for free a few days later. Whether she ever spoke with Veronica, Keenan never knew.

A few days later, there was a now-familiar "cop knock" at the door. This time, Keenan ignored the knocking, which was to serve him with papers for yet another TPO. From Faith.

Beyond the stress of these court cases, Keenan's entire dating life seemed to halt and stutter. His career, nor did his family take a beating, but his love life was bound by these cases and what it said about him as a person. There were women he met during this period who were very successful that would immediately shy away when he told them about the impending cases. Keenan was not one to hide information when someone has a right to know. He figured that the one who was supposed to be with him on a long-term basis would see him for who he was and stay by his side through this madness.

To temper the storm he was weathering, he reached out to his good friend Stacy, who had relocated to St. Croix with her newborn. He was all too eager to get away from the negativity and the events surrounding his last twelve to fourteen months of dating. Stacy was more than welcoming, and within a couple of weeks, he was on his way to the Virgin Islands.

His bags were packed and he was early to the airport, so he made a sudden decision to stop and get a haircut on the way. As he drove to the barbershop, he chatted with his friend Gary on the phone.

"So, what's your plans for St. Croix?" Gary asked. "Party at the resorts?"

"Nah, I'm just going to enjoy nature while I'm down there," Keenan said. "I need a mental break." He glanced in the rearview mirror. "Oh, shit," he said.

"What?" Gary asked over the speakers.

"It's fucking Tanya. She's directly behind me. I can see her in my rearview mirror."

"That's a sign," Gary said. "Keep it moving. Keep her in the rearview mirror."

"You think so?"

"Oh, yeah," Gary said. "Let the past be the past."

"Huh," said Keenan. He took a few random lefts and rights, but kept his focus on getting to the barbershop, bullshitting with Gary along the way. He was going to Rolfy's, which was in a strip mall off of Buford Highway. He pulled into the strip mall and found a parking space close to the door. Then he turned his head and saw a familiar white European crossover behind him, blocking him in, waiting for the car next to him to move.

"Oh, *shit*," he said again.

"What, Tanya's still following you?" Gary asked. "I thought you lost her."

He heard Gary's words in a daze as what was almost certainly Veronica's car pulled into the spot next to him. He looked to the left and caught a full second of eye contact with her.

"It's Veronica!" he yelled.

"Brother, get the hell up out of there right now," Gary said.

He put the car in reverse, quickly. "What the fuck? What the fuck?" he said. He was forbidden to be within twenty yards of her, and she was about twelve feet away.

"Nothing good is gonna happen if you don't move quickly," Gary said.

"What the fuck?" he said again, backed up, and sped out of the parking lot.

"Guess you're not going to Rolfy's," Gary said, and laughed.

Turning back onto Buford Highway, Keenan laughed, too. "Not going to jail, either," he said.

"What are you gonna do about your haircut?" Gary asked.

"I'll figure it out," he said, feeling his heart rate slow down after that rush of adrenaline. It was still early enough for him to find another barbershop and get to the airport on time.

St. Croix was his favorite island, truly, because it felt the least like a tourist spot. Stacy had family there, so when she introduced him around, he was immediately treated like a local. Everyone's gentle friendliness worked on him like a medicine, along with the turquoise water and beaches of fine, soft sand.

Stacy was working, so he kept to himself mostly, soaking in the beauty of the pink-and-red ocean sunsets with only his own company. He took long swims through the warm, perfect waves and felt the island work its powerful healing on him.

On the flight back, he tried to hold on to the peace he had found on the little island, but his own issues came hurtling back to his mind. He was so sick and tired of people using him and getting played! He was trying to offer his very best, and it was never enough. But he knew he had his own responsibility for the mistakes and pitfalls he had experienced since divorcing his ex-wife.

He came back to the States with the determination to focus on his own personal health and career goals. *Enough was enough,* he thought, and for Keenan, the time had come for him to stop and ask himself if it was the "other person," or if it was him. He knew that it was almost an unavoidable question to ask if you want to be in a relationship or to be tied to a purpose.

These were questions that he sorted through as the airplane returned him to the legal fallout simmering in the Fulton County Courthouse.

Faith's Limbo

ONCE AGAIN KEENAN had been drawn into a vindictive cycle with women who were much better at getting their revenge than he was. Maybe because at the end, his heart was not in it. Hadn't he canceled his civil and criminal case against Veronica when he was urged to by his own lawyer and Faith?

Emotionally exhausted, he decided not to hire a lawyer for Faith's case, and beyond that not even to show up himself. Last time, he had played by the rules and all he'd gotten was a judgment against him and a mountain of attorney's fees.

He asked for a favor from Raj.

"You want me to do what?" Raj asked.

"Go to court and see what happens," Keenan said.

"Because you're not going," Raj said, to confirm the latest madness.

"No, I'm not going! I never want to see the inside of Fulton

County Courthouse again. I'm not spending my hard-earned money on a dipshit lawyer. I'm not putting on a suit and having my character assassinated. I'm not taking time off work."

"But you want me to?" Raj asked.

"You have more flexible hours. I'll, uh, buy you lunch," Keenan said.

"Aw, thanks," Raj said. "What else?"

"Ha, ha," Keenan replied. "Do it," he said. "I'll owe you."

Raj finally agreed. The morning of Faith's court case, Keenan sat at his desk and tried to look busy, but his mind was fully occupied with what was going on at the courthouse. At lunch, he met Raj for tacos at a Mexican restaurant and prepared himself for the news.

"Okay, so the case was delayed another fifteen days," Raj said as he sprinkled hot sauce from a paper cup over his first taco el pastor.

Keenan felt disappointed. Would this ever end? But on to more important questions. "Did she look around for me?" he asked.

"Oh, yeah, she looked around for you. You weren't there."

"Ah," Keenan said. "Did they say anything specific?"

"Just some legal bullshit. At the end, though, the petition was definitely delayed. Your girl was pissed. I watched her walk out of the court. She looked angry from behind," Raj laughed. "I see why you wanted me to go."

When fifteen days passed, he didn't even bother asking anyone to show up for him, so no one from his world was there to witness it when the TPO was denied. Faith sat alone with her mouth half open, tears in her eyes. After the judge banged the gavel, she headed directly to the clerk of the courthouse to file a criminal warrant for his arrest.

Faith's Criminal Warrant Application Hearing

Though no one reported back to him, Keenan had a gut feeling that Faith was probably not done with him and continued to check the court system's online public records to ensure that nothing else had been filed against him. A few days later, he felt a sense of sudden dread as he saw that Faith had indeed filed a criminal-warrant application in court on the same day that the temporary protective order was dismissed by the judge. Faith was bound and determined to mess with his life.

Because Keenan had moved, he was never served with papers. He knew if he was not served, even the criminal warrant might be thrown out due to that technicality. He decided again to keep letting it ride. Raj couldn't be there this time, so he called up his lawyer friend Monica.

"I have a huge favor to ask of you," he said.

Like Raj, Monica watched the criminal court case from the audience then reported back. "They waited and called for you," Monica said on the phone, "then they seemed like they were going to drop it. Then Faith presented them with some paperwork, I think related to Veronica, then there were two lawyers huddled up talking to the judge," she finished. "I don't know exactly what they were up to, but there might be a warrant out for you." She sounded concerned. "You should call them."

Keenan sighed. "I will," he said. "I've got to take care of a few things at work first."

He got back to work, and after ensuring that all of his tasks were completed for the day, he reluctantly shut the door of his office and called the courthouse.

"I need to see if there's a warrant for me," he said quietly, hating to say those words at work.

"I'm sorry, sir, but you need to come down in person for that information."

Okay. He cleared off his desk slowly and headed over to the courthouse. When he parked his car near the courthouse, he left the key to the ignition behind his license plate just in case, then walked into those doors that he had sworn to avoid forever.

The courthouse was empty when he walked in except for him and the court officers. He went to the clerk. "I, uh, had a court case today that I missed," he said.

"Hm, let me check," said the clerk. "Oh. Yes. Court is still in session. You can go right in."

He walked into the courtroom. It was as quiet and empty as a library after finals. He said, "Hi, I'm Keenan Green. I missed my court date today."

The judge looked him up and down. "Oh, yes, the no-show," he said. "We have a warrant for your arrest for stalking and trespassing. Bailiff?"

"You're under arrest," the bailiff said, his words echoing loudly in the hushed and peaceful courthouse.

Keenan's heart fell to his shoes. He honestly figured he would have had a chance to just reschedule the court date. *I should have brought a lawyer*, he thought to himself as the bailiff zip-tied his wrists. "Standard procedure," he said, then led him into a van to take him to the holding cells across town.

He'd never been to jail before in his life. No excessive drinking, or fighting, or gangs, or drugs. And now he was going to have to sit behind bars, if only for a few hours, because of another relationship gone bad. But he was a grown man, and he could handle it. He stared down at his black cap-toe oxfords, so out of place on the grimy van floor. Then he took a deep breath and tried to fight off his claustrophobia.

He remembered how Faith had playfully put him in a headlock for a selfie while they were on a hike in the woods, and how uncomfortable it had made him. The city outside the windows looked strange and different in the waning light of the autumn afternoon. Inaccessible. His body moving mechanically, he allowed the police to lead him through processing, where he was fingerprinted, photographed, led to a crowded cell, and fed a cheese sandwich that tasted like wax.

With no family in town, he wound up calling his ex-wife to bail him out. She did it without an angry word. Thank God for her. Besides the favor of a lifetime, he could look to her easy willingness to have his back as evidence that he wasn't the monster these women were making him out to be.

By evening, he was home with a hearing scheduled for February of the following year. He took an hour-long shower and crashed into his king-sized bed, relishing all the comforts of his home as if it were a palace. As he closed his eyes, he hoped that his imagination would not take up this experience and feed it back to him in even more horrifying ways. He was truly living a nightmare—all the more so because it was the same horrible circumstance that he thought he would never face again.

He had been trying so hard not to have to hire a lawyer, but it seemed unavoidable. He needed help. This time, he tried to choose someone who would be able to manage the long, painful, and expensive process of defending his name. He decided to choose a woman lawyer this time, and found his match in Ms. Patel, a child of South Asian immigrants who specialized in family law.

This time, however, it was all preparation and no case. He spent thousands of dollars to have Ms. Patel periodically inform him that the case was not on the books yet. At the point of a year's passing, the lawyer attempted to earn her keep by advising him to lie low and wait. "Just live your life," Ms. Patel advised him. So he did. And living his life, as he understood it, meant dating and meeting new women, too.

As he drifted in Faith's limbo, Keenan felt that his dating life was as chaotic as the Queens club scene in *Coming to America*.

Back on the dating site, he met Brie for lunch, then dinner. She had skin the color of honey, green eyes, and the athletic build of a track star. He decided he needed to see her naked body between some hotel sheets and planned a weekend away.

"Do you want to go away this weekend?" he asked the next day on their date.

"Sure," she said, but slowly. "I should tell you, though."

"What?"

"I have herpes," she said.

* * *

He met Michelle online because he was looking for a partner to try Chicago step dancing. He found a Chicago step club, but it was all the way in Tucker, Georgia. To his delight, Michelle was game for it, even when the day was just pouring rain.

"You really good to meet tonight?" Keenan asked on the phone.

"Sure," she said.

What a sport, Keenan thought, and the two of them had a blast learning the new dance at this out-of-the-way club, with the rain creating a sexy intimacy between them. After that, even though she was traveling, she called and texted all the time. Keenan didn't mind. When she got back into town, Keenan picked her up at the airport and took her to lunch at a popular seafood restaurant.

"So, tell me more about what you do," Keenan said.

"I told you I work for the court, right?" she said. "I'm the head administrator for the Fulton County Courthouse. I hire and fire everyone, take care of the IT needs, all the judges in Fulton County."

Uh-oh.

"Um," Keenan said, "just wondering. Would it be a conflict of interest if I have an open case in your jurisdiction?"

"Absolutely," she said, holding eye contact. Then she shrugged. "But we can be friends." She told Keenan that in spite of her role, she understood about court trouble--she had a cousin in prison and a brother that got in trouble all the time. They finished lunch and hugged a goodbye.

A few days later, she called him. "I did look your case up. It's definitely in my courthouse."

He didn't hear from her much after that.

* * *

Keenan expanded his online dating search to Raleigh and found Heather, a Spellman graduate. She answered his messages, and when he talked to her, he found she had the cutest little stutter. "There's a medical term for it," she said. "It's a mild disfluency."

Heather was an eye surgeon who made close to a million a year. She owned some property in Atlanta so was there frequently, which was why she was open to dating someone a bit far from home.

They talked all the time, with a lot of that time being Heather's invitations to go visit her in Raleigh. When they finally met up, the sex was explosive. She reminded him of Tanya the way she expertly gave head. It was always the classy ladies who were so decadent in bed—this Roman-orgy style of lovemaking even if it was just the two of them. He was into it.

He bought them concert tickets for Joe, who was performing in Charlotte. Hearing Joe croon about his desire to leave his player days behind for the perfect lady made Keenan look at Heather in a new way. He took her back to their hotel room in Charlotte and he gave her his best shot.

They luxuriated in a long, slow sixty-nine for what seemed like hours, until Keenan finally turned her over and skillfully finger-fucked her until she squirted. Then she wrapped her legs around him and he stretched out her delicious pussy with his rock-hard dick.

They weren't in love, but they were loving it.

Keenan was planning to go to California for the holidays that year, and was telling her about his plans in early December.

"I'm getting my plane tickets this week," he said while visiting her in Raleigh.

"Why don't you get them now to get the rewards?" she asked.

"I don't have an airline card," he said.

"Just use mine then, and pay me back," she said, so he did.

The next day, Keenan called to let her know the date he would pay her back, and Heather suddenly seemed confused. "Wait, you don't have any credit cards at all?"

"No," he said.

"Why don't you have a credit card?" she asked.

"I don't know," he said. "I just use cash all the time."

"Hm," she said disapprovingly. "I can't believe you're in your forties and you don't have good credit."

"Yeah, well," he said, making a bad situation worse, "I'm actually getting rid of my house, also. I'm underwater, and if they don't reduce my principal, I'm just going to walk away from my house and rent for a while."

"What do you mean?" she asked. "I've never heard of that. Who doesn't pay their mortgage?"

Then she hung up the phone.

Shocked, he called her back. "Why would you hang up the phone on me?" he said.

"I don't know," she said in a voice that sounded stunned. "I was raised to have good credit. I need to evaluate this relationship."

Keenan paid her back, and they never spoke again.

* * *

One day in a coffee shop while working on his laptop, Keenan saw a woman with perfect eyebrows over intoxicating brown eyes and got her number. The next two days they chatted on and off, and he invited her over to watch a movie. When she got to the house, she slipped on the floor.

What the fuck?

And she was a chiropractor.

Did this motherfucker just slip and fall in my house trying to set me up? Keenan thought. *What the hell? I need to get her out of here.*

But all he said was, "Are you okay?"

She popped right back up and they watched a movie like they planned. She even put her hand in his lap. But he sent her on her way, holding her elbow firmly as she walked through the foyer.

* * *

He had been seeing this woman, Candy, for a few dates at that point. She was an RN with an easy smile, short hair, and big, soft-brown eyes. She came over one evening before their planned dinner date.

"Would you like a drink?" he asked.

"Sure," she said, all smiles. So, he poured her a glass of wine.

She drank it while he continued to get ready. When he emerged from the bedroom fastening his watch, she was seated on the couch, frowning. Her half-empty glass was on the side table.

"I'm feeling really tipsy," she said. "Did you put something in my fucking drink?"

"No!" Keenan said, shocked.

"Well, I feel fucked up," she said.

He called her a rideshare service, all apologies, and she stumbled out the door and into the car with his help. When he came back inside, he looked at the wine glass on the side table, went straight to the kitchen, and started opening drawers. He took the wine glass into the kitchen with some barbecue tongs, and carefully placed a freezer bag over it. Then he put it in the back of the refrigerator.

Evidence.

It stayed there for about a month before he relaxed.

* * *

He was spending a lot of time with Ruby. She had long, dark, wavy hair, really sensitive nipples, and the sexiest pout. He loved kissing her and the sex was fun, but Ruby was struggling with what she wanted to do with her life and career. She was unstable financially, and it bugged him a little bit. It wasn't something that he wanted to be involved in long-term. Besides, she had a whiny, baby voice that could get on his last nerve.

* * *

When he met Serena, she was just one of the many women he was dating. Like Veronica, Serena was a medical doctor, only she worked in the emergency room, while Veronica was a pediatrician. Also, like Veronica, she had a bit of a wild side. They did have an intense bonding experience on their first date. The plan had started out ordinarily enough.

"Do you like the roof at Ponce City Market?" he asked her.

"Love it," she responded.

So they met at Ponce City Market to eat gelato and take in the view. As they were gazing out over the Atlanta skyline, Serena's phone buzzed. She saw that it was family and excused herself to pick it up. Then her face suddenly turned very serious.

"Okay," she said quietly. "I'll be there right away." She slipped the phone back in her pocket as if she were stunned.

"What's wrong?" Keenan asked.

"I have to go," she said. "My sister just had a seizure and they're taking her to Grady Hospital."

"Oh, my God, I'm so sorry," Keenan said.

"I hate to ask, but do you think we could do this another time?"

"Of course," Keenan said.

As they drove back to her house, Serena shared a few more details with Keenan. Her sister was autistic, and this was not her first seizure. Her mother and father were divorced, but still friendly. Her mother was currently riding with the ambulance and her father was on his way.

"Look," Keenan said, "I don't want to drop you off at your house. Let me just take you to Grady Hospital."

"You don't mind?" Serena asked.

"Not at all."

And so, hours after meeting Serena, Keenan found himself in a hospital room being introduced to her mother and father. Her sister had experienced a severe seizure and was on a ventilator. She was not quite in a coma, but it was clear her condition was life-threatening. Serena's mother hugged him, and her father shook Keenan's hand and thanked him for bringing his daughter to them as soon as possible.

He got out of their way and scrolled through his phone in the waiting room until Serena was ready to go. At her house, she wrapped her arms around him at the door and whispered, "Thank you," in his ear. It was heady stuff.

Only a few days later, they had their makeup date at Ponce City Market. Her sister was improving, she told him, and the good news seemed to have cheered her up immensely. He found that she was really easy to talk to. She wasn't his usual type—a little shorter, with slender arms and a thick, round booty. She was dark-skinned and had a wide forehead and a sweet face, especially when she smiled.

They had the same taste in TV shows, so when she would invite him to come over and watch TV, he was always glad to go hang out. Only a week or two after their first date, they were at her house watching a comedy TV show, laughing together at a skit in which Peele strapped several babies to his body.

"Would you let me borrow your baby to get out of a fight?" Keenan asked her.

"You'd have to wait a while," she said. "I'm going to have a baby someday, though. I had my eggs frozen."

He was next to her on the couch at her house with his hand on her bare thigh. He slid his hand in underneath her tight shorts and started playing with her pussy. All thoughts of frozen eggs flew out of his mind as he stroked her hot, swollen clit and kissed the side of her neck. She smelled so good.

She started making these little squeaky noises, like a rabbit. He didn't mind. He eased her shorts down her round thighs and plunged his face into her hot mound, licking and sucking as she arched her back. His jaw ached by the time she came, but it was worth it to feel her thighs thrash about as he hung on for dear life, with two fingers as deep into her as he could get them.

She took him upstairs to her bedroom and she sucked his cock, but he could tell that she wasn't really into it, so he flipped her over and fucked her hard from behind. That's what started the squeaking again.

Serena

KEENAN STARTED SPENDING more and more time at Serena's house, since she never wanted to go over to his place. He wasn't sure why, but one possible reason could have been that she had certain habits she couldn't indulge in at his place.

One morning, when he woke up in her bed, she was already awake and outside. As he came down the stairs, she was coming inside via the sliding glass door. To his surprise, Keenan saw that she was smoking a blunt.

"Do you want some?" she asked.

"No," he said, barely even awake. "You smoke?"

"Yeah. Does it bother you?"

"No," Keenan replied quickly, but it did, a little. She was an ER doctor, after all.

"Do you want an omelet?" she said as she put out the blunt in a little ashtray Keenan had never noticed.

"Sure," he said. "You cook?"

"Some things," she said.

Keenan forgot all about the blunt. It was nice to be hanging out with someone who knew how to cook. Veronica had cooked sometimes, but Faith absolutely hated it. Serena cooked him an omelet with a delicious spicy flavor and then gave him a thick, green beverage.

"What's this?" he said.

"It's good for you. It's a superfood smoothie."

He wasn't sure about it, but when he drank it, he could feel his body absorb the nutrients. *For a pothead, this girl was healthy.*

He quickly found out that she liked to smoke and then have sex, and she definitely seemed like she was getting a lot out of it. After a few more passionate nights of squeaking followed by a healthy breakfast at her kitchen table, he found himself deeply into Serena. Of course, they weren't exclusive; that wasn't his goal after all the trouble he'd had, and it didn't seem like she wanted anything serious, either.

They were lounging in bed together one weekend when an idle thought drifted through Keenan's brain. "Have you ever been in a threesome?" he asked, stroking the skin along her shoulder blades.

"No," she said. "Have you?"

"No. Nothing too crazy. Never anything gay. I was married a long time."

"I had a lesbian experience once," Serena said.

"Really?" Keenan said, shifting his position slightly.

"Yeah. I went to a hotel to sit at the bar—"

"Which one?" Keenan asked.

"Midtown. Anyway, I was sitting at the bar, and this woman was sitting next to me. She wanted to buy me a drink, but I already had one. So she invited me up to her room to smoke. Then after we smoked, she went down on me."

"Were you into it?" Keenan asked.

"It was okay," she said. "But it's not something I would chase after. I'm strictly dickly," she said, and slid her hand down so that she could grab Keenan's erection.

"Show me," he murmured, and she spent the afternoon demonstrating her preference for dick.

He'd booked a vacation to Jamaica with Ruby of the sexy pout, but by the time they went, he was only thinking of Serena. Jamaica was hot and crowded, much more of a party scene than serene St. Croix. They had booked an all-inclusive at Montego Bay, and even though Ruby looked sexy as hell in her short little skirt when he met her at the airport, he wasn't feeling it.

On their first night, they wandered up and down the hip strip and ate at a world-known restaurant with Jamaican vibes. She was picky about the meal, and it annoyed the shit out of him.

"Why would you come to Jamaica if you don't like jerk chicken?" he said. It took the fun out of the night, and when they went back to their hotel room, he went to bed and turned off his light while she was still in the shower.

Ruby slipped into bed, then touched his shoulder. "Baby?"

He kept his breathing deep and even, and eventually, she sighed and turned off her own light. He drifted off, but something woke him up in the middle of the night. He grabbed his phone off of the nightstand. There was a text from Serena.

"How is Jamaica?"

"It's okay," he texted back. "This girl doesn't even like the food here."

"How can you not like Jamaican food?" Serena texted back.

"I know!"

Ruby snored slightly beside him while he texted back and forth with Serena for an hour. Eventually, he went back to sleep, and when he finally woke up, Ruby had already made her way to the beach. He took his sweet time getting ready, then joined her on a strip of soft sand. They didn't talk much.

"I think I'm going shopping," she said as the afternoon wore on. "Do you want to go?"

"Sure," he said.

They browsed the touristy shops on Gloucester, then, while Ruby was dragging him to yet another store of silly souvenirs, he begged off.

"I'm going back to the hotel," he said, but he actually went back to the beach. It was near sunset, and the western edge of the horizon was streaked with red and pink, in sharp contrast to the deep blue of the sky overhead and the ocean stretched out before him. He sat on a little cot swing and called Serena.

"What did you do today?" she asked.

"Some shopping. Do you want me to bring anything back for you?"

"A grinder!" she said, and had to explain to Keenan that a weed grinder was a device to break up the cannabis buds into crumbs that could be smoked.

"Okay, sure," he said, and laughed.

The final day they were in Jamaica, he and Ruby didn't even pretend to hang out. He went downtown by himself. At a place called Mez, he found more weed paraphernalia than he knew existed. He bought two grinders, since he wasn't sure which one she would like better, and a silly pot-leaf bandanna for himself, just to get into the mood. After shopping, he wandered around with no real goal other than to relax and enjoy the scene. He followed the sound of live music and wound up on the edges of a reggae festival.

Jamaica is a place to party, he thought, and wished again he was there with Serena instead of Ruby. *Oh, well.* He took a funny selfie of himself with the bandanna and sent it to her. She would think it was fun. Serena was all about fun.

When he came back, they started seeing more and more of each other, going out and having a blast together. He took her and her family to see New Edition at Chastain Park Amphitheatre, along with many other concerts that summer.

"Let's go on a trip together," he said sometime in June as they were cuddled up on the couch watching a Caribbean TV show.

"Where? Jamaica?" she asked.

"Nah," he said. Jamaica was fun, but he wanted to go somewhere different with Serena. "How about the Dominican Republic?"

"Sure," she responded, her eyes lighting up. For a week or so, planning the trip became one of their favorite things to do together. At work a few days later, she texted him a link with the message, "Let's stay here."

He clicked on the link. The Perfection Punta Cana, he noted, had twenty-three pools and a staff that was well known for their hospitality. The sprawling resort was made up of several different buildings to house the luxury suites, including the massive three-story main building where Serena wanted a suite. He imagined fucking her from behind while looking out over palm trees and the ocean.

He was in. He couldn't wait for September.

In the meantime, the romance and fun continued, but it seemed like her energy was changing. He noticed it first when they went out salsa dancing, which was quite often. Serena took dancing a lot more seriously than he did. She had been at it a long time, had regular partners, and was part of the salsa-dancing community. She explained a lot of the culture to Keenan and knew the nights when the really good people would show up to dance. To be honest, it took a little of the fun out of it for Keenan. Going salsa dancing with her was not really a date.

One night, she introduced a random man to Keenan as her salsa-dancing partner and whirled away on the dance floor to the familiar sound of Hector Lavoe, leaving him at the bar. He got so bored and irritated that he left. She didn't see him go.

The next day she called him. "Hey, where were you? What happened? Why'd you leave?"

"Because you were busy dancing with everyone else."

She laughed. "Everyone dances with everyone," she said. "You should have just found another partner."

He understood her attitude toward salsa dancing, but it seemed like she was starting to have the same attitude toward everything they did together. While they never argued, he would try to talk about a relationship and she would say it was too soon.

At a month, she said, "I've just known you for a month."

At two months, she said, "I've just known you for two months."

Keenan knew deep down that once a woman uses the phrase "I've just known you," she can use any time period she wants—a month, a year, ten years—and never be ready for a relationship.

Also, he admitted to himself, he was not super comfortable about how much cannabis she smoked. One weekend, when he was staying over, he came downstairs and saw a strange mess that looked out of place on her elegant glass-top coffee table. In addition to a very normal pile of several issues of *Money* magazine, a laptop, car keys, and a water bottle, there was also a blunt wrap and a scattering of prescription bottles with her sister's name on them. While the label said they were filled with capsules, they were actually filled with plastic-wrapped buds. To his shame, he also saw one of the weed grinders he had bought her in Jamaica. *Man, this is weird*, he thought. He snapped a photo and sent it to his friend. "Check out this ER doctor with her drugs," he texted.

He was still seeing Ruby and casually dating other women, but for the most part, he was focused on Serena. He had clothes there and a massage table that they would use for long, slow, sensual massages with so much touching that it was hard to tell when the massage ended and the sex began. She also loved to bring him into her shower, where he would bend her over in the hot spray and take her hard. She loved it. She had no stomach at all, just thick thighs and a little booty. The fact that she was so fit and healthy made her irresistible to him, even though she treated him like a side piece more and more.

By the time of the trip, they were on the rocks, and Keenan admitted to himself that he wanted more than she was willing to give. He could not help himself but ask her sometimes, "What are we doing? If this isn't a relationship, do we need to stop talking?"

Sometimes, he got fed up enough to go and get all of his stuff, but there was never any yelling or fighting, and they always drifted back into seeing each other.

She smoked her stinky blunts around him all the time. He had become used to it, in spite of himself. Maybe this trip to the Dominican Republic would bring them closer, he thought, or maybe it was just one last fling.

It was not a good sign, then, that even at the airport she spent more time chatting with a random coworker from the hospital who happened to be there than with him. Keenan sat patiently, half listening to their work gossip, and hoped for the best. He reminded himself that they were staying at the Perfection Punta Cana, with a staff that treated everyone like they had just won an Oscar.

It worked. As they neared the resort, all thoughts of Serena's airport friend vanished and they checked in on a cloud.

Keenan took a shower first, enjoying the marble walls and soft lights of the bathroom, and lounged in his terrycloth robe on the plush, king-sized bed while Serena took her turn. When she emerged, she sat down on his side of the bed and pulled at the belt he had loosely tied, opening his robe. She wrapped her hand around his dick, which was already hard the minute he'd seen her step out of the shower. He pulled her down onto the bed and started kissing her hard, grinding his hard dick on her soft, round thighs. She opened her legs and was already wet enough for him to push into her easily, holding both of her wrists in one hand. They didn't often fuck in the missionary position, since she liked it so much from behind, but Keenan was feeling it. He came fast, but he was pretty sure she didn't.

"Did you come?" he asked her as they cuddled on the bed, drowsy.

"Yeah, baby," she said. He wasn't convinced, but let it go. Before he was done holding her, she got up again to take another quick rinse.

"Are we in a relationship?" he blurted out before he could stop himself.

Serena sighed, and stood there naked in front of him without saying a word. Finally, she said, "Why are you trying to ruin this trip?"

She went into the bathroom and closed the door. He heard the water running. When she came out, all she said was, "I'm headed to the jacuzzi."

After she left, he laid there and guilt-tripped himself for saying anything to ruin the vacation. He gave himself a pep talk, looked out the windows at the beautiful world that was waiting for him to indulge, and decided to join her at the jacuzzi.

She was right where she'd said she would be, deep in conversation with another man. When he got in to join her, she left to swim some laps. *Damn.*

But when they went salsa dancing that night, they seemed to find their rhythm both on and off the dance floor. She was wearing a short red dress that made her ass look amazing. He loved dancing with her since she was so skillful. It made him look like a better dancer than he was. She spoiled him with that; she'd ruined him for dancing with other women.

"Do you want to try something new tomorrow?" he asked her as they sipped cocktails at a tiny table by the dancefloor.

"Sure. What?"

"Horseback riding," he said.

"Really? Okay," she said, not terribly enthusiastic. He'd signed them up for it on a whim and already kind of regretted it. But it was a new experience for both of them, so they decided to go for it.

The next day, he quickly discovered that Serena hated horseback riding. "This is uncomfortable," she said. She barely managed a smile when their host took a picture of them on the horses, which were standing close together for the shot. "Hold hands in this one," the photographer said, and they complied. Keenan glanced down at the back of her hand. It was covered in tiny bumps.

"Are you okay?" he asked.

"I'm breaking out," she said grimly. "I think there's fleas out here. Something's biting the shit out of me."

"Smile!" the photographer said.

When they finally dropped the horses off, they were presented with a bottle of wine that had a picture of them holding hands on the horses for the label.

"This is an aphrodisiac," their host told them. "It's a wine blended with herbs and honey to make your bed hot!"

"I hope it pairs well with Benadryl," Serena said dryly as they took an off-road four-by-four back to the resort.

"Do you have any?" Keenan asked.

"No. Will you get me some?"

Keenan wandered through the hotel lobby toward the gift shop while Serena showered. The two gift-shop attendants looked about twenty-one and had the same impeccable resort manners that everyone did here. In a flash, he found himself joking and laughing with them, relaxing in a way he wasn't really able to with Serena. Impulsively, he took a selfie with both of them and sent it to his brother.

"I've got your Benadryl," he said when he walked back into their hotel room.

"Why are you sending me pictures of yourself with the girls from the gift shop?" she demanded.

Oops.

"I meant to send it to my brother," he said. Not much of an explanation, he knew.

All she said in response was, "Huh."

She slept that night covered in lotion and Keenan left her alone. He read the ingredients on the back of the wine bottle as she slept. *Con hierbas y miel.* He liked the label. It was a nice picture of them, if you didn't know too much of the backstory.

The next day Serena was much improved, and seemed to have forgiven him for his flirtation with the gift-shop girls. Or forgotten. They decided to make it a spa day, since the horseback riding had been rough on their bodies. Besides the beach, this was really the main attraction of the resort, and they made the most of it.

The moment he stepped through the doors of the resort spa, his stress about Serena melted away. There was something about this place and the setting that made him feel like he was an emperor. He could hear the continual muted splash of the cascades and the jets of the pools, jacuzzis, and aqua-treatment stations that filled the space. He let go of his concerns and allowed himself to enjoy the physical sensations of the steam room, the ice pool, and a sensation shower that jetted water from every possible direction.

After taking the waters in every way possible, they both stretched out on deeply padded massage tables and let the masseuse expertly knead out every lingering muscle memory of the previous day's ride.

When they returned to their room, it was more than natural to just keep the physical sensations going. Serena rode him hard while wrapping her hands around his throat. That time, he was sure she came. He turned her over and returned the favor, sliding his thumb into her thick ass while he drilled her. She squeaked even more when he was rough.

On their final day at the resort, they took a catamaran out to one of the barrier islands for a beach day. Separated from civilization, the barrier island beach had a wild and natural energy that was contagious. Drinks only amped up the playful and relaxed vibe. Keenan watched the snorkelers out in the shallows for a while as he and Serena lounged in the resort beach chairs, then he got into a pickup football game with some other guests. The day was brilliantly blue, from the ocean to the sky, and as he ran in the sand, he felt a brief moment of the elusive vacation bliss that had been hard to catch on this trip. It felt damn great to toss the football around on a picture-postcard beach with his pretty lady watching from the side.

Only she wasn't watching. She was talking to another dude.

Just like that, the vacation popped out of bliss mode and returned to its regular semi-stressful program. He didn't stop playing, but tried to stay close enough to at least catch a bit of their conversation. This man was clearly using the time to get to know her and ask her little personal, flirty questions.

Then he heard her say, "We're not together. We're just friends."

Oh, okay, Keenan thought. So, she didn't claim him to anybody. In fact, she made it a point not to claim him.

He caught a pass and ran toward the opposite end of the beach like he didn't care. The physical act of running helped to flush out the bad feeling of defeat and embarrassment, and the hard blow to his self-esteem.

All he had wanted to do was be with a woman who wanted to be with him. One of the things he really liked about Serena is that he knew she wasn't with him just for the sake of being able to enjoy some great experience, like going to a concert or going on vacation. They had split the bill for this trip—she bought the plane tickets and he paid for the excursions and resort. She did things with him for the sake of being with him and enjoying his company, or so he had thought. Now that he had witnessed her behavior over the course of the weekend, he realized he'd been wrong, and it hurt.

To rub just a little salt in his wounds, when they returned, they ran into the same guy at the airport from the beach, and the two of them exchanged numbers in front of Keenan.

I'm probably not going to talk to her anymore, Keenan thought to himself.

But she still wasn't quite done with him. A couple of weeks later, she called him out of the blue.

"Guess what I just bought," she said.

A six-foot bong, he thought, but just said, "What?"

"A new European convertible!" she squealed. "Want to see it?"

"Sure," he said. *Why not?* He guessed he was still someone to show off to, if nothing else.

"Come outside, then," she said. "I'm right around the corner."

Keenan walked outside, and Cameron followed him, curious. A moment later, the long hood of her brand-new mineral-white sports nosed around the corner. She had the hardtop up, for some reason. She drove slowly up the street to Keenan's house, then pulled over and rolled down the window.

"What do you think?" she said from the driver's seat. Keenan and his son Cameron stood on the lawn. She put the top down so they could see the pristine interior with leather seats of natural brown.

"Nice car," Keenan said neutrally.

His son Cameron's admiration was a little less reserved. "Can I have a ride?" Cameron asked.

Serena smiled widely. "Sure," she said, so super generous with her new status symbol.

Keenan watched from the lawn as the two of them rode down the block together with the top down, then went back into the house. When they circled back, he was surprised to see she came in with his son.

"Do you want to watch a movie or something?" he said, since it seemed that she had invited herself over.

They holed up in his bedroom, but he didn't even put something on before she was taking off his shirt. This woman had moods, and today's mood was horny. Of course, he loved to fuck her, even when it was pretty clear he was being used for dick. He put his hand over her mouth to keep her squeaking down, since his son was home. It was easier when he flipped her over so she could bury her loud head in a pillow while he thumbed her ass and slammed the shit out of her pussy until he unloaded in her with his own stifled groan. She was so good.

Soon after, they got together for a barbecue at House in the Park with both his friends and hers. It was a sociable, easy day spent eating plate after plate of grilled meats and vegetables, surrounded by their nearest and dearest. At sunset, they packed up together.

"Do you want to stay over?" she asked.

"Sure," he said.

When he came in, he noticed the bottle of wine from their trip was missing. He had offered her the bottle of wine with the romantic picture of them on the label when they returned from the Dominican Republic. She seemed happy to have it at the time and placed it prominently in her living room on the mantel.

"Where's the wine bottle?" he asked. "Did you drink it?"

"No," she said, extra casual. "I put it in my bedroom." She wasn't lying; he saw it in her room on a dresser. The label with their photo was facing the wall. That ruined the mood for Keenan, and in the morning, he double-checked that none of his clothes were still in her closet. *Was this the last time?*

A few days later, she called. "I miss you," she said.

"I miss you, too."

"Come over."

"Okay, but I have to leave early and go to the courthouse."

His two-year time limit with Faith's warrant was drawing to a close, and he was finally going to get this heavy load off of his mind. He took a shower in the morning at Serena's, anxious to go to the courthouse. When he came out of the shower, he saw her squatting down in the doorway of her bedroom, petting her cat.

"Why don't you pet me that way anymore?" he said, half joking.

She just looked at him. He continued to get dressed, and then on his way out the door, she said, "I don't think we should see each other anymore."

So, he thought. *Finally.*

"If that's how you feel, okay," he said.

He gave her a hug and left, going directly to the courthouse to confirm with the district attorney that the charges Faith created two years prior were dropped. He had to go to the solicitor's office and file some paperwork, and then received the official dismissal that day. It seemed his time in legal limbo had finally come to an end.

Little did he know that he would have to deal with yet one more legal battle to defend his reputation.

* * *

The next few days were a blur of getting his stuff back, a few mean texts back and forth, and a drunk salsa night to blow off steam. It was better, he thought, to be done with Serena. The fact that she smoked weed and was an ER emergency physician was never something he had been particularly comfortable with.

He tried to put her out of his mind and focus on the event he would be attending with Monica, a lawyer friend he knew in the city. Monica's cousin was a doctor and chief administrator at the same hospital Serena worked at, and had invited her to a fundraising gala. Monica knew how nice Keenan looked in a suit and asked him to be her date. They stood there chatting with Monica's cousin after the silent auction.

"So, how was your trip to the Dominican Republic?" Monica asked.

"It was okay," Keenan said cautiously, "but I don't think I'll be going on any more trips with Serena."

"It didn't work out?" Monica asked.

"Nah. She smokes a lot of weed," he added, comfortable enough in Monica's presence that he spoke as if they were having a private conversation. Her cousin's eyebrows shot up to her forehead, and Keenan quickly changed the subject.

"Keenan," Monica whispered when her cousin joined other guests, "you know Serena is a subcontracted doctor at my cousin's hospital."

Keenan felt a moment of *uh-oh*, then shrugged it off. It was none of his business if she got caught. Maybe it was even better.

In fact, over the next few days, he continued to think about how she was an ER physician and smoked weed every day. She was truly putting people in danger. Maybe the right thing to do was to report her, regardless of his feelings. If she was a banker or even a lawyer, he wouldn't think twice about it; it's people's choice what they do. But doctors are supposed to be saving lives.

He still had the card from when he had last contacted the medical board. In spite of a nagging feeling that he was being drawn into a vicious cycle and that his motivations were too cloudy, he could not stop himself from calling Agent Smith's number. She advised him to contact Risk Management at Serena's hospital.

So, he did. It was a very brief conversation, and he was relieved to have it done. Now, he thought, maybe he could just stop thinking about it and forget that he ever knew her.

A week or two later, on an unseasonably warm November day, Keenan went to pick his son up from school. He dropped him off at a coffee shop to hang out with his friends and decided to take advantage of the mild weather by going on one last jog along the Beltline for the season. The trees along the meandering pedestrian path were red and yellow, still concealing back porches and windows. He knew that soon the trees would be bare with the exception of some stubborn holdouts, the leaves long lost of any vibrant color but still hanging on.

People along here must miss their privacy in winter, he thought, *or maybe they appreciate the view.*

After the run, he picked up his son Cameron and they went to the health food market. Since there was a car wash on the same block, Keenan made a spontaneous decision to drop off his car, which was dirty from the previous day's brief rain shower. He then walked back across the street to the health food market where his son was waiting for him. There at the buffet was Serena.

"Isn't that Serena?" Cameron asked as she walked past.

So, Keenan tapped her on the shoulder and said, "Hello, Serena. Nice to see you."

She stopped and said, "Is it really?" Then paused and added, "Hello," to Cameron. She seemed really cold, but Keenan didn't know why. They left and went to stand in line. There were multiple lines open, and most had three or four people waiting. He and Cameron got in what looked to be the shortest one. Serena was nowhere in sight.

Suddenly, she reappeared next to them. "I read your book, you fucking stalker," she said.

When they first started dating, Keenan had given her a first draft of a story he'd written about the troubles he'd gone through with Veronica and Faith. She never read it, he realized, until they stopped seeing each other.

"Stay away from me," she added, although she had come up to him and his son in line. "I know you reported me."

People from the other lines began to glance over. She *was* quite loud. But from the words she was saying, it seemed like he was the aggressor, even standing in line with his son minding his own business. Some of the women in other lines looked at him with suspicion. He could see the people in the store taking a side mentally.

"What?" Keenan said.

"Yeah," she said. "I had to go take a drug test."

"I don't know what you're fucking talking about," Keenan replied, "but you shouldn't smoke weed and then go to work as an ER doctor. Getting high before trying to save someone's life."

"What are you talking about? I know you called the hospital on me for some bullshit," she said accusingly.

He pulled out his phone and found pictures of the grinder. "What is this?" he asked.

She knocked his phone out of his hand and it smacked the floor hard, cracking the screen.

"What the fuck!" he said, moving toward his phone. He picked it up quickly without seeing the crack. A large man at the front glass doors wearing a security shirt began to walk toward them.

"I'll wait outside," he told Cameron. He stood outside the glass doors, then pulled out his phone, saw the screen, and felt a wave of fury. He walked back in to tell security, "She cracked my screen."

"Stay away from me!" Serena screamed over and over again. He realized the best thing they could do was leave.

Sure enough, a few weeks later, he was hit with another order of protection. He decided not to go with Ms. Patel this time; she had been expensive and not worth it. Driving in the city the next day, he saw a sign that said "Goodman Law" and decided to call. He was calling other lawyers, too, but Goodman called him back.

On a Saturday. That was cool.

They met at a coffee shop near Keenan's house. Goodman seemed like a younger version of Mr. Smith, his powerhouse lawyer from the first case. He had the same commanding aura, and he listened carefully to Keenan's tale of woe and of the three women who had filed four TPOs against him.

"Can I get a copy of your book?" he asked.

"Sure," Keenan said. "I'll send you everything." He sent every bit of information he had from the cases with Faith and Veronica.

A few days later, Mr. Goodman called him back. "There's no grounds for a TPO," he said with a confidence and certainty that Keenan very much liked to hear. "And have you reported her pot-smoking to the medical board as well as the hospital?"

"Yes," Keenan said, grateful that this lawyer was not only supporting his case, he was supporting his decision to report her.

"Come to my office next week," Mr. Goodman said, "and we'll start preparing your case."

Another Day in Court: This Time with Serena

KEENAN ARRIVED WITH Cameron for his court date dressed in what he had come to think of as his "court suit." He'd spent a long time selecting a tie that morning, and finally decided on a muted gray-blue. It was calming. "Just wait out here," he told Cameron, who looked a little nervous. Cameron would not be allowed into the courtroom as a witness until it was time for him to testify. Keenan hadn't necessarily been excited about bringing his fourteen-year-old son into this mess, but Cameron had insisted on being a witness. Mr. Goodman arrived early—a good sign.

"Now, the first part of this is going to be rough," his lawyer told him as they settled in. "Just be patient and wait for me to get started."

This wasn't the first time a lawyer he hired had said these exact same words. Keenan was prepared, or at least he thought he was. He put on his blandest expression and allowed himself to be put through the wringer again. Even in his stressed-out state, he couldn't help but notice that Serena's lawyer, Ms. Seaman, was a bit of a battle axe compared to Veronica's lawyer Ms. Kennedy, who had looked like a straight A popular blonde girl turned lawyer. He put his old nemesis out of his mind and tried to focus on what Broom Hilda was saying.

" . . . Because she's the third person in the last three years to file a stalking and/or protective order against Mr. Green. Very similar conduct, very similar behavior, and it placed her in extreme—"

Keenan's lawyer Mr. Goodman stood up. "I would object to the nature of her comments regarding similar behavior without— I mean we're getting into relevance and hearsay and multiple issues pertaining to that particular matter."

The judge allowed it, but Keenan was relieved to see his lawyer jump up and fight back within the first five minutes of the trial. Mr. Goodman sat back down and glanced reassuringly at Keenan. Ms. Seaman called Serena to the stand and the real character assassination began.

Serena was dressed in a conservative gray business suit with a pencil skirt and white silk blouse. Her doll-like face was somber and she walked with purpose to the stand, her low-heel pumps clicking with every step. She looked like a school principal about to chastise a rebellious student. She settled into the witness stand while Ms. Seaman glanced down at a sheaf of papers and commenced the questioning.

"How do you know the respondent, Keenan Green?"

"We met through a match dating site."

"And when did you all meet?"

"We started dating in July until October."

"What caused the demise of the relationship?"

"Well, from the moment we started dating I was concerned with the fact of—by the first couple of weeks he wanted a very serious relationship and I felt that I was just trying to slow things down and get to know each other and almost on a weekly basis he was always wanting to have a conversation about being official."

Ugh, Keenan thought. *Then why were we never exclusive?*

Her lawyer seemed to read his mind, because her next question to Serena was, "Were you all dating exclusively?"

"We were," Serena replied.

What bullshit is this, Keenan thought. They never dated exclusively. How could she even state that under oath when back in the Dominican Republic he had been "just a friend" to any single dude who happened to ask her?

Then she started talking about the calls and the texts. Keenan squirmed slightly in his seat. They'd spent weeks breaking up, and hearing his call log and text messages verbatim in the court was about the most embarrassing thing he could imagine.

"Okay," her lawyer said. "So what happened after you broke up with Mr. Green?"

"Well," Serena said, "within the first couple of hours of breaking up I received a call from him. I received maybe two calls that day but I also received a call from my own phone number that I didn't answer. That's the first time I've ever received a call from my own phone number."

"When you say you received a call from your own phone number, can you be a little more specific?" her lawyer asked.

"When I look at my phone it says my name as if I'm calling myself."

"And that had never happened previous to October 12?"

"It had not."

"And what else happened?"

"Well, I began to get, you know, continued calls from my own phone number that I wasn't answering and then eventually I think I received a 1-800 phone call and I answered that because I didn't recognize it and it was actually Keenan on the line through a 1-800 phone number."

"Did you all have a conversation?"

"We did have a conversation. He expressed to me that he wanted reasons why I didn't want to be with him and I didn't have any specific reasons and I said I just wanted to end it and then he became upset and he demanded his belongings back."

It was easy now, sitting in court and hearing his breakup dissected, to realize that he'd been more hurt than he had allowed himself to believe. Their split had been surprisingly bitter considering the short time they were together. It was hard for him to admit that he'd had strong feelings for Serena, because he always kept seeing other women. But she did get under his skin. Just like Veronica, in so many ways. Why was this one type of woman so attractive to him?

They were all really smart, he realized. God, Veronica had been so smart. He loved intelligent and successful women who had some sort of mildly dangerous edge. Was he attracted to a certain type of "bad girl"? Serena was a pothead. Veronica worked her way through college as a stripper and churned out scripts for pills like she had her own printing press. Faith ripped him off for $600. But "bad girl" was not quite the right term for these women. They were clever and sophisticated, and when he surrendered to his worst impulses and allowed himself the smallest moment of love-sick revenge, he found himself at the mercy of a superior adversary. He was the knight and they were the queens. Even if he won this case, he would always lose if he played their game.

When Serena at the prompting of her lawyer went over the call

logs from what he thought of as "the drunk salsa night," his confidence in the outcome of the trial began to crater.

There was no doubt that he had drunk-dialed and texted her
that night. That awful night. He had been out salsa dancing at the
salsa dancing club—just missing the feeling of dancing with her.
It was a painful reminder to dance with other partners—the same
moves that had seemed so graceful and effortless with her now
felt mechanical. He wound up doing shots of tequila at the bar
instead of dancing, and the rest of the evening had been . . . messy.
He wondered if the judge had ever drunk texted or dialed an ex
from a different number.

"The twenty-first, I had eleven calls. On the twenty-second,
thirteen calls," she said.

"And the eleven calls that you received, where did those numbers come from?"

"The twenty-first was the one I'm saying it came the multiple
two-one-five numbers and my own number and his number on
into Saturday because that night he—after sending me the pictures
of himself at the salsa club—said that he was stranded, he went to
another club, and that he lost his keys and wanted to ride share to
my house. So when I didn't respond he just started calling from all
of these different numbers to try to get me to answer the phone."

His lawyer stood up. "Objection, Your Honor," he said. "Spec-
ulation again as to the number issue."

"Sustained," the judge said.

Undeterred, Serena's layer continued.

"And what did the last text message say at two a.m.?"

"It said, 'Let's see what happens when I report your weed addiction to the hospital and medical board.'"

"What did he text on October 26, after you specifically told him
that you did not want to hear from him anymore?"

"He texted, 'You were still rude to me. You hung up on my face. Here's a quote from the famous Nate-Dog to make you laugh. Hey, hey, hey, smoke weed everyday.'"

Keenan's lawyer seemed to sense his increasing despair at the picture being painted of him, caught his eye, and nodded slightly. The game wasn't over. It had barely begun.

"When were you called in by your work to be drug tested?" Ms. Seaman asked.

"They notified me on November 3. I was tested November 5."

"What were the test results?"

"I tested negative."

The rest of the examination, Keenan could tell, was directed to the specific legal language of the protection-order statute and what she and her supervillain lawyer wanted from the court. It was like a memorized call and response. The rhythm of it depressed him.

"Did his contact occur without your consent?"

"Yes, it did."

"And did his conduct place you in reasonable fear of your safety?"

"Yes, it did."

"Are you asking the Court to order him to undergo a psychological evaluation?"

"Yes."

Keenan felt his eyebrows go up. So those were two different evaluations? Clearly, they were out to convince the judge that he was not only guilty of harassment, he was stark-raving mad. "And can you tell the Court about your attorney's fees that you have spent and your cost incurred in litigating this action?"

"How much?" Serena asked.

"Yes."

"Counsel," the judge interrupted their sing-song litany, "let me get to the basis of this later if we're going to get there. Let's handle attorneys' fees later and get through this first."

That's a good sign, Keenan thought. *They only get attorney's fees if they win.*

To his relief, with this admonishment from the judge, Serena's opening testimony had drawn to a close. His lawyer had promised him that this would be the worst part, and now it was over.

Mr. Goodman lifted his six-foot frame out of the seat to cross-examine with a serious and intelligent look on his face. Keenan was relieved that he had found a lawyer who was prepared to go to battle for him.

First, Mr. Goodman demolished her call logs by pointing out that almost all of the alleged calls had occurred before she had told him to stop contacting her. Then he turned his attention to the text messages. He confirmed again that October 26 was the first time that Serena had specifically told him not to call or text anymore.

"And the messages that he sent you after you actually told him to stop, with the exception of—after you told him to stop . . . going back, I see one, two . . . two messages actually after you told him to stop," Mr. Goodman said.

"Correct."

Keenan was feeling better and better. Now, his lawyer turned to the incident at the health food market. She admitted that she had approached him and had slapped his phone out of his hand.

"He reaches in his pocket. I don't know what he's pulling out," she said.

Yeah, right, Keenan thought.

"Did he actually threaten you in any way?" his lawyer asked.

"He didn't threaten me, no," she responded.

"Was his son with him?"

"His son was with him."

After confirming that Keenan never tried to hide from her the fact that he had reported her, Mr. Goodman finally asked what Keenan thought of as the million-dollar question.

"Have you ever smoked marijuana?"

"I have," she said.

"Do you still smoke it?"

"I smoked it on occasion to help me sleep."

Suddenly, Ms. Seaman was on her feet. "Your Honor, I object to the relevance of this questioning."

Keenan held his breath. This was the real crux of his case at the TPO trial. It was entirely possible that the judge would sustain the objection and leave the fact that she actually was a pothead ER doctor completely out of bounds.

"Your Honor," Mr. Goodman said, "the entire line of questioning goes, if she's accusing my client of making false allegations and calling her at work and harassing her about it, that's one thing. But if the allegations are true, that's another. Especially if she's a doctor."

"I'll allow it," the judge said cautiously. "I don't know if it's appropriate to call her employer about it, but I think he should investigate the validity of the claim."

Keenan felt a thrill of relief go through him. His side was going to be heard. Serena now looked less like the stern principal and more like the kid who had done wrong. As she explained her "light" and suspiciously past-tense marijuana habit, she talked faster and faster. The judge seemed unimpressed.

"So we'll sum it up like this," Mr. Goodman said. "You still smoke marijuana, is that correct?

"I don't smoke currently."

"What do you mean 'currently'?"

"I don't understand."

"You said you smoked two months ago?"

"Well, it's—he was implying that I was smoking and high at work which is not about a claim. I'm an ER doctor. I have to be alert and, plus, I don't get breaks. I work ten hours straight and if I was smoking, it would be on my clothes and I would be obviously high at work. So that's the reason for calling—my point is, the reason for calling my job was not to report because I smoked marijuana, he smokes marijuana as well. It was to attack me because he didn't threaten to report it to my job until I told him I didn't want to see him anymore. Then he produced photos that he took some time in the course of our dating life. He was stacking evidence for just an occasion."

Mr. Goodman ignored this and continued to hammer home the fact that she was a self-confessed marijuana user, in spite of the continued attempts at objections by Ms. Seaman.

When it was time for the redirect, Ms. Seaman did her best to put the focus back on Keenan's supposedly vindictive motivations for reporting her. She pointed out that Keenan had bought her weed grinders in Jamaica, and that he had only first expressed his concern in those breakup texts. She tried to claim that he smoked marijuana.

He wasn't too worried about this redirect, because it was so blatantly untrue. Except for at the very beginning of the relationship, he'd always been vocal in his discomfort with her smoking. He was a grown man in the twenty-first century, and of course, knew people who used cannabis. What had increasingly bothered him was not the smoking, but that she was an ER doctor. She wasn't teaching a ceramics class.

Was being hurt a part of his decision? Of course. But it wasn't all of it.

Serena was finally finished and sat down, her black pumps clicking with a little less confidence. Keenan gathered himself. It was his time.

"Mr. Green," said Serena's lawyer as soon as he sat down and was sworn in, "you had several petitions for protective orders filed against you from December 2013, correct?"

Wow, she really wasn't wasting any time in attacking his reputation. "I have," he said.

For the millionth time, he regretted giving Serena the first draft of his book. She had used it as a building block for this whole court case. If he hadn't shared it with her, she never would have known about Veronica or Faith, or been inspired by them to put him through another round of hell. Nothing could have been further from his intention, yet in hindsight, it seemed almost inevitable.

He spent the next few minutes in court arguing the details of the no-contact agreement, the actual TPO with Veronica, and the other two attempts by Faith. At each turn, Ms. Seaman tried to get him to admit that he was a stalker.

"I do not have a history of stalking," he insisted. "I have had a few frivolous petitions filed against me."

He felt like he held his own through the regurgitation of his old, private life. He even had to explain once again how his near-death experience motivated him to go to Veronica's house and leave that accursed note on the door.

"And Ms. Rubio is a doctor, correct?" Ms. Seaman asked.

"She is."

"And you threatened to go to the medical board after she broke up with you?"

"I did go to the medical board after we stopped seeing each other, yes."

It was so strange to be discussing his previous case with

Veronica years later in court again, with Serena front and center sitting and watching. He half expected to see Faith and Veronica walk in arm-in-arm and take a seat. Maybe this wasn't a courtroom at all. Maybe he had died and this was his judgment day.

"And this would be the fourth petition for stalking against you since 2013? That's a question. Or are there more?" He could hear a slight hint of a sneer in her voice.

"Yes, that's it," Keenan replied. "That's it."

To his surprise, Ms. Seaman did not ask him any further questions about his relationship with Serena, the incident at the health food market, or the facts surrounding his reporting of Serena to the medical board. All she tried to do was establish him as a person with a history of stalking.

She sat down, and Mr. Goodman stood up to question him. He felt himself relax just a tiny bit. He knew what was coming now.

First, Mr. Goodman questioned him about the number of protection orders that had been filed against him. He was able to explain not only what happened with Veronica, but also Faith and her devious attempt to hire Veronica's attorney and file in revenge for him demanding his $600 back. Faith then filed a fictitious criminal application which was denied and dismissed by the district attorneys office after two years of refusing to prosecute it. He felt as if he were on trial for his entire dating life and not merely this bad, brief episode with Serena.

"So, to be clear," Mr. Goodman concluded, "you've actually had more frivolous TPO's filed against you that were dismissed than TPOs that went into effect against you?"

"That's correct," he said, loud and clear.

His lawyer then moved on to his experience with Serena, and he was finally able to state into the record that they were non-exclusive. He saw Serena's face wince just slightly when he said it. It was time to tell his side, and she knew that her behavior wasn't so innocent.

"We saw a series of messages that she alleges that you had sent to her. Did you send those messages?" Mr. Goodman asked.

"I've sent some messages to her, yes," he said. No way to deny it. With his lawyer carefully guiding him, he went through the ugly details of their breakup again. It wasn't so bad now that he was telling his side.

Then they moved on to his decision to report her.

"We're shown two numbers that you called from," Mr. Goodman said. "One was a 1-800 number. And that's when you had called and you were asking for your things back. Do you recognize that number?"

"Yeah, I went downstairs, my phone was dead at the time and I did call her from the 1-800 number. The reason I called her from my job was because I needed to talk to her. I was attempting to get my possessions back."

Then, Mr. Goodman presented the pictures he had taken of her sister's prescription containers, weed grinder, and blunt wrap on her living room coffee table.

"I didn't have any intent behind it besides just to confide in a friend," he stated. "And I was dealing with some conscience issues to be real frank."

"So you had seen her use marijuana?" his lawyer asked.

"Yes, absolutely. Several times."

"You had seen marijuana in the house?"

"All the time."

"And how did that make you feel?"

"I was kind of like, you know, I don't—I have children. I have an eighteen-year-old that goes to Morehouse, I have a fourteen-year-old. I don't keep alcohol really in my house and I don't smoke marijuana or anything like that. I never grew up smoking. I grew up in California but never grew up doing that. I actually had it in my household, I remember seeing a plant in my household and always resenting my stepfather being a smoker. So, to be frank, it kinda made me feel leery, especially really leery that she was an ER doctor. My father is really sick, he has bone marrow cancer right now. I had been to an ER just two years ago and at the ER I can't imagine that if my physician was high or had been high, I wouldn't want that."

He discussed how he had first called the Medical Board, using the same contact from when he was dealing with Veronica, and then at their suggestion he had called Risk Management at Southern Regional. "It didn't have anything to do with her," he concluded. "It had to do with her patients."

Mr. Goodman then proceeded to discuss the incident at the health food market. He had Keenan walk through his day step by step to show that their meeting was nothing but a random occurrence. Keenan felt the judge's attitude recalibrate in his favor with every detail he shared of his day. There was clearly no intent on his part to do anything but buy groceries at the health food market and cook breakfast for his growing son.

When Ms. Seaman rose to cross-examine him, he began to dare to hope that he might win this case. He was already getting a strong sense that his lawyer was just more skilled than Serena's, objectively, and that feeling grew stronger as she asked questions about his trip to Jamaica, when he had playfully texted Serena a picture of himself wearing a pot-leaf bandanna at a music festival and bought her the grinders.

"Your Honor, objection," Mr. Goodman said.

"Not sure what the relevance of this questioning is," said the judge, already inclined to sustain.

"The point is," Ms. Seaman said, "you say, 'I'm against marijuana,' yet you're in Jamaica smoking marijuana, taking pictures of yourself."

"He's stated that he wasn't," the judge replied.

Wow. The judge seemed to be moving to his side.

"I think there's a very good distinction between taking pictures while you're in Jamaica of people smoking marijuana versus dating someone smoking marijuana," Mr. Goodman said. "And I think it's a fine distinction."

"I would agree," Ms. Seaman argued, "but he continued to date her. Now he's testifying that he has this objection and consciousness against marijuana smoking, and he was resentful."

"That's not what I heard from him," said the judge, contradicting Serena's lawyer once again. "I heard he's got an issue with an ER doctor smoking marijuana when she's responsible for other people. I'm not sure I'm hearing an overall objection to it. But I heard him saying, 'I don't do it. I've got a son.'"

"Your Honor, which is contradictory to these pictures that he sent her," Ms. Seaman argued.

"Where he said I don't do it?" the judge asked.

"No," Serena's lawyer replied. "He testified that he didn't do it, but he clearly in the picture is smoking marijuana."

"I'm not smoking marijuana in the picture!" Keenan said emphatically. They didn't even have any pictures of him in Jamaica as an exhibit. *Nice job, Ms. Seaman*, he thought. It was not very good planning on their part if some unsubmitted picture was the cornerstone of their argument.

Mr. Goodman called Serena to the stand.

"Doctor Price, there was a photo that was introduced earlier of a prescription bottle with—filled with what appeared to be marijuana. Do you recognize that photo?"

"Yes."

"Was that your marijuana?"

"It had some marijuana in it."

"But was it your marijuana?"

"Yes."

"Did you smoke that marijuana?"

"Did I smoke it?"

"Yes. Did you use that marijuana?"

"I already admitted to the court that I smoke on occasion."

"I'm asking, did you use the marijuana that was in the pill bottle that we displayed to the court?"

"The picture in August?"

"Yes."

"I probably smoked some of it, yes."

"Now, that pill bottle was a prescription bottle, correct?"

"Yes."

"Do you know whose prescription bottle that was?"

"That's my sister's."

"Why did you have that prescription bottle?"

"Because my sister comes to my house sometimes and she has a chronic medical condition and she has prescription bottles."

"Do you prescribe her any drugs?"

"I do not."

"That's all," Mr. Goodman said. "Thank you."

Then Cameron came up and testified in a soft voice that they were shopping for breakfast when they saw Serena, who then had called Keenan a pussy and smacked the phone out of his hand.

"Was he pulling the phone out of his pants?" Mr. Goodman asked.

"No. He already had it out," Cameron said.

"He already had it in his hand?"

"Yes," Cameron said.

So much for not knowing what he was pulling out of his pocket, Keenan thought.

Ms. Seaman barely cross-examined Cameron.

"Cameron, you previously met Dr. Price, correct?"

"Yes, sir," Cameron said. "I mean, ma'am."

Keenan watched a thin line of perspiration appear on his son's forehead. Cameron hadn't shown any sign of nervousness yet, but now he looked uncomfortable. Ms. Seaman continued.

"And isn't it true that she advised several times during that interaction at the health food market, stop calling me, stop calling me?"

"Yes," Cameron said, avoiding any honorifics.

"That's all I have."

Cameron stepped down quickly. Keenan caught his son's eye and smiled, relieved that it was over and that Cameron hadn't been berated by Serena's lawyer. He'd forgotten some of the details of Serena's temper tantrum—like being called names—it was good that the judge had heard it from his son and not from him.

Keenan checked his watch. Nearly three hours had passed since this circus began, and they still had to do their closing arguments. No matter the outcome, this experience had been punishment enough. Ms. Seaman went first, but her closing argument did not quite have the strength of her remarks at the beginning of the trial, doubtless because so many of her accusations had fallen completely flat.

Then his lawyer stood up.

"This case," he said, "boils down to a very simple act of revenge on Dr. Serena Price's part. Dr. Price knew Mr. Green had gone through this before. She knew it had affected him so much that he had written a book about it after having been subjected to multiple illegitimate TPOs. After he reported her to her work for using marijuana, that's when she used the very same process he had told her about against him."

He continued, "For a TPO to go into effect, you need more than just 'You're tired of someone calling you.' You need reasonable fear. And Your Honor, in this case, there's been no demonstration of that whatsoever."

Mr. Goodman completed his remarks and sat down, smiling briefly at Keenan, who didn't even dare to smile back. He thought his lawyer had gone beyond excellence in defending his case, but in the end, there was only one opinion that mattered: that of the judge.

The judge began, "It is very clear that unless there's a safety issue, I don't have anything to do here," she said. "Counsel for respondent makes a good point—this is not an unwanted text-message statute or unwanted phone-call statute. The time does come that the phone calls and text messages become threatening in the fact they don't stop. The time comes in cases, so if somebody sends somebody flowers and says, 'I love you, miss you,' but they've been told twenty-seven times to go away, I take that as starting to get threatening. I'm not there in this case, so I'm deny-ing the request for TPO."

Keenan felt joy run through his body. He had won!

The judge continued, "As for the report he made to her employer disclosing illegal drug use, she admitted it on the stand, so it was not a false report. I don't find that that amps it up for safety. For now, I don't believe this statute is met. I don't believe this is a safety issue. I think a lot of the texts had to do with the altercation at the health food market. I believe they had to do with the report made to her employer, which she was angry about. I would be, too, but I do not find it gives rise to the stalking statute. This petition is denied."

To Keenan's surprise, when the judge finally banged down the gavel, a spontaneous wave of applause erupted in the courtroom. Perfect strangers were actually clapping their hands for him! Something about this case had caught the sympathy of the people sitting there, waiting their own turn at justice.

A bit dazed at his sudden win and adoring public, he stood and shook hands with Mr. Goodman while Serena and her lawyer ducked out.

"Guess she won't be getting those lawyer fees out of me, after all," he said to Mr. Goodman.

"No, you only have to pay me this time," Mr. Goodman laughed.

Feeling strongly vindicated and more than a little relieved, he hugged his son.

"Were you nervous?" he asked.

"Not too bad at first," Cameron said. "But then Ms. Seaman's so ugly, I thought she was a man."

Keenan couldn't help but laugh. "Is that why you said sir?" he asked.

"Yeah," Cameron said. "That's when I got nervous. It was bad. I had to go."

"We're both going, right now," Keenan said.

In that moment he made a silent promise to never stoop to these women's level again. Each time he gave in to the temptation of revenge, he paid too high a price, and Cameron witnessing a woman literally smack a phone out of his hand was the last straw. He would always be the bigger man from now on, no matter what unfair or hurtful behavior he experienced.

They strolled out to the parking lot together.

"Isn't that Serena's new white convertible?" Cameron asked.

It was indeed Serena's car, and she was parked right next to Keenan. In spite of the vow he had literally just made, some devil inside him started working up a mouthful of saliva for a satisfying spit. But he stopped himself before he could really get something going. No, no, no more revenge.

Just then, his phone buzzed. It was a text. He pulled out his phone. It was from Serena.

"`My stalking petition was denied,`" it said.

"Serena just texted me," he said.

"Really? Why?" Cameron asked.

He shook his head, slowly. "I think it was an accident," he said, and laughed a little. See, he didn't have to seek revenge. He could just wait for karma to work things out.

"Let's get out of here, Dad," Cameron said.

"You did so great up there," Keenan said.

"Thanks," he replied. "I'm hungry."

"Me, too," Keenan said.

* * *

He had the chance to demonstrate his commitment to the high road very soon after the court win, when some sore losers started blowing up his phone. Veronica had apparently gotten married, because someone calling himself her husband left him a psycho voicemail. "We're coming to get your ass," he said, along with some other threats.

Okay. Blocked.

A couple of days later, he answered a call from yet another unfamiliar number.

"Keenan?"

"Yes?"

"Um, so I hear that—this is Officer Cantone—I hear that you're going through the same stuff that you're going through with Serena that you went through with Veronica and that other lady. You just don't know how to stop, do you?"

What in the fuck? He listened for a second to this officer of the law harassing him about his love life, then hung up on him and blocked his number, too.

It didn't even make him mad. He was so over it.

The Nightmare Is Over

THAT DECEMBER, KEENAN was on his way to an afternoon coffee date with a woman who lived out in McDonough. He had just enough time to get there when his phone buzzed.

"Hi, Keenan," a familiar voice purred through the speakers of his car.

"Tanya?" Keenan asked. *This was a surprise.* He pulled over to chat with her without distraction.

"I just want to ask you something," she said, as if they had spoken last week and not almost two-and-a-half years ago. "What would make a man who was honest with you be a liar?"

"What would make a man what?" Keenan asked.

"What would make a man who was always honest with you suddenly turn into a liar?" she repeated, as if she was his guru or it was a trick question.

"I have no idea, Tanya," Keenan said.

"Can I talk to you?" she said.

"Isn't that what we're doing?" Keenan replied at the side of the road, already late to his date.

Tanya told him the full story. It had not worked out with her precious Robert, and she had moved on to a gentleman who was a C-suite executive—a vice president of something. They even rented a house together. Her vice president, however, had lost his job shortly after moving in together. Instead of telling her what happened, he was still "going to work" every day in his corporate attire with his briefcase in his hand.

"He would come home every night at six," she said. "I'd ask him, 'How was work, honey?' And he'd say, 'Fine. The usual.' I had no idea."

To pay the bills, her out-of-work VP was going to Tanya's own family. Her mother refused him, but her father, a doctor, gave him a sizable loan, which he used to manage household expenses for months. When that ran out, he went to Tanya's friend's husband. Not only did the husband refuse, he made sure Tanya found out.

"I went to my mother and told her, and that's when she told me that he had asked her for money, too. She told me she'd refused, but I should check with my dad," Tanya said. "Our whole life was a lie."

"Is he still living there?" Keenan asked. He was now officially thirty minutes late. The texts from his date had started to roll in. He tapped in "Almost there," as Tanya spoke.

"He doesn't have anywhere else to go," she responded. "It's so stressful. Can I come over?"

"I'm on my way to a date!"

"Okay, so maybe in a couple hours."

He had a rushed meet-and-greet with a mildly annoyed lady, then was back at home to greet Tanya with open arms.

It was pretty clear that she'd come for more than just a shoulder to cry on. She took sex from him first for comfort or relaxation, but then fell into a more un-self-conscious arousal and really let herself go. *No one could give head like Tanya,* he thought vaguely as he watched the top of her head bob up and down on his cock. He put his hand on the back of her head until he heard her choke on it, then she sucked hard at his shaft with a slick up-and-down motion that took him to the stars.

Afterward, she curled up into his arms and they both dozed while watching some random movie.

"Let's go salsa dancing," she said drowsily. "I need another lesson. It's been years since our cruise."

"And you haven't gone salsa dancing since?" Keenan asked, laughing.

"No. Do you believe me?"

"No."

"Well, it's true," Tanya said as she dozed off.

He was still into the lady from McDonough, though. Her name was Lynda, and she was an assistant principal at a local middle school. She was light-skinned with big, brown eyes and long, wavy hair. She was in decent shape with large, soft breasts and skinny legs. They mostly talked on the phone.

Keenan had decided to stay in for New Year's Eve that year. Cameron was at his mother's, and Kelvin was staying with friends. He had just finished watching the ball drop alone when his phone rang. It was Lynda.

"Happy New Year!" she said, sounding a little loud and tipsy. "Do you want to pick me up from a party?"

Hm. A party I wasn't invited to? Nah. Unless it was an emergency.

"Are you okay?" he asked.

"Oh, yeah, baby," she said. "It's New Year's Eve, and I want to fuck."

She said that clearly enough. "Ooookay," he said, pulled on some shoes, and drove across town to a random house where people were streaming out in their New Year's Eve hats and party dresses.

Sure enough, there was Lynda in the driveway, slugging a bottle of spring water in her high heels, looking luscious. Her tight New Year's dress still gave her the perfect cleavage. She tossed the bottle, slipped a lipstick out of her glittering party purse, and reapplied it in two expert dashes. Then she finally saw him. He was glad to get to see her all dolled up, and her sexy party vibe was contagious.

"Don't you look delicious," Keenan said, feeling suddenly aware of his sweatpants for many reasons.

"Thanks, baby," she said with a flirtatious smile.

Unbidden, a thought suddenly came to his mind about the massive amount of cash that he had just saved himself by staying in on New Year's Eve. It was as if he had popped up for the good part of the night through no effort of his own. It wasn't a bad sign for the New Year.

Another good sign was that she slid out from under the shoulder seatbelt and ducked her head into his lap, pulling down the elastic of his sweatpants and sucking his dick.

"Hey," he said, laughing and enjoying it. "Not tonight. There's checkpoints."

She complied, pouting, and reapplied her lipstick in the passenger mirror. As soon as they got inside of his house, she started taking off her clothes. "Don't need this anymore," she said, and shimmied out of her dress. Her ample breasts looked pretty tasty in the black pushup bra she was wearing. Then she reached one hand behind her back and they tumbled out, looking even tastier. Watching her stand there in just panties and heels, he felt like he had hired a stripper. He noticed that he had lipstick smears on the front of his sweatpants. *Happy New Year,* he thought.

"Come on," she said, and Keenan took her up to this room naked and bouncing. As soon as he shut the door, he started kissing her deeply, massaging her glorious nipples as she moaned underneath his mouth. "Ooh, fuck me," she said, the alcohol fueling her New Year's horniness. He put her flat on her back and gave her what she wanted.

In the morning, she made pancakes wearing Keenan's robe, and they ate naked in his bed.

The week after New Year's, he finally made it out to her house for dinner. One sure advantage of living in the country was the size and grandeur of the homes out there, almost all built within the past ten years or so. As he drove the quiet, well-paved roads, he saw the occasional obscured roof and chimney, but not much else.

When he slowly turned in at her mailbox, a rather imposing dog with brindle markings came running and barking down her long, winding driveway. This is how he discovered she was the proud owner of a vigorous, young Presa Canario. He resembled a shorter Rottweiler with a wide stance between his front legs that lifted his chest like a bulldog.

He pulled in and saw Lynda standing by the house in black cigarette pants and a tight, white sweater. To his relief, Lynda had the dog well-trained; it ceased barking and sat patiently beside her as he got out of the car.

"This is Muffin," she said, laughing. "Just kidding. His name is Zeus."

When they went in, Zeus trotted over to his outsized dog bed by the fire to continue his interrupted lounge. Keenan glanced at the walls and saw pictures of a smiling young boy grown to almost-man in graduation robes.

"That's my son," she said. "He decided to go away to college. I don't know why."

She had cooked salmon with asparagus, and they drank Pinot Grigio, which for a moment reminded him of Veronica, but he shook it off. No more energy to that. All he knew about Pinot Grigio was that it paired well with the salmon. He took in another forkful of the pink flesh, and Lynda's phone buzzed on the table. She glanced down.

"I have to take it," she said. "It's my son."

She disappeared into the kitchen for barely a moment, then returned to the large dining-room table. They were seated next to each other at one corner.

"Everything okay?" Keenan asked.

"Oh, yes," she said. "Just, he's coming home this weekend. Sorry."

"Why are you sorry?" Keenan asked. "That's nice you get to see your son."

"I just wanted you to stay the night," she said.

He looked into her Bambi eyes and smiled. "I'll leave before breakfast."

She was insatiable. It seemed like New Year's Eve had just been a prequel. She wasn't into anything too crazy—just wanted to be fucked hard and long and again. He had no choice but to stay the night, switching condoms four times. As he was slipping off the last condom, he kicked one under the bed somehow, out of laziness probably, because he didn't want to go to the bathroom and he was busy with satisfying her.

He slept for two hours, drove home, and went back to bed.

When he woke up, Lynda had blown up his phone with calls and texts. He sat up in bed, still drowsy and fucked-out, and called her back.

"How could you?" she hissed on the phone, uptight, so unlike the wild animal he had been pleasuring all night.

"How could I what?" Keenan said.

He finally got the story out of her. Zeus had sniffed out the condom under her bed. While she sat with her son drinking coffee in the kitchen, the dog fetched the used condom and brought it to her.

"Do you know what my son said to me?" she said, sniffy, pissed, and half-crying. "He said stuff like this is why he went away to college!"

So, it was all Tanya all the time then, and in addition to dinners and movies, he found out she wasn't kidding about wanting to go dancing. A few weeks later, they decided to meet at the salsa club. Tanya danced with him a couple of times, and she surely hadn't improved, but hey, they were having fun.

He saw Serena across the room but didn't pay her any attention. He felt grateful again to his lawyer for fighting so he didn't have to slink away from the places he loved.

As for Tanya, she didn't care about executing a bunch of steps with every man in the place. She didn't even dance with anyone else and was much more interested in just being with Keenan, like a real date. It was refreshing. As the night went on, they sat with their heads closer and closer together at the neon-lit bar.

"You're so sexy when you want to be, Tanya," he said as she looked up at him over the rim of her glass.

"Well, you're sexy even when you don't want to be," she replied, smiling.

He was about to put his hand on her thigh when he saw a woman with long straightened hair and obviously fake breasts marching up to them with a troublemaking look in her cat eyes. He recognized her as a friend of Serena's from the last day they had spent together the previous year at House in the Park.

"Excuse me," she said, ignoring Keenan and staring straight at Tanya, who suddenly had a very neutral expression on her face, "but you should know this man is a stalker."

"Excuse me," Tanya replied haughtily. "Do I know you?"

"You should just know he's a stalker," she repeated. There was a brief pause as Tanya didn't respond. She started again. "He's had multiple—"

"Actually," Tanya interrupted in a professional tone of voice, "I've known this man for years. I know everything about him. This is a very old friend of mine, and I'll make my own judgments, thank you."

The woman flounced off, and Tanya asked Keenan, "What was that about?"

He put his hand on her thigh. "Some bullshit," he said. "I'll tell you later, if you're interested."

"Not really," she said, and tilted her head toward him in a certain way that made it impossible for him not to kiss her. Her lips had puckered slightly at the moment he bent down his head, and it reminded him of the fish in the koi pond. *In these shallow waters,* he thought, *why not just fish to have a good time, then let them return to the pond with no hard feelings?*

They made out at the bar, and Keenan found all thoughts of Serena had vanished completely as his life resumed its regular rhythm of catch and release.

"Let's get out of here," Tanya said, and Keenan quickly paid the tab and helped her with her coat. They walked out to his car, even though Tanya had driven herself, so they could continue with what they started at the bar.

She kissed him while unzipping his pants, wrapping her hand around his dick as his own hand reached to grab her sexy breasts. He slid his way out from the driver's side as Tanya let her front seat go all the way back. She was wearing garters and stockings under her swinging skirt because she liked to flash them when she turned on the dancefloor.

Under him on the passenger side, she wrapped her legs around him as he pushed her panties to the side and drove his dick into her, making her moan. She gripped him tightly, and he could feel the scratchy garters on his own thighs. She felt so good, he wondered why he had ever messed around and tried to fall in love.

"Baby, I've got to go," Tanya whispered. She tucked herself all back in and made her way to her European coupe. Keenan watched her headlights drift out of the parking lot as he got himself together for the drive home. He closed his eyes for a second, feeling himself out a bit. Yes, he felt okay to drive home. He found a bottle of spring water in the back seat and drank it down, then pulled out of the parking lot a few minutes after Tanya.

He saw the headlights in the distance safely on their side of the road, until the last instant when the other driver suddenly pulled into his lane. He swerved into the soft shoulder, and in a flash lost control of the car. Keenan felt an odd sensation of tumbling as the car rolled into a drainage ditch, and then the world abruptly stopped.

When he came to, he was being wheeled on a gurney into some emergency room. He looked groggily at the sign passing above him. It said Southern Regional Hospital.

"Wait, what?" Keenan said, but nobody heard him. His brand-new designer men's dress shirt had been cut off of him, and he was already in a hospital gown. He saw an IV in his arm.

"Not here, not here!" he said, but again his words were ignored and they rushed him into a waiting bed in the emergency room. "Okay, not Serena, not Serena," he muttered to himself fervently.

Then he heard the sound of a newborn baby on the other side of the curtain. *Was someone delivering right now in the emergency room?*

"Ms. Rubio, you have a brand-new baby girl," he heard a voice say, and then he heard the unmistakable brainy cadence of Veronica talking to her new baby. "I'm going to treat you so much better than Matt," she declared.

From his hospital bed, he saw the nurse walk by carrying the newborn. *Was that Amy?* She glanced at him and frowned. "Oh, it's you," she said, and went back to caring for the baby.

"Don't worry, the doctor will be with you soon," said another nurse walking up to him. *Candy?* "Hey, you put something in my drink!"

"I swear, I didn't," he moaned. "You can check my refrigerator." *Wait, had he thrown out the wine?* He sniffed suddenly. "It smells like Las Vegas in here," he said.

"Oh, that's Dr. Price," Candy said, and then Serena was standing over him with bloodshot, squinty eyes.

"What was I doing?" she asked nurse Candy.

"You were preparing the patient for emergency surgery," Candy said helpfully.

"Ah, yes, give him the knockout shot," Serena said. "I'm going to step out for a toke. Come on, Zeus," she sang out cheerfully. The Presa Canario trotted after her, a used condom in his mouth. Francis appeared out of nowhere, bitch slapping Keenan with her left hand's ring finger brushing against his nose, scraping his nostrils as her hand pressed by.

"Noooo!" Keenan said, as he suddenly felt the shot penetrate his skin.

Then he woke up.

He was still in his car where Tanya had left him, his dress shirt wrinkled but otherwise untouched. He patted the cuffs lovingly, then turned on the wipers to clear the heavy condensation from his dashboard window. The club was quiet and long-closed in the dim, gray light.

"It was just a dream," he said to himself, and chuckled. Glad he got that one out of his system.

The End

Acknowledgments

Remembering always that "Every good and perfect gift is from above" (James 1:17). I am grateful to God for being with me while I completed this project, just as I am grateful that he was with me during the life events that inspired it. I am also grateful to everyone who played a role in bringing this book to life.

About the Author

Ke'Aughn Caver is a motivated tech entrepreneur and small business owner with a passion for mentoring others in the field of technology. Raised in California, he graduated from the HBCU Clark Atlanta University. Mr. Caver stayed in Atlanta after college to get married and start his career. He raised two young men and has traveled extensively throughout the Caribbean, South America, and Europe.

Made in the USA
Middletown, DE
26 July 2023

35783947R00179